THE PRINCESS
OF CANNON BEACH

A Novel by

KATHRYN JAMES

ISBN: 978-0-557-16395-3

James, Kathryn [1946–   ]
The Princess of Cannon Beach / Kathryn James—1st ed.

Manufactured by Lulu.com
Text and cover design by redbat design
This book is printed on recycled paper

10 9 8 7 6 5 4 3 2 1

AUTHOR'S NOTE

This is a work of fiction and in light of today's knowledge impossible; but the age-old question "what if" is always intriguing. More than that, when a life is suddenly and brutally ended, it can be heartening to ponder what "might have been" for a young and vibrant person denied the chance to find out.

Regarding the translations of Russian names and terms, since there is no definitive method of transliteration from Russian to English, I have used my own discretion in choosing whenever possible the spelling that most simply demonstrates how to say the word in English, yet still keeps its Russianness.

PROLOGUE
NEDDY—1960

I promised I'd do it, and now I shall. For too many years we were so busy. Our children married, moved, took new jobs, and gave us grand-babies—an even dozen! The flow of our lives left no time for the dust-covered past. But now I'm alone, except for Henry's last gift, my trusty Newfoundland, Raven. As my great bumbling companion and I comb the beach for treasures, my mind is crowded with memories of the people I loved.

And, as I said, I promised I'd set it down for the children. At sixty-three I don't feel the least bit old, but more than most I should know how fleeting life can be. Still, it wasn't until I lost my Henry so suddenly that I remembered my own mortality.

It won't be easy, this task of telling my story. I suppose that's really why I've put it off so long. I wonder what they'll do, my magnificent children, when they find out the truth?

Who would I have been, what life would I have had, if my magical-seeming childhood had not ended the way it did?

ONE
TATIANA—1911

I was born Grand Duchess Tatiana Nikolaivna Romanov on 11 June 1897, second daughter of Nicholas Alexandrovich Romanov and his wife Alexandra, formerly princess Alix of Hesse-Darmstadt. I had three sisters and one brother. My father, Tsar Nicholas II, was emperor of all the Russias, and my mother, his empress.

Reeled off like that, it sounds like a boast. A skeptic would read no further. But for me, those proud names and titles are simply an identity, and an admission of truth that has been shrouded in death, lies, and deception for too many years.

Looking back down the path of time, I see now that there are seminal moments in my life, moments that plotted the course for years to come. The most significant of these was the birth of my brother, Alexei Nikolaevich Romanov. He was the long-awaited heir to the Russian throne, the heart of all our hopes for the dynasty and our nation. He was also a hemophiliac.

Before his birth I have almost no memory, only a collection of impressions; the sun-brushed frigid water of the Finnish fjords on my toes, a summer-blue sky, the scratching of palms and smell of spices from the Crimea where we went in spring, bright exhilarating cold and delightful fear as I rode a flying sled down an ice-hill in the St. Petersburg winter. I remember the coziness of sleeping with my sister Olga, Olenka, on trains as we went from one estate to another. I recall the sound of my father's voice as he read to us, and my mother's smile. The rest of my first seven years is a haze of laughter, caring hands, kind voices, and safety. But after Alexei's birth there was no safety, and I never saw my mother truly smile again.

. . .

It was, of course, not Alexei's fault. Much larger factors were already at work and my father, a kind man who lived for his country, wasn't pragmatic or ruthless enough to surmount them. He understood that Russia was at a crossroads when he assumed the crown, and knew just as well that European powers, as well as many of his own countrymen, thought it time for monumental change. But he believed Russia was different from Europe. Despite our attempts since the time of Peter the Great to turn our faces to the more democratic West, my father never wavered from his more Eastern conviction that only through the consistent strength of the autocracy and its power to exert its will over all Russia, could he bring about reforms to the bygone serf-based wealth system the aristocracy clung to so tenaciously. The serfs had been freed by Alexander II, but the relationship between peasants and masters, workers and bosses, had changed little. By 1904, the year of my brother's birth, it was patently obvious that there had to be another solution—but this was beyond my father's comprehension. Driven by an innate fear of violence (his grandfather had been blown up before his eyes and died in agony), he wouldn't listen to those he referred to as radicals. His past had already closed the door on compromise and redirection.

But on the day my brother arrived in the world, I jumped from my chair, upsetting the checkerboard.

'What are you doing?' demanded my sister Olga, just one year my senior and my best friend.

'Olenka, Papa! I hear him in the hall!'

The door opened, and Olga fairly danced into his embrace.

'I thought you two might want to hear about a surprise,' he said, taking us both onto his lap.

'Is the baby here? Is it?'

'Yes,' Papa chuckled. 'You have a little brother. Now, what shall my four little bunnies do when they have a great rowdy boy in the house?'

'Play all the games boys like,' I answered. 'Anastasia will like that especially.'

'But you're a princess,' Papa said, pretending to be stern. 'Such games are not for ladies of the court.'

'I'll not be a lady of the court,' I replied firmly. 'I'll marry a Cossack adventurer and tour the world.'

Papa laughed. 'Before you run off to the steppes, perhaps you'd like to meet your brother.'

'Now? Can we see the baby now?'

'We'll let him and his mother rest a bit,' Papa said gently, 'so perhaps this evening before bed.'

'What will his name be?' Olga asked. 'It must be a grand name, he'll be the tsar and get to tell everyone what to do.'

'His name will be Alexei,' Papa informed us, as he put us down gently and stood up. 'It's an old name, a traditional name, for a tsar who must lead a modern nation.'

I felt a little brought-down. 'But he's younger than me. Will he really be able to tell me what to do?'

'Tatiana, I think no one will ever be able to tell you what to do and get away with it.'

I could hear his chuckle as he went down the hall.

· · ·

A few weeks later, I urged the hands of the classroom clock forward to no avail. Papa said being a pretty princess who did needlepoint and sang songs wasn't good enough in this day and age. So my sisters and I had to study Latin, English, French, Russian, and German as well as mathematics, science, and literature. I liked to learn things, but now I had something more fun to do.

As soon as I was released I went straight to the nursery. My fascination with my baby brother hadn't faded as it had for my sisters. Maria said he cried too much and didn't like it at all when I told her she'd been a real crybaby, too. I think Olga was a little jealous because Papa doted on him so—she'd always been his favorite. And Anastasia, who'd brought him a ball the first night, was impatient for him to be able to play boys' games with her.

At the nursery door I heard voices but no crying and, assuming Alexei was asleep, tiptoed in. *Maman* stood on one side of the bassinet, Papa on the other. Their backs were to me.

'It's not your fault,' Papa was saying.

She was shaking her head fiercely. 'But you know it is. This curse comes through me. I'm the instrument of this innocent boy's doom—'

'Alix, you mustn't think that way.'

'Who then, Nicky, who but me?' Her voice grew high-pitched and she sobbed.

'It does no good to do this to yourself, my love. Now we must put our sadness aside and help our boy.'

I gasped. '*Maman*, is something wrong with Alexei? Is he sick?'

Both of them turned. My father looked only sad, but in my mother's eyes there was a grief, an inner torment, a terrible pain so powerful I was frightened.

She stared at me and the look in her eyes changed to horror, as if she was seeing a monster. 'God help me,' she wailed. 'What if it's in you too, or Olenka, or Maria, or Anastasia? Oh, Nicky, what've I done to them all?'

I stood petrified as she stepped toward me, her hands like claws. I'd never seen more than a stern look from my mother in my life, and wanted to flee this stranger with the haunted eyes.

But I couldn't, because there was something else in those eyes, and her whole body seemed to speak of defeat.

I ran into her arms and she clasped me convulsively to her, so hard I couldn't breathe. She murmured over and over, 'I'm sorry my baby, I'm sorry. Forgive me, forgive me.'

Then Alexei cried and she released me so abruptly I fell. All her focus was on the baby in the bassinet.

It was Papa who helped me up and reassured me. 'Your brother is going to be... delicate.'

I watched my mother gather Alexei into her arms. He was the same baby I'd fallen so in love with. He still had a silken downy fuzz on his head that glowed in sunlight like spun gold and his brilliant blue eyes goggled comically as he tried to focus, just as they always had. He burped, much too loud a sound for such a tiny body, but this time I didn't laugh as I always had in the past. This time it was different.

'But,' I said, my eyes filling with tears, 'Nurse Shura says he's full of life and God's love.'

'And so he is, my little bunny,' Papa whispered. 'Now, go and find Anna Vyrubova. Ask her to come to me.'

I ran to do his bidding and found her in the small parlor working on some lace, humming a love song as her needle flew. She was my mother's companion and I'd never cared much for her, she seemed too foolish and silly to be a grown-up. But she loved my mother and made her smile. I remember thinking at the time, my mother desperately needed a smile.

· · ·

Anna did everything she could, but nothing assuaged *Maman*. When she did smile, it was for the baby, and it wasn't the carefree happy smile I remembered. Her world was one little boy. Nothing else mattered, not her duties with the court or what was going on in the world the rest of us inhabited.

The year 1905 had been terrible. My grandmother, Dowager Empress Maria Fedorovna, had called it the year of nightmares. It began with a worker's revolt, and after it was put down people called it Bloody Sunday—if they were sure Papa couldn't hear them. Then, Papa's brother Serge, the husband of *Maman's* older sister Ella, was blown up by a terrorist bomb in Moscow, right outside the Kremlin, and I heard Dr. Botkin say, 'He was blown to bits, poor bastard, there was nothing left of him.' I suppose I remember it so well because Dr. Botkin never used that kind of language. Papa and *Maman* weren't even allowed to go to his funeral because of the danger.

After that it seemed everyone was tense and either shouting or whispering about the war with Japan and a railroad strike. Finally, after a lot of the shouting, Papa was persuaded to create the Duma. And he was determined to get back to his usual routine, to appear in public again so the people would know their world was stable. He wanted them to know they could count on him.

One morning in November he entered *Maman's* boudoir in breeches and shirt, lacking only his formal regimental jacket and decorations. His gaze fell on *Maman*, wrapped in a filmy dressing gown, lying on her couch, eyes closed.

'Alix. Get dressed. We must go.'

'I can't,' my mother murmured.

'Count Vladimir says you must do this.'

Count Vladimir Fredericks was a Finnish nobleman in charge of protocol for the court. No one questioned his decisions about dress, correct manners, or appropriate behavior. At almost seventy he was still handsome, and my sisters and I had heard plenty of giggling and whispered allusions to his success with the ladies. He was the repository of royal secrets in the extended Romanov family, and he kept us from making embarrassing mistakes. He'd told my mother the day before she had to make this appearance.

'But yesterday Alexei fell off the ottoman,' my mother

pleaded. 'Surely you see, Nicky, I can't leave him now.'

Alexei was two. He was a curious and eager baby, but his tumbles always stopped my mother's heart. Sometimes he could sustain a bump that seemed to signal disaster, but be fine, and other times begin to hemorrhage without reason.

'Alix, you must.'

'He struck his elbow. If he starts bleeding into that joint it will be agony. Don't you remember, Dr. Botkin explained when that happens there's no place for the blood to be absorbed and—'

'Alix, he was fine two hours ago at breakfast.'

My mother turned her eyes to him, pleading.

'You know the count wouldn't ask you...' my father began, trying to insist, but when his voice trailed off I knew he wouldn't. Once again my mother wouldn't appear, and there would be talk saying she didn't love her people, didn't care for the crown she wore. The silence in the pretty lilac room that was my mother's sanctuary grew tight.

'Papa, perhaps I could go,' I said, a little breathlessly, clutching my older sister's hand, 'And Olga too. She loves parades.'

Papa seemed to think for a moment and then called Count Vladimir.

'Your Majesty?'

'Could Olga and Tatiana attend the review... in the empress's place?'

The old gentleman took one look at my mother and knew he was beaten. 'Both of them, yes. That would do. But there's no time to waste.' He turned to Olenka and me. 'It will be a terribly long day in the saddle,' he warned.

It didn't matter, we saw *Maman* relax and almost smile with relief. We assured him we wouldn't let him down. And when we came to meet Papa, both of us in our uniforms of the regiments we'd been given at birth, all our sashes and orders of rank properly placed, we were rewarded again.

'You look beautiful, my bunnies,' Papa said with his warm weary smile. 'Now come with me and be grand duchesses.'

It was a grueling day. The weather was drizzly and we were damp in the first hour, but the troops' enthusiastic greeting and crowd's cheering warmed us and kept our backs straight. We went home proud and exhausted to find Alexei still happy and well. It had been a good day.

Somehow, as time went on, and even in a court that fed on gossip, Alexei's hemophilia remained a secret. I see now it created a kind of isolation around our family and within each of us. There was an odd theatricality to our lives. For days we listened to that little boy suffer, or lay awake at night hearing him moaning, not daring to mention it between us. It was a matter of fact that the routine of the palace went on as usual despite his afflictions. And each time he recovered from the latest hemorrhage, we played with him, laughed with him, teased him, and never spoke of his illness.

All of us would have done anything, given anything, to end his ordeal, but the doctors who streamed through the palace left us with the same grim prognosis. And then, hard as it is to believe, the simple and adoring Anna Vyrubova, the guileless darling companion of my mother, brought into our world a man who wore the guise of a healer and was in truth a destroyer. Grigory Rasputin.

.   .   .

Olga and Anastasia were playing cards, Maria and Alexei had set up an elaborate house of blocks with wooden soldiers on all the ramparts, and I was holding a skein of yard for *Maman* when Anna Vyrubova flew into the room unannounced.

'He's coming!' the pretty plump Anna exalted.

My mother dropped the ball of yarn. It was dark red and I remember vividly how it rolled across the floor, unwinding over the gleaming hardwood.

My mother raised her hands to her lips in a prayerful pose. 'When?'

'Tomorrow,' Anna said. 'I asked him and he said, tomorrow for tea. Just like that. I told you we were best of friends. And tomorrow you'll see it's so.'

Now we were all paying attention because we knew whom she was talking about. All of St. Petersburg knew of the humble Siberian *sterets* and healer, Grigory Rasputin. He'd appeared from nowhere and was said to be a devout and simple priest who could see into your very heart and know how God himself felt about you. Despite his humble birth he was the darling of every important salon in the city and hostesses gloated when he appeared at their social affairs.

Our little Anna was completely beguiled by him and claimed him as her personal confessor and friend. I was skeptical of this, even though I was ten. She was too simple a person to have such an important man as a friend. But now she'd managed the impossible, a small family gathering with the great man here at Tsarskoe Selo, and my mother was beside herself.

She'd heard about the mystical power of Rasputin's faith, but this wasn't what attracted my already-devout mother to him. He was a healer. And as she sat, listening raptly to Anna prattle away about every word the great man had said, I let my eyes fall on three-year-old Alexei and hoped that all I'd heard about this mysterious man from the steppes was true.

The next day Olga and I were kept after class by our German tutor because we'd been talking and giggling too much. Herr Weiss didn't take such breaches of his discipline lightly. But we'd been infected by the mood of hope that had emanated from my mother, and when we were finally released, we rushed down the corridors to the small parlor and came to a skidding stop. We caught our breath, straightened each other's hair, and made sure our dresses were in order. On the other side of the door we heard Alexei's laughter.

Jim Hercules winked at us. He was a powerfully built black man, and he attended the entrance of any room my father was in. Despite his grand Ethiopian costume he was an American, and had worked for our family ever since I could remember. He brought us jars of his mother's guava jam when he came back from his vacations at home.

We slipped into the room. Alexei was playing with his little spaniel, and Papa stood by the fireplace, teacup in hand. Anna was pouring tea. My mother sat on a sofa with a man in a dark peasant blouse and baggy pants tucked into a pair of boots so crude and worn I'd not seen the like even in the stables. But the amazing thing about the scene, and the reason it's so clearly etched in my memory, was the expression on my mother's face. She was smiling and nodding, eagerly agreeing with everything the priest was saying.

She saw us and beckoned. 'Come girls, come and meet Father Grigory. He's going to help your brother.'

Now the reason for her smile was clear, but as I crossed the room I stole a peek at my father. His expression was pensive.

'Father Grigory, my eldest daughter, Olga, named for the beauty in Pushkin's novel.'

Olga curtsied as she'd been taught.

As I waited for my introduction, I was assailed, repelled, by a terrible smell. It was a strong, dirty, unwashed stink, an animal odor emanating from the celebrated Siberian priest.

He held out his hand in something between a greeting and blessing of my sister, and I saw he was grimy, his nails black with dirt, his shirt filthy with grease stains and sweat marks. His hair was lank and unwashed, and his beard unkempt and full of crumbs from the muffin he'd been eating, as well as grease and bits of older food.

'And my second daughter, my Tatiana, who has all the loyalty of Pushkin's heroine, the sister of the fair Olga.'

This was my mother's standard introduction and as she

spoke I made myself meet our guest's gaze.

In that split second, when his attention fell on me, I had the sensation that his pale eyes were at once piercing and caressing, simple and cunning, dreamy and yet intent. But I also saw something else, something dark and predatory in the depths of his look that made me take a step back, and had *Maman* not been holding my hand, I'd have run from the room.

'She's your image,' Father Grigory said to my mother, 'a proud and regal beauty—truly the look of an empress even though she's a young and fragile flower... un-plucked.'

My mother nodded, pleased by his flattery of her and myself. But I heard menace in his words, and when he said unplucked, I was afraid of him. He smiled at me and I felt as if he'd touched me in a rude and probing way. He chuckled and returned his attention to my mother.

She sent Olga and me to get our tea while it was still hot, which released Anna from her duties. 'Isn't he magnificent?' the dumpy little woman gushed in a whisper. 'I always feel God's presence in his eyes.' Olga agreed and I felt strangely wrong. It was as if I'd done something bad because I'd found only darkness and fear in his gaze.

For the rest of the visit I remained as far from him as possible. But as the adults talked and my brother and sisters played, I found the priest's taunting eyes on me and each time I felt mortified, as if I harbored some evil secret he alone had discovered.

· · ·

From that day forward Rasputin was part of our household. No one except me, it seemed, saw anything but an innocent holy man.

Rasputin—I cannot call him Father Grigory as the rest of my family did—had tremendous hypnotic power. When he stared at a person they'd usually acquiesce to his will. A simple soul like Anna Vyrubova needed only to hear his voice on the phone and an expression came into her eyes that showed she was ready to do as he said. That he could hypnotize a small boy was no surprise. I don't think he ever tried to mesmerize my father and mother. That he could help Alexei was enough. He called them Mama and Papa to their faces, saying they were the mother and father of all Russia and her people. He fooled them with feigned simplicity, never letting the bestial look creep into his eyes when they could see. For them he was a saint, and Alexei the proof.

He burrowed himself deeper and deeper into their hearts, becoming so much a part of the family he was allowed into our nurseries and playrooms. Oh yes, he made mistakes. Outside the palace, in the social world of St. Petersburg, he was a rampant rogue. He roistered through the finest restaurants and salons, lewdly exposing himself in public, drinking until he vomited, and using language in front of one and all that shocked even the most accomplished roué. With women, all women, rich and poor, old or young, he had his way. Many were willing—to be his lover could make one famous. But some, the stories told, had not been willing partners.

My parents would hear none of this kind of talk. They had by then, in order to protect my brother, retreated so far from the real world that they were shielded from his perversions. If word of his actions reached them, they put it down to malign and jealous gossip. And if there had ever been a chance they would see him for the charlatan he was, Spala put an end to that.

. . .

When I was fifteen the country celebrated the centennial of the battle of Borodino, the burning of Moscow by Napoleon, and the eventual defeat of the French army. The emperor and his empress, as well and all the children including Alexei, had to be on display for weeks.

By then it was easy to see the toll Alexei's illness had taken on my parents, mostly my mother. If it's possible to have your heart break and still live, this is what happened to her. Her heart was weakening from the strain of watching her child in pain and knowing she'd been the instrument of his affliction. In addition, she suffered from sciatica.

My mother's strength was failing, bulwarked only by her indomitable will. She rationed it carefully, and always with Alexei in mind. Olga, Maria, Anastasia, and I knew we'd lost our mother years ago. Only for one little boy was her smile bright and her voice cheerful. Oddly, we didn't blame her or resent him as we might have. No one who'd seen him suffer could. In the subtly macabre atmosphere created by his illness and handicap, we drew together in tacit battle to protect him. There was never any kind of plan between my sisters and me, but somehow each of us found a way to do her part.

Olga, Papa's favorite, turned her efforts to keeping up his spirits. I did what I could for *Maman*, and she often said I fulfilled her wishes before she even asked. Anastasia, always the trickster, became Alexei's boon companion who played with him the boy's games he loved and she preferred. And Maria, the prettiest of us, helped him pass the hours he was confined to bed. She knew every card game, word game, and board game that could fill a long dull day, and even learned the war games he loved to play with his lead soldiers. I remember she always laughed and called herself General Maria.

We couldn't fix our little brother, though sometimes for a week, even a month, he seemed to get better. And the time of the centennial was a magical reprieve from his suffering despite the constant demands. Alexei took his place with us and reveled in the pomp-filled celebrations and long days. We appeared before cheering crowds who all seemed to adore their royal family. After the exhilaration and exhaustion of the events that had taken us from St. Petersburg to Moscow and the battlefield of

Borodino, we reluctantly, but also gladly, boarded our train for the peace and escape of Spala.

Spala was a place to play. It was a dim run-down old hunting lodge hidden down a long sandy road. Lights had to be lit all day to banish the gloom and the old furniture was comfortably worn. It was a refuge, a place far from our typical world. My sisters and I would run wild, playing in the stream that meandered through the yard, and venturing into the deep and protecting woods where we constructed forts and had secret places to dream and read alone.

Maman and Alexei went for rides in the car that usually ended in a picnic. And dear Papa would hunt with the locals and lesser gentry, all shabby at the heels but never without a fine gun and a good dog. After a day away from governmental and family demands, soaked in fresh air, he'd come home smiling and laughing to tell us about his adventures.

At Spala, Papa wore a simple uniform with a Russian tunic belted outside his trousers and old comfortable boots. *Maman* might go all day and never really dress. Shoes were regarded as unnecessary, not to mention hats, gloves, and parasols. Family was everything.

For three weeks we ran wild through the woods and invented games to play on the lawn with Alexei. He was eight that year and eager for activity. He could be imperious and insisted on being first; always the general, the tsar, or the fiercest Cossack. But his laughter was pure, often directed at himself, and it took him over completely. I saw too that when he played he tried to position himself so he couldn't see my mother, or whomever had been designated to be his watchdog that day.

Some adult was always there, *Maman*, Anna, or one of the loyal sailors who carried him when he was too frail to walk, reminding him to be careful, slow down, take it easy. And it wasn't that he intended to disobey the warnings; he simply wanted to avoid the concerned looks that always followed him.

He was a master at getting us so involved in his games we forgot to worry about him, but that one adult never forgot and he never stopped trying to pretend he was a normal boy. It might have made him irritable and sullen, but though he did have a temper there was too much sunshine in his spirit to turn him bitter. And at Spala we were all carefree children, just like him.

Then one day when my sisters and I came in from the woods a hush filled the old house, even though daily chores were going on as usual.

Anna met us in parlor. 'Your dear mother wanted him to get some fresh air, only a ride in the motorcar, just the three of us. But after a short time we saw he was in pain and we, your mother and I, tried to shield him from the bumps and swaying of the car as we returned, but the poor angel was suffering terribly by the time we reached here...'

The wildflowers Olga had picked for *Maman* slipped from her fingers. The bag of mushrooms Anastasia had gathered no longer seemed important.

'But he hasn't fallen,' Anastasia insisted. 'Not since the boat and that was weeks ago.'

'You know that has nothing to do with it,' Olga said gently.

'But it's not fair,' my littlest sister said, tears filling her eyes. 'He didn't even have fun. It's not fair!'

For eleven days Alexei grew worse. He was hemorrhaging into his abdomen and the joint of one hip. His knee drew up against his stomach to make more space for the blood in the joint but when that was filled the real agony began. *Maman* never left him, and I never left her. The doctors could do nothing, but no pain medications could be given. Finally, when my baby brother had begged God to let him die and then became so weak he no longer spoke, but only lay on his side, eyes half-closed, and moaned with each breath, my mother said they must find Father Grigory. And even I, as much as I hated him, wished him there to ease what I was sure was the final suffering of my little brother.

A telegram was sent to Siberia. Rasputin was finally tracked down in his home village. *Maman* and I waited at Alexei's bedside for the end we knew would come.

I can't remember wishing for his death. I do know I prayed for an end to his suffering. Papa was there with us through the nights but when dawn came the footman would arrive to call him. And I shall never forget watching my father rise from his knees to go out and meet his hunting companions. Squaring his shoulders and putting a horribly bright smile on his face as an actor dons his makeup, he made himself go through another day of denying his son's suffering, pretending he was simply on vacation.

It was Monsieur Gilliard, our French tutor, who brought the telegram from Siberia. And I know it by heart because my mother repeated Rasputin's words over and over, like a mantra, her only hope against the doctors' predictions.

'God has seen your tears and heard your prayers,' she whispered hour after hour. 'Do not grieve. The little one will not die.'

They gave him the last rites and as the priest chanted I watched my mother's lips as she repeated the words of the telegram, not the prayers. And then she sent the doctors and priests away. The telegram had also told her not to let them bother Alexei too much. With her little boy's hand in hers she continued her vigil. I too waited, and as the light of morning crept into the room, and my mother's lips continued to move in silent prayer, I saw my brother relax just slightly and draw an easier breath... And then another.

Miraculously, he survived; and slowly, very slowly, he got better. But he was now crippled. The leg never again worked properly. And this was another thing to hide from the world.

. . .

From Spala we went to the haven of Tsarskoe Selo near St. Petersburg. The Alexander Palace there was the center of our world, the base we called home. Here we could protect Alexei's now-permanent disability from the public, and Papa could still spend time in St. Petersburg fulfilling his duties.

At this point Alexei couldn't walk, his leg was still bent, and it seemed impossible that it would ever function again. Wherever he went he was carried by a sailor of the Imperial Navy, a companion who was to stay with him almost to the end. That he was a delicate child, people knew; but from the way he reveled in state occasions and always had questions for visiting dignitaries and potentates, it was the general opinion that his frailty was no more than a minor inconvenience he would outgrow.

The ordeal at Spala had affected my mother terribly. Her hair had become almost completely grey and she hardly walked at all. She and Alexei spent whole days on the divan in her beloved lilac boudoir reading to each other, chuckling and chatting together. He thought he was helping her pass the time while she was laid up with her bad back; and she, after the terror of Spala, was cherishing every moment with her son.

When she had to leave, she entrusted his care to his sisters. Olga was too sensitive to be much help; she cried too easily. Anastasia, encouraging him to get well, shared his complaints over the inactivity. Maria was still his bedside companion, and I was his night nurse.

When he was restless I sang him old folk songs, simple repetitive melodies that lulled him to sleep as I massaged his sore leg. He wasn't a complainer, but I could see him growing frustrated, waiting for this affliction to pass as he'd been told it would. He knew all the horses in the stables, their names, habits, and quirks. And he'd tell me which ones were right for me, and which ones he was going to claim for his very own when he was able to ride. Though I hated the lie, I hadn't the courage to dash his hopes of leading a normal boy's life. In those quiet hours when the rest of the family was asleep I'd sit beyond the glow of the light and listen to him spinning his dreams with silent tears slipping down my cheeks.

His world was so small, so restricted, and so guarded. But his tutor, Pierre Gillard, saw that his pupil was growing restive and angry, and it was he who convinced my mother to let him have some small freedoms to keep his spirits up. He was happier, but she grew more drawn and silent with worry. I wonder how she did it, how she let him sit on even a docile old horse, or tussle with his dogs.

Now Rasputin had her complete confidence. Whenever he was in the palace she seemed stronger, and when he was away she pined. She wouldn't believe he drank to excess, grossly exposed himself in public all over St. Petersburg, and consumed women like candies. She and Anna were his most devoted followers and I felt myself drawing away from them, disgusted by their blind adoration and inability to see past the mask of the gentle, self-effacing holy man.

'Tatiana, where is my pincushion?' *Maman* asked one evening as we gathered in the small parlor before the fire. Papa was going to read to us as he always did when he was home.

'Where were you this afternoon while I was with Papa?' I asked, quickly checking the usual places.

'Oh, of course! I left it down at Anna's little house.' Mother sighed, resigned, then cast her eyes over the piece she was working on and let it drop into her bag.

I knew that look. She needed a particular needle and didn't have it. She wasn't one to make do when it came to her crewelwork.

'I'll run down and fetch it,' I said, throwing my shawl around my shoulders. 'It will only take a moment.'

As I stepped toward the doorway to summon an escort, I saw Alexei frown. 'It's already late and it's time for *Robinson Crusoe*,' he said, disappointment in every word.

'Papa can start reading without me,' I assured him with a grin. 'I'll hurry back.'

Ivan the footman stood at the door and Papa gave him a nod of consent. As I slipped out into the corridor I saw that *Maman* was already sorting thread in anticipation of my return.

It only took about ten minutes to walk down the path to Anna's little house. It was sheltered in a birch grove just past the pretty pavilion around the curve of the oval pond, out of the palace's sight. Ivan had brought a lantern and we easily made our way. I remember I asked him how his son, who'd been suffering from a chest cold, was doing.

We stepped up onto the small porch and he knocked. To my surprise it was Rasputin who opened the door.

'I came for *Maman's* pincushion,' I said quickly.

'Come in,' he said as if it were his own home, taking me by the arm. 'Anna will be so glad of a little visit.'

I called a greeting to Anna and hurried to her, forcing him to release my arm. As I entered the tiny parlor I heard the door close.

'Darling Tatiana, so kind of you to come and see me,' Anna chirped as she disentangled herself from a heavy blanket she'd had over her knees and around her feet.

'This place is so terribly drafty,' I said, helping her up. 'It's a wonder you can stand it.'

'Oh, dear me, I don't mind one bit. When I'm here I can be of service to your mother at a moment's notice.'

'Tonight it's I who am to be of service,' I said, glancing around the small over-crowded room. '*Maman* left her pincushion this afternoon.'

'Oh, well, dear me, she was sitting right there by the fire. I always make her take this chair, it's so much better for her back. Now, where could it be... let me see...'

I spied it on the floor beside the chair. 'Found you, you sneaky thing,' I chuckled. 'No hiding from me.' I kissed Anna, insisting I had to hurry back and she not see me to the door but stay in the relative warmth of the parlor. I dashed out into the hallway.

Rasputin stood by the doorway in his dirty shabby cloak.

'Where's Ivan?' I asked, wary.

'I sent him home. His boy is ill.' A lazy smile curled his lips as he combed his beard with his fingers. 'I'll chaperone you back to your parents.'

'But I couldn't disturb your visit with Anna,' I insisted.

'We were all finished, and I'm looking forward to your father's reading. The tsarevich is so enjoying the book. His first time hearing it. Such a pleasure to share that with him.'

I had no choice. I clutched my shawl tightly around my shoulders as he opened the door with a flourish and called a cheery goodbye to Anna.

I was almost running down the path but he stayed my pace, firmly taking my arm.

'How thankful you must be that the tsarevich is getting better,' he said, reminding me who it was that should get the credit for that blessing.

'I'm very grateful for all you've done for my brother,' I replied, with the stilted and emotionless tact I always used with him. He chuckled and put his arm around my shoulders, enveloping me in his stink. I made a face.

'What, little empress,' he crooned, bringing his lips close to my ear. 'Do you not like the aroma of the people, the perfume of the children of the tsar?'

I closed my mouth firmly and said nothing.

He stopped and in two quick steps pulled me off the path and pushed me against one of the pavilion posts. 'You think yourself too good to talk to a simple healer?' he snarled.

Never in my life had hands been laid on me. I was indignant. I was a grand duchess and no dirty peasant was going to treat me like a recalcitrant dog. 'You call yourself a healer,'

I snapped. 'If you were truly endowed with the power you'd not have let him suffer for eleven days. Take your hands off me, charlatan.'

'Don't like my hands on you?' he hissed, banging me against the post. 'You think I've no power? You dare to call me a fake?'

The pincushion popped from my hand. Then he threw me on the flagstones of the pavilion and clamped his filthy palm over my mouth as he climbed on top of me.

His cloak was open and I saw he was almost naked, his torso and private parts exposed. He expertly rucked up my skirts and forced himself between my legs. When I realized what was happening and saw the pure fury and madness in his eyes, I was terrified.

He laughed softly as he entered me and gasped with the rhythm of his assault. 'Like doing your imperial mother herself. Now I know what it's like to fuck an empress.'

I tore my eyes from his reptilian mesmerizing gaze and saw, just beyond the ends of my fingertips, my mother's pincushion. I stared at that homey little object until he was finished.

'Now, little empress,' he said, venomous menace entwined with a syrupy sweet tone, 'you'll pick up your mother's pincushion. You'll take it to her. And you'll tell her nothing. And,' he added as he pulled me to my feet, 'you'll remember the price of your arrogance to the man who holds your brother's fate and your mother's heart in the palm of his hand. If you think you've seen your mother suffer, you're wrong. If you give me away I'll take from her the one thing she has left, the thing that only I can give her. Hope.'

He released me, and in a businesslike manner, put his clothes in order. I swayed to a pillar and only with its support was I able to stay on my feet.

'Here,' he ordered sharply, holding the pincushion out to me. 'Take this. Fix your hair and dress. If you dawdle they'll ask questions.'

Even before we entered the parlor the sound of my father's voice came to me. '"A little after this my ink began to fail me,"' he read, '"and so I contented myself to use it more sparingly, and to write down only the most remarkable events of my life, without continuing a daily memorandum of other things." And so ends Chapter Eight. Tomorrow we shall go on.'

There was a protest from Alexei and with the breaking of the spell of the tale the group noticed Rasputin and me standing at the door.

'Father Grigory,' my mother exclaimed with warm delight. 'Children, look who's come to hear your prayers.'

'You were a long time,' my father observed.

I stood, the pincushion in my hand, but could think of no words.

'You know what a chatterbox dear Anna can be,' Rasputin said with an indulgent smile. 'If I hadn't intervened, she'd have kept the poor girl the whole evening.'

'We thank you for rescuing her,' my mother said lightly. 'Anna is dear to me, but she does love to visit.'

I handed my mother the pincushion.

'What's this?' she murmured. 'It's damp here.'

'I dropped it. I'm sorry, *Maman*, I didn't mean to do it, but...' Tears filled my eyes.

'Tanushka, my sweet,' she reassured me, her eyes on the little peach-shaped orb, 'there's no harm done.'

'*Maman*?'

'Yes, child?'

Rasputin's eyes, mild and innocent as a babe's, fell on me.

'May I have a hot bath? It's cold out... I'm chilled.'

.   .   .

For the first time in my life, in a world where I was literally surrounded by people almost every hour of the day, I was completely alone. For all that I've painted a picture of my family as intimate and sheltered, we lived in a palace that required hundreds and hundreds of people to maintain it on a daily basis. The hallways and rooms were never empty. There was always someone going and coming, cleaning and repairing, or doing some service for us. Footmen stood at every door so we didn't have to open them for ourselves, maids slept in our rooms so our needs could be met at any hour of the day or night. The bustle of a busy establishment was something I took for granted and the comfort of all those people who smiled as they passed, or chatted and laughed in another room. It made you feel as if you were always protected and safe.

But now that shelter was gone. Rasputin watched me, enjoying my suffering and fear. He'd wink at me, or grab his crotch, once he even exposed himself to me when he knew no one was looking. My dreams were nightmares about Rasputin. I was haunted by the memory of his hands on me, the lust in his eyes, and his crawling, menacing, slithering voice. The more I thought about it, without the balance of the good counsel I'd usually sought from my family, I came to believe it had been my fault. If I'd been more polite, hadn't lost my temper, perhaps I wouldn't have angered him.

I withdrew into myself, let instinct carry me through the hours. Alexei was on the mend and during the day my focus was on him. I was trying to become invisible to scrutiny. But one day Olga teased me, saying that if I no longer wanted to be the 'Governess,' as they all called me because I usually took charge of things, she'd like to apply for the job. After that I began to monitor my behavior more closely and be sure I appeared to do as was expected, was normal, for me.

Then one morning my little maid chided me for learning to ride astride. She was a sweet thing and very traditional, so I smiled at her and said lightly that it was the modern thing to do.

She shook her head and replied that it was unladylike, it took away my femininity and that's why I'd missed my monthly flow. She warned me in her simple country way as she left with the laundry that if I continued with this masculine pursuit there was no telling what might happen.

I may have been brought up in the sheltered and unrealistic atmosphere my class dictated, but I was sufficiently worldly to know that riding astride didn't cause the cessation of menstruation. And I also knew what did.

My mind reeled, but I forced myself to keep my composure and went into the bedroom to get my French book. Olga was recovering from a hard cold and the smell of menthol drifted from her bed where she was propped up on pillows with a huge sensible handkerchief in hand. She snuffled hoarsely that I'd be early and Monsieur Gilliard would still be with Alexei.

I teased her and said I was going to the classroom to work because her honking nose blowing distracted me. She gave me a smile and a small lethargic wave as I left.

It felt like miles down the corridors to the schoolrooms. Everyone I passed seemed to see my terrible secret. I felt they were all staring after me, some shaking their heads in disappointment and others snickering in scorn. I was almost running when I reached the last hallways and burst into the quiet room, near panic.

'Oh!' Monsieur Gilliard exclaimed.

I froze. I'd expected time alone.

'Well, well, Your Highness,' he said with his gentle humor. 'I'm so glad you're eager to begin your lessons.'

Pierre Gilliard was not an imposing man. He was slight and soft-spoken, his features nice but unremarkable, and his coloring bland. His devotion to our family was unquestioned, and as Alexei's tutor he was party to his condition, making him a true intimate. Despite the fact he was just thirty years old, he was steady, dependable, and always calm.

'I thought you'd be with Alexei,' I stammered.

His forehead creased in a frown and he clenched his fist. 'The tsarevich has a caller this morning.'

'Oh, a caller,' I murmured, hardly paying attention.

'That filthy mountebank of a priest. You'd think now he's the darling of St. Petersburg he might at least bathe before he comes into the presence of the empress.'

It was the last straw. Rasputin was here in the palace this morning. I broke down completely. I cried hysterically, babbling terrified nonsense, begging this kindly man to protect me.

He led me to the window-seat, made me sit, and took a place a respectful distance along the bench. Then he waited, offering his handkerchief, until I had gained some control.

Smiling kindly, he urged me to tell him why I was so frightened. And I did. His evident scorn for Rasputin had somehow made it possible for me to trust him and I laid the whole nightmare at his feet, including my latest fear that I was pregnant.

When I'd finished, he sighed and began to pace the floor. Back and forth he walked, hands clasped behind his back, lips pursed, crossing and re-crossing the old Aubusson carpet deliberately and silently.

My eyes flickered restlessly over the carefully shelved leather-bound books in their grand cases, the maps and ornately framed landscapes on the walls. As the tall clock ticked, my heart pounded, and I looked anywhere except into what I feared would be the accusing eyes of Pierre Gilliard. I'd placed a huge burden on the slender shoulders of a very kind man, and was terrified of his opinion.

With a sharp nod of his head he stopped pacing, faced me, and steepled his fingertips. 'We must confide in Count Fredericks.'

I was instantly warmed by his use of the word we, but horrified at the suggestion. 'Please Monsieur,' I begged, my voice ragged and deep from weeping, 'don't make me expose my shame again.'

'Your shame!' He ripped his glasses from his nose. 'My God, your Highness, how can you speak so? That man is a beast. Everyone but your dear mother—God bless her, I understand her need—knows he's a wretch and a pig. I'll not allow you to feel ashamed. Do you hear me, your Highness? I'll not allow it!' He checked his emotion, restored his glasses, straightened his tie and collar, and smiled apologetically. 'Surely you see,' he went on, returning to his usual scholarly demeanor. 'The count is the only one who can help us. He's been covering up—' He stopped abruptly and his face flamed red.

'Scandals?' I asked, and managed a smile.

'He'll know what to do,' he finished with a small shrug.

'While you and I alone are completely ignorant,' I added, seeing the sense of it.

'He walks about this time,' Monsieur said, checking his pocket watch. 'Perhaps we'll take our literature out into the park this morning. It's cold, but clear, and fresh air will be good for you after spending time in your sister's sick room.' And suiting his action to his words he took up a book from his desk.

'Thank you Monsieur,' I said.

'No, your Highness, it is I who thank you for placing your trust in me. You've given me great honor by your confidence. I'll not fail you. Now, get your cloak. Our studies await.'

. . .

The count was where we thought he'd be and when we approached he was at first a little annoyed. He preferred to take his exercise alone. But he soon saw why we'd chosen to interrupt him. My debt to Pierre Gilliard grew as he explained my situation.

The count swore a few times under his breath and then turned his attention to me. 'Your Highness, I've never known

you to shirk your duty, and have often seen you grasp the importance of a situation when others didn't. If I may be so bold as to
speak my mind; I hope you see that this child cannot be born.'

I nodded. The disgrace to my family would be terrible, but
that might be avoided or at least dealt with by a trip abroad
and a convenient marriage. Worse, I understood that a helpless
little being subject to blackmail would inevitably become the
pawn of all manner of political and religious factions, not to
mention a powerful playing card for his or her father.

'I think, Your Majesty, you're coming down with something—something contagious. You were in Petersburg for the
festival three days ago were you not?'

'Yes, I was.'

'And you mingled with some of the participants?'

'Yes.'

'Then it's possible you've caught something that should be
kept from your siblings. I'll leave the details to Dr. Botkin.
And by the time he's sure you're not contagious, I think we can
have things properly arranged.'

I hunched in my cloak, engulfed in guilt, trying not to cry
again. I said nothing.

'I'm an old man, Your Highness, and have lived a grand
life. I've seen much, and you must believe me when I tell you
this is a thing you can and must overcome. You must put it behind you and go on.'

'I know, for the sake of my family,' I said trying to sound
brave.

'Yes, but more for yourself. He's a slinking coward and the
shame is solely his. Now, the courage must be yours.'

The three of us continued to walk; a shattered and ruined
princess and her knights; one a prim tutor with a moustache
and receding chin he tried to hide with a high collar, and the
other a rapidly fading charmer who knew too well the foibles of
mankind. And for the first time since Rasputin had grabbed

me in the darkness of the pavilion, I felt as if I might survive.

. . .

In two days I was sequestered in a suite not far from the count's, under the care of Dr. Botkin, who'd sufficiently scared my parents without causing them undo anguish. And I was prepared for a common and seldom-dangerous procedure with a skilled doctor and discreet nurse.

When they applied the ether I thought it would be a matter of hours until I saw them again, not of days. I'd been assured I'd be up and about in a week, when in fact it was a month. No one made a mistake. Things simply went wrong. When I was returned to my family I knew I was lucky to have survived and that I'd never have children.

Another level of deception was added to my life. The count, an expert at the art of dissembling, seemed not to remember at all the arrangements he'd made or risks he'd taken. When I saw him he chided me with a kindly smile to take care of myself and put on some weight now that I was better.

Between Pierre Gilliard and myself, however, our secret became a circumspect friendship, and I was the only one privy to his quietly ardent feelings for Alexei's nurse, Shura.

As I recovered I came to understand what had happened to me. Women who carried hemophilia had a tendency to hemorrhage more than others. My sister Maria had given my parents quite a scare when simply having her tonsils removed. And after my experience, it was clear that I too carried the same curse as my mother.

But poor Dr. Botkin, my third confidante, was beside himself and could hardly face me. He, after all, had been in charge of the operation and when it went awry, took all the responsibility. It wasn't until I was up and walking for exercise, more than a month afterward, that I managed to find myself alone with him in the park.

'You must stop blaming yourself,' I insisted. 'Thank God you'd been through it before with Maria. You saved my life.'

'But, your Highness, to take away the chance for you to have a child, such a sacrifice...'

'Look over there,' I said to him, pointing to our right. 'What do you see?'

'I see Princess Anastasia pushing the tsarevich on the swing, and your mother watching from her chair.'

'Do you know what I see?'

He shook his head.

'I see a little boy with his leg so badly damaged from his affliction he'll have to wear a brace to walk. I see a baby whose first word was careful. I see that laughing face twisted in agony for days and nights without end. I see my own son doomed to that terrible life, and myself broken and destroyed like my mother. I think perhaps you've given me the freedom to love, to marry, and find happiness in complete safety.'

He stopped walking and stared at me. 'But it wasn't certain. Your child might have been spared.'

'I couldn't have brought a child into the world with that sword of Damocles hanging over him,' I said flatly.

Dr. Botkin smiled with relief and patted my hand.

Alexei laughed with delight as the swing swept higher and higher.

'Careful,' my mother cautioned. 'Careful.'

TWO
TATIANA—1918

The beginning of World War I postponed the inevitable end of my father's reign—for a short time. The incredible outpouring of national support from the people kept alive his belief that they truly loved him and all he needed was a victory to restore their faith in the autocracy. Both he and my mother couldn't envision how their beloved Russia would manage without the autocracy's strength, though at seventeen I could see they were clutching at dreams. And the war, with the need for all Russians to put aside their differences and defend their homeland, restored their faith in the rightness of their fantasy.

The whole country was seized with patriotic zeal, and we of the royal family were no different. All four of us girls, as well as *Maman*, attended the Red Cross course and became nurses. This wasn't a ceremonial distinction like the generalships of regiments we'd been given over the years—this was the real thing. From the day the hospital opened in Tsarskoe Selo my mother was its most dedicated employee. To tell the truth, I think the hard work distracted her from the fact that Alexei had gone to the command post with Papa and was out of her sight. And I saw that after so many years of standing helplessly by as her son suffered, she was glad to be a comfort to other mothers' sons.

Olga, after only a month, couldn't take the stress of the wards and spent most of her time with the convalescents or doing boring administrative duties.

I found the time I spent with the recovering officers, as we weren't allowed to associate with the rank and file, little more than a social event without the pretty clothes and dancing. And though I received a darling French Bulldog puppy from one of the men as a thank you for my efforts, I soon decided I wanted to do more of the real work. So I left Olga to her recovering charmers and made my way back to the wards.

Maman was in the thick of the operating rooms, and after I discovered the anonymity of my uniform, I was back there too. One nurse in a grey dress with a white headpiece looks much like another. A doctor wants his orders filled. The face of the woman who hands him the scalpel or brings the bandage material is unimportant. Olga threatened to tell *Maman* because of the impropriety, but I reminded her not unkindly that when she'd been trysting with her Mitya, Dmitri, I'd kept her secret.

My older sister had been much in love with Papa's young cousin. He'd practically grown up in our household after he lost his parents and they'd known each other since they were small. I know, because she'd confided to me in tears one night that her adoration of Rasputin had caused Mitya to break off the romance. She'd been crushed by his refusal to see things her way, and it had affected her nerves.

From childhood we'd always been close. And though I'd never told her about Rasputin, we still understood each other and saw the changes growing up brought about. I was able to persuade her that my work with the doctors meant a great deal to me, and she agreed to say nothing. Though at the time even I didn't fully comprehend it was the ability to be taken at face value, not always bulwarked by name and rank, that gave me such a feeling of self-worth.

. . .

But the freedom given by my uniform had another side. When I was in the wards the patients spoke openly as if I were no more than a piece of furniture. I heard things about my father that were hard to bear, and as the war went badly for us and we were beaten on many fronts, the talk grew angrier. My father was characterized as a butcher. My mother, because of her German heritage, was an agent of the Kaiser trying to bring the country to surrender. And Rasputin wasn't only playing them both like puppets; the soldiers said he was sleeping with my mother! From a very few I even heard he used my sisters and me as his sex slaves. In this context, that the common soldiers saw Rasputin for what he was gave me small comfort.

And their talk did open my eyes to some truths. My father didn't know how to regain the military's allegiance, and my mother was utterly influenced by the Siberian monk. The fact they both loved their country meant little to men dying by the thousands. My father was the tsar, the emperor; he was supposed to fix things—if he couldn't there were those who said they could. These were the people my father referred to as terrorists, but they called themselves Bolsheviks, Mensheviks, Communists, Marxists, and all manner of other names that made them sound like members of some club rather than men who plotted to overthrow the government.

The political situation grew more volatile. My father was consumed by the war effort. Left in charge of the home front, my mother was pressured from all sides and consistently took the wrong advice. Only Rasputin and those who respected him, or pretended to, were within her trusted circle. Something had to be done.

That was when my cousin Dmitri, my father's own cousin and a Romanov (the same Mitya who'd cared for Olga) came together with Felix Yussoupov, a scion of one of the richest and most powerful families in Russia, to take matters into their own hands. They decided if they assassinated Rasputin the monarchy might turn its course from his disastrous advice and survive. They settled on the night of 31 December 1916 for his murder. But he wasn't that easy to do away with. Poison didn't work so they then shot him, clubbed him, and threw his sheet-wrapped body into the Moika River where it vanished under the ice. It was three days before he was found. The autopsy showed there was water in his lungs, proving he'd still been alive when he went into the frigid water.

When word reached my mother she was devastated and completely panicked. Striking out in terror, her fury against Felix and Dmitri was monumental. The one man who might have saved her boy's life was gone. She called for their deaths, insisting my father have them hanged. But Papa, in one of the rare moments he went against her wishes, didn't punish them severely. Dmitri, a soldier, was posted to the Far East, and Felix exiled to his family estate.

The rest of the monarchists hailed the pair as heroes. There was a veritable avalanche of advice and opinion that thundered down on Tsarskoe Selo, enveloping my beleaguered father in demands for action. Only one comment in that Brobdingnagian crush of words do I remember—from Monsieur Gilliard. When he was told the circumstances of Rasputin's death, I heard him murmur, 'The devil was hard to kill.'

My mother buried Rasputin on the grounds of Tsarskoe Selo, and truly mourned him. I understood the dread she now faced, but there was no sorrow in my heart for the rapist and liar. I did as was expected and attended his internment service with a solemn face. Across the grave, I met the eyes of Monsieur Gilliard, and saw the flicker of triumph in their depths. No matter how my mother felt I would bless Felix and Dmitri for as long as I lived.

.   .   .

About the second week of March, Alexei, Olga and I came down with the measles. Papa was back at the front and *Maman* threw herself into nursing us. We had high fevers and knew nothing of the events outside our sickroom for more than two weeks. When I began to sit up and take notice, just as my sisters Maria and Anastasia were getting sick, I laughed at Olga because she had a shaved head. She pointed out mine was the same. Our beautiful long hair had been sacrificed to the fever, as it was the custom to shave off the hair in these instances, though to this day I'm not sure why.

As we slowly recovered and became used to our bald pates, I saw that *Maman* was upset. Papa had abdicated. Knowing the war was in shambles, and afraid to rip his country further asunder with an internal struggle, my father had given up his throne. But what my mother couldn't comprehend was that he'd passed the crown on to his brother Michael rather than to his son.

She didn't understand that Papa knew he and she would be sent into exile, and that Alexei would be left alone in the hands of strangers. The thought of his frail son trying to survive without the protection of his family was something he couldn't face.

All the while she cared for us and prayed for Papa's return, *Maman* had about her a look of baffled mystification. Her world had been turned upside-down and she knew no way to right it. Her friends and advisors shunned her to protect themselves. And many of the servants left or took advantage of the situation to show their disrespect. The mobs in the city turned ugly and we were in a state of near-siege. We were officially placed under arrest, but that event didn't change things much. Ever since the disaffection of the general public, we'd lived in a circumscribed world. The guards inside the park kept strangers out, as always, but the fact there were now guards outside to keep us in made little change in our daily lives.

The thing that made me realize we'd turned down a completely new path was the day Alexei had to be told he'd never be tsar. *Maman* had tried for days but her courage always failed. The self-deceptions and fantasies she'd spun for him were based on his becoming well and taking the throne—to admit the end of one dream brought her too close to facing the end of another.

Finally, she persuaded Monsieur Gilliard to break the news to him. The unpretentious tutor had become a true friend and advocate for my brother, often risking my mother's wrath when he insisted Alexei be allowed to do more for himself and be more independent. He and my mother fought, but it was always worked out between them because they both had the interest of the same thirteen-year-old boy at heart.

When the professor left Alexei's room I was waiting and he nodded for me to go in. My brother was bewildered and downcast, but I did get a weak grin for my bald head.

'They might have left you a topknot,' he observed, hastily wiping his nose on his sleeve. 'Then we could have pretended you were a Cossack.'

I pulled my shawl around my shoulders and perched on the end of his bed where his little spaniel, Joy, was napping. 'So, now you know. Papa has given up the throne; and for you too.'

'He'd never do wrong,' Alexei said staunchly. 'He'll explain it all when he comes home.'

'I agree. Will you mind terribly not being tsar?'

He pondered my question like an old sage, and then said, 'It never seemed Papa had a such a good time being the tsar—except for getting to go on maneuvers with the troops. It looked to me like most of it was a bore, people always asking for things and telling him what to do. I don't think I'll mind so much not having to do that. But...'

'What, little brother?'

'Do you think when I get better, I mean really better, even my leg and all, I might be a soldier or a sailor?'

His eyes were so big and blue, his boyish hopes, despite his suffering, so simple and clean. It made me feel like a cheat, like a trickster, not to tell him the truth. But I backed down in the face of his dreams.

'That's a grand plan,' I said. And then added, rubbing my shaved head, 'Now that I no longer have to be a grand duchess, I'll be free to marry a Cossack instead of some boring old prince, and then I'll run away to the steppes and raise horses.'

He laughed. 'And I'll come and visit you and your Cossack when I'm on leave.'

Later that night I was awakened by a noise I don't recall. My little bulldog, *Tortino*, growled, and as I looked to where Olga slept soundly I realized the light in the room was far too bright to be cast by the flickering ikon lamp in the corner. Outside the windows there was a glow. I slipped out of bed, clutching my little brindle dog, to peek through the curtains.

There was a leaping flare of fire out in the grounds, and though *Maman* had tried to protect us from the frightening news of threats to our safety, the maids were always chattering about dire events. My first thought was that we were under attack, but the guards who paced below our windows showed no sign of alarm. They paused, watching the flames.

I cautiously opened the casement just a few inches.

'High time they sent that Holy Devil to hell,' the taller of the pair said.

'Wonder what the German witch will think when she hears the Bolsheviks dug up her lover and torched him?'

'He was a heretic,' the tall soldier admonished seriously. 'He belongs in the flames.'

They were talking about Rasputin! My eyes went to the glow of the fire and I realized it wasn't far from the small chapel where we'd buried him a few months ago. I stood there in the dark and watched until the fire burned low, feeling as if a chapter in my life had truly come to an end, and thinking the only kind thoughts I'd ever had, or ever would have, about the Bolsheviks.

. . .

As we left the sickroom behind and started paying attention, we could see hints of a new world. Our guards had been changed. The new men who walked the grounds were uncommunicative and hostile. If they gave us information it was usually some dire prediction we couldn't believe, or didn't dare to. Even after we'd gotten to know them, due mostly to Papa's diplomacy, we never spoke of anything important: only small talk about families, weather, and food. And I remember they liked the dogs.

Our friends and remaining loyal servants were all agreed it was only a matter of time until we'd be sent into exile. Papa had hoped the Provisional Government would let us go to Livadia, our estate in the Crimea. But when that option was denied, we were sure we'd be allowed to go to England. Papa's dear cousin would take us in.

Maman began to tell us wonderful stories about her childhood visits to England and how she and Papa had courted there under the indulgent eye of her grandmother, Queen Victoria. She also set us to sewing diamonds and other precious stones into our corsets and stashing them in other places a well. We poured paraffin into an ink-bottle, then filled the paraffin with stones, and even put ink into the top of the bottle so it appeared usable. We also made candles in biscuit tins, and hid diamonds in those, too. Our excuse for making candles was that the power to the Alexander Palace was very inconsistent since the Bolsheviks had taken things over. As we sewed, *Maman* declared she wasn't about to go into exile a pauper in need of a handout. Thus, with needles in hand and dreams of England, we wove our fantasy of hope and accommodation.

Through Monsieur Gilliard, who came and went in the

village of Tsarskoe Selo, there was always news of Royalists who wanted to effect an escape. Papa and *Maman* called this kind of talk foolishness and declared confidently there'd be no need for that sort of thing. It was necessary, they asserted, for the revolutionaries to make our lives a little difficult—just to keep face—but as soon as arrangements were made, we'd be on our way.

My father was deeply sorry that his dynasty had fallen. He carried the weight of failure personally, having been the one who marked the end of a three-hundred-year-old reign. But honestly, I don't think he minded not being the tsar. He wore only the simplest of uniforms and spent all the time he could outdoors, chopping wood, making plans for a garden, and even riding his bicycle around the grounds on good days. As we children recovered we went out to work in the garden with him.

Our lives weren't a picnic, and we had to mind our ways at all times. There were people in the new government who were ready at a moment's notice to execute Papa and send the rest of us to prison. But Alexander Kerensky, the man in charge of our daily life, was doing his best for us. He seemed to be able to convince those most against Papa to be more lenient and wait, while he did all he could to keep our lives as normal as possible.

But as the days of our confinement drew on, fewer and fewer friends were allowed, or had the courage, to visit under the eye of the government. They were all trying to make their own plans to expatriate to Europe. We were allowed the use of fewer and fewer rooms, our meals were bland and repetitive, the days long, and I looked forward to lessons. They at least made demands on us. Monsieur Gilliard set us on complicated problems to keep us occupied.

Then in August, when the garden was lush and we were just beginning to enjoy the fruits of our labor, it was announced we'd be moved. At first, we thought we were on our way to England. But Alexander Kerensky told Papa this wasn't to be the case. We were going somewhere else within Russia.

Poor *Maman* was weeping and silent the last night. Tsarskoe Selo, specifically the Alexander Palace, was her home, her sanctuary, where she'd raised us. Now she had to enter the unknown. She'd lost the drive and courage she'd shown during the war, and seemed to lose as well her concentration and grasp of the situation. She became overwhelmed and weepy whenever a decision was required, and soon simply gave up, turning to the comfort of her bible, fingering the lavender ribbons while the departure plans went on around her.

Olga and I had been checking lists all day, making sure every scrap of my mother's world that could come with us was packed. Books and trinkets, pictures and favorite furniture made quite a pile of odds, ends, and treasures in the vast central hall. But to poor *Maman* it represented only the barest little bits of the world she'd shared with my father, her prince, the only man she'd ever loved. It was the strength of that deep and passionate ardor they had for each other that kept her going. Without Papa she'd have broken down completely.

I sat beside her, my *Tortino* in my lap, and fondled his funny ears. He looked up into my face with his constant smile as if to say, 'Don't worry, I'm your friend and I'm here, everything will be fine.'

I wasn't so sure of this, and was grateful that along with some of our loyal servants, Shura, Dr. Botkin, and Monsieur Gilliard were going with us. *Maman* and Papa might not listen to talk of rescue or escape, still believing this inconvenience was no more than a step on our way to England, but Monsieur had learned things that made me doubt.

It was as if I was seeing my parents for the first time. And perhaps I was. The bright and safe world I grew up in was gone; Rasputin had taught me that lesson long ago. Now my parents had to face that same fact, and it was clear they were unwilling or unable to do so with any kind of valid perspective. They were from the privileged class, related to all the crowned heads of Europe, and the thought that this ordeal was anything but temporary was incomprehensible. Sitting there among the boxes and trunks, I vowed to listen to Pierre Gilliard and with his help, make an alternative plan.

Maman wiped her tears with a sodden handkerchief and watched Papa and Olga deal with a guard who'd decided it was necessary to open one of the trunks yet again.

'Such a pair those two,' *Maman* said affectionately. 'I wonder what he'll do when she marries.'

I was shocked that she could think if something so silly, so naively romantic at a time like this. And was bothered by the idea that maybe my plans for escape were just as foolish. But I kept my forebodings to myself.

In the dark hour before dawn they came to take us away and we were trundled rudely to the railroad station, our belongings treated with even less respect and care than ourselves. *Maman's* tears flowed afresh every time she heard the crash of a box or the splintering of wood as the few remaining bits of her world were hurled into a baggage car. As the train rolled out of the station there was talk we'd be back. I didn't believe it. And as we traveled we learned we were bound for the city of Tobolsk at the western edge of Siberia. Yes, the tsar and his family were being exiled to Siberia—not that anyone actually called it that.

·   ·   ·

Though some thought it a grand irony that we were sent to Siberia, Alexander Kerensky had carefully selected Tobolsk as his final good deed to our family. The railroad was two hundred miles to the south, thus putting it out of the path of revolution. It was a prosperous town, content with its lot, and its climate was good.

However, when we arrived after the train trip and a week

traveling on the river, it was discovered that the governor's house was in terrible condition. And so we were given a reprieve and spent a carefree week living on the boat, walking the dogs, and picking flowers in the late summer weather. When we did move in and the weather turned wintry, the room I shared with my sisters was frigid.

Pierre Gilliard took up residence in the city and came every day to tutor us. He was a great source of diversion for us children, though Olga and I were technically finished with schooling. He also became my conduit to a royalist group determined to rescue my family.

There were many Monarchist factions in Tobolsk. However, Monsieur Gilliard met with them and assessed their ability to help. He soon decided most of them were poorly organized or led by people with agendas that would place my father and Alexei in grave danger. He settled on a band who wanted the entire family out of the country completely. With no hostages to fortune, my father then could, in safety, begin a campaign to regain the throne. Gilliard agreed with them philosophically, and also because there was simply no question of my father putting any of us at risk.

It was at this time that I met Nadezhda Osipov and her grandfather, Kuzma. Both of them had found work in the house itself, Kuzma as a handyman and Nadezhda as a cleaner. It was she who met with me and we began to formulate a plan. I, of course, had to take my father into my confidence, but we agreed to say nothing to the others. He was sure this was all an unnecessary exercise, and I often heard indulgence in his tone when we spoke of the plans. But I didn't care, as each day passed the depth of the trouble we were in became more and more clear to me, and the only person who seemed to understand was my newfound ally.

Nadezhda was resourceful. Her education wasn't deep, but in matters of deception and perception, she had skills

I'd never dreamed of. She seemed to know, simply from a slight conversation, who could be trusted and who couldn't. She could talk her way out of, or into, anything she wanted. And there was one other thing about her, discovered by Pierre Gilliard before she came into the house, that made her my perfect co-conspirator—she bore a twin-like resemblance to me. So much so that on some occasions we'd switch places so she could walk in the yard with Papa to exchange information while I, in her garb with a scarf to cover my shorn head, scrubbed the floor in her place. Even Olga, who knew me so well, walked by more than once without even noticing it was her sister kneeling on the tiles.

My parents vetoed every plan that separated us from them. Finally, it was Nadezhda who thought of using my sisters' and my short hair to disguise us as boys, all orphans and novices, being taken from one monastery to another by a goodly priest and his wife.

The battle between the Bolsheviks (Reds) and Monarchists (Whites) was consuming the country and swung radically through different districts, neither side making conclusive progress. Stay where we were, or make a move, we were in danger. At least out of our prison we had a chance. But once free of Tobolsk we had to present to both sides an innocuous face, and for that Nadezhda's plan was perfect. Even my mother, forced by Papa's frank words to face things she'd been denying, was willing to consider this option. We even started the preliminary arrangements. But just as things were taking shape Alexei became ill. This was one of those times when there was no warning, no event to cause the hemorrhage; the bleeding just began and hours later, he was in agony.

This was the first time Nadezhda had witnessed a disease like his. Our secret was out, and though it was still simply referred to as 'an illness' in the house, my brother's suffering could no longer be hidden. Nadezhda hovered around outside his door worrying so much the guards became angry with her and barred her from the house for several days.

Then everything fell apart. Our jailors decided we must once again move. There was no consideration for Alexei—the guards simply insisted Papa had to leave. Finally, though I know it tore her apart, my mother chose to go with Papa. Alexei had to stay behind under my care, with Olga, Anastasia, Monsieur Gilliard, and Shura to help. On 26 April 1918 my parents and Maria left. I was in Alexei's room when they went and didn't even get to say goodbye, as he'd finally fallen asleep holding my hand. All my parents could do was silently bless us both from the doorway.

From that day forward I felt the weight of responsibility. Anastasia was bored and Olga weepy without Papa to bolster her courage. The real patient, accustomed to inactivity, was probably my easiest charge. And as he mended, his other sisters could do more to help him, and I finally got some respite.

One morning early in May I'd left Alexei playing checkers with Anastasia. Olga was napping in the parlor as she'd stayed up late reading to him the night before. After I'd checked in the kitchen to see what we might concoct to tempt his appetite I slipped into the room I shared with my sisters. My loyal little *Tortino* leaped into my arms, licked my face with his sloppy tongue, and made no complaint about how I'd neglected him.

'Oh, my sweet boy,' I whispered into his fur. 'What should I do without your love?'

The door opened and I braced for another crisis with my sisters or a rude confrontation with one of the guards. But when I saw it was Nadezhda my hopes soared.

'You're back!' I whispered, jumping to my feet, *Tortino* clutched against my chest. 'Do you have news? I only know they arrived in Ekaterinburg two weeks ago.'

'I've heard from my grandfather,' she assured me as she drew off the blue glasses she wore to keep others from noticing our resemblance. 'He passes in and out doing errands for the guards. Everything is censored.'

'That's why *Maman's* letter didn't sound like her. What did Kuzma tell you?'

'They're installed in the house of a merchant named Ipatiev. It's said he was given one week to vacate the premises. As soon as he was gone they erected a high fence around it. Your family will be in two bedrooms and a dining room on the second floor. The guards on the first.'

'What else?'

'They're not kindly treated, but are unharmed. And they're very closely watched, even as they move about between their rooms. And...' She shrugged, folded the blue glasses against her hip, and let herself be distracted by a few books beside the door. 'What are you reading now?'

'Finish it all,' I commanded.

She sighed, still not looking at me. 'They've painted over the windows with white paint.'

'Why ever for?'

'So no one on the inside can wave or signal to the outside.'

'Now we're truly going to prison. We've lost our chance.' I sank to the floor weeping and rubbed my cheek against *Tortino's* brindle fur.

Nadezhda dropped to my side and put her arms around me. 'You mustn't despair,' she said. 'We're already making plans. People are already there.'

The door burst open and Anastasia ran in. 'Alexei's bored and so am I. Checkers is stupid. Where's the chess set?' She stopped and peered at me, then came closer. 'Tatiana? Are you crying? Is it Papa or *Maman*? Is it? What's happened?'

'Hush, little princess,' Nadezhda chided. 'Don't make such a fuss. Your sister's only tired from all her nursing and has a headache.'

'Tatiana never cries,' Anastasia said with great assurance,

'not since that time she was ill. Not even when I mashed her fingers in the door.'

'You slammed her fingers in a door?'

'Not on purpose!' Anastasia laughed.

Nadezhda smiled at my capricious sister. She might be seventeen, but she'd lost none of the rowdy enthusiasm that made her so dear and such a good friend to her brother.

I wiped my eyes and got to my feet.

'You two look so much alike,' Anastasia said. 'It's a little eerie, you know, like a—what's that thing Monsieur was reading about in that tale? A dop- dop-'

'Doppelganger,' I supplied.

'Are you a ghost, Nadezhda?' she teased, her fears forgotten.

'If I were a ghost,' Nadezhda said dryly, 'I wouldn't be scrubbing floors for a living. I'd go about in a fancy gown of the latest Petersburg fashion.'

'Ah, but then we should never trust you.'

'Why not?'

Anastasia quoted the old proverb. 'The devil is always dressed in the latest fashion.'

'Not always,' I murmured, as the other two laughed.

'Anastasia!' an imperious voice came from the sick room. 'What's all that giggling?'

Anastasia picked up the box with the chess pieces. 'I'll tell him you're a ghost, Nadezhda, come to haunt us,' she laughed as she left the room.

I went to the window and saw Monsieur Gilliard and Shura sawing wood, as the tutor and my father had done almost every day. And I thought, what's the point? Soon there'll be no one to keep warm.

'Is what Princess Anastasia said true?'

'About what?'

'That you never cry?'

'There's no point in it, is there?' I watched Monsieur

Gilliard stacking the wood to be split, struggling with its weight. 'You learn that very quickly, when you're alone and no one comes.'

'I can't imagine your mother and father ever allowing you to cry alone.'

'Oh, I was in the care of someone they trusted. Someone they believed would never hurt me.'

'What is this? What are you saying?'

I got a grip on my emotions and set *Tortino* in the bed. 'Never mind Anastasia, she was a child then. It was nothing. I was ill but also growing up. She simply associates the two things together. Nothing more than that.'

'You're lying,' Nadezhda snapped. 'I thought perhaps we knew each other. But I see now it's only the accident of the looks.'

'No, no,' I said, taking her arm as she turned away. 'It's just I've never had a friend. Only my sisters. And then…'

'You were left alone with this person of trust?' she asked. Her eyes, darker grey than mine, questioning. 'And because of this person they're separated from you. I see that. You love them, but there's always a reserve, always a distance, a door that remains closed.' She studied me for several moments before she spoke. 'Was this so dark a shadow?'

'The devil reached out and touched me,' I said softly. 'Within the lights of home he laid his hands on me, used me, and left me unable to denounce him. And then he mocked me for it every day.'

Nadezhda gave a curt nod. 'And this rapist, did he leave you with a child?'

For a moment I wanted to deny what she'd guessed. But then I looked out the window, at the spring sunshine, the pile of wood.

'Yes,' I admitted. 'But I did have a friend. And he's never let me down.'

She came to stand beside me. 'Such a proper little man,' she said as she watched my tutor and the sweet woman who'd been a part of our family since Alexei was born. 'No one would guess the courage that abides in him.'

'I had an... operation,' I told her, 'and it went wrong. I almost died. There will be no babies for me. The one blessing from all that hell.'

'Not to have children?' Nadezhda was a little shocked. 'Why is that a blessing?'

Alexei crowed with victory in the next room and Anastasia called him a cheat and demanded another game.

'I carry that disease. That's why I almost died. But at least I'll never bring such a curse on an innocent child.'

'It's terrible the way the tsarevich suffers,' Nadezhda murmured, and her eyes went to the ikon corner of the room as she crossed herself.

'He has hemophilia,' I said flatly, never having uttered that hopelessly appalling word aloud in my life. 'And one day it will kill him. He'll go on like this getting more and more crippled, or bump his head and become an imbecile. Sooner or later he'll die, probably in agony. And all we can do is stand by and watch.'

'This is what has broken your mother's heart and puts such sadness in your father's eyes.'

We embraced.

'And now you must tell me your secrets,' I said with a weak smile, trying to lighten the somber mood.

'My secret? Oh that's easy. One day I shall learn English and know so much about you I'll take your place. I shall become the grand duchess and you'll clean the floors!

'And will I get to live with your dear grandfather and become a fearless guerilla fighter like you?'

Nadezhda smiled as she thought of Kuzma Osipov, who'd raised her alone. 'Oh, well, then I guess you must stay a princess. I couldn't give up my grandfather, even for all the diamonds you have hidden in your corset!'

. . .

From that day forward I had a friend. And though we had to be very careful about how much contact there was between us, it lightened the load of my responsibility to know Nadezhda was there. It was a blow to me when she disappeared.

I was told one day she'd no longer be coming and could probe no more. If she'd been arrested by the Bolsheviks I might make trouble for her with my inquisitiveness. Monsieur Gilliard knew nothing either. He was now closely watched and strictly avoided anyone working for our freedom.

The last communication I'd received from my mother was completely noncommittal but reminded me to take care of the patient as she'd instructed. This had nothing to do with my brother but was a reminder to dispose of the jewels she'd left in our care in the proper manner. This we'd already done. And as Alexei's health grew slowly better I didn't know which I dreaded more, going to join my parents or remaining in Tobolsk without them.

Not that it was ever my decision. One afternoon we were informed we'd leave that night and told to pack only what was easily carried. We left the governor's house with little more than clothes, books and the dogs. Then we were jammed into the back of a truck for a bumpy two hundred mile ride to the railway.

When we reached the station, I put Joy and *Tortino* into Anastasia's care. Olga had charge of Alexei, and the guard who had grudgingly agreed to carry him. I tried to be sure all our things were loaded on the train. But before I could count, we were unceremoniously shoved into one car while Monsieur Gilliard and Shura were put in another. They waved at us, smiles on their faces and we returned their casual salutes. What did it matter if we could not travel together? They would be there at the end if the journey, just as they always had.

Then, as the train pulled out, Anastasia spotted several of our boxes still on the platform and threw herself at one of the guards, insisting they'd forgotten our things. He knocked her back against the seat, laughing at her desperation, enjoying her panic as yet another piece of her world slid out of reach.

When we arrived at Ekaterinburg we were hustled off the train. I was carrying *Tortino* and lugging a huge suitcase down the platform. It was raining and we sank into the mud to our ankles as we walked. The guard carrying Alexei was none too careful, but I could do nothing for my brother and was proud of him for his stoicism. Anastasia had his little spaniel under her coat, protecting him from the rain. I'd seen that Monsieur Gilliard and Shura were being kept on the train, but was sure they'd be with us soon. We slogged up the streets and despite the weather people stopped to stare. From every window and doorway a shadowy face peered at us, curious and hostile. When I saw the tall fence around the Ipatiev house, my heart sank and I had a powerful urge to drop my heavy suitcase and run.

And then, right at the gate, I saw Nadezhda. She was wrapped in a shawl against the wet and the raindrops on her blue glasses sparkled in the lantern light. She flashed me a grin and it gave me courage. My brother, my sisters, and my parents were depending on me. I kept walking.

. . .

As soon as we reached the top of the stairs my mother snatched Alexei from the guard, weeping and thanking me repeatedly for taking care of him. I was stunned by her reaction, until I realized she'd never expected to see him again. But then I also realized she was making this display of affection and weakness right in front of the gawping guards; paying no attention to their derisive comments, his handicapped state, or their pointed discussion of her pretty daughters. And in the moment when I'd been about to cast my responsibilities off on my parents, I saw they were no longer capable of carrying them. We were truly prisoners.

In only a few days my worst fears were confirmed: my parents had given up. But in the terrifying boredom of the Ipatiev house, who did not? The painted windows created a constant fog, and in that fog our bored jailers tormented us. Papa was tentative, thin, and pale, the polite smile on his lips never reaching his eyes. My mother wept constantly and patted us often, eyes vacant. She hadn't even the strength to keep up appearances. And we had lost Pierre Gillard and Shura — they were denied entrance to the house.

We couldn't lock the bedroom doors. Some days the guards left us alone for hours, others they escorted us from room to room, even to the lavatory, and took great pleasure in our mortification when we had to face the lewd drawings of my mother and Rasputin they'd scrawled on the walls.

It was the imbalance that was so nerve-wracking. Sometimes they listened to our every word, others grew suspicious if we were silent. There was nowhere to find an hour's peace, no respite from the constant uncertainty. And if a precious moment of solitude happened, knowing it couldn't last took away the courage it might have brought. We passed the days reading Tolstoy, Pushkin, and Turgenev aloud around the dining room table. *Maman* sat in a straight-backed chair by the window and read her bible, lips moving, her fingers twisting the lilac ribbons whenever one of our jailers came too close.

It was four interminable days before I could speak to Nadezhda alone.

'They call it The House of Special Purpose,' she murmured.

'Is that a bruise on your cheek?' I whispered.

'I scrubbed that filth off the walls in the bathroom and one of those pigs didn't like my work.'

'Oh, my friend, you mustn't take such risks.'

She shrugged. 'Gilliard is still here, but they're trying to make him leave. Except that because of the fighting there's nowhere to go.'

'We hear guns sometimes.'

'They're still far away. I must visit with your father. Today.'

Eyes locked on the open bedroom door, we crouched in a corner and exchanged our clothes. Then I took up the scrub brush while Nadezhda slipped down the corridor under the guards' noses to my parents' room.

As I scrubbed, the guards chatted with each other and checked on my progress from time to time. Oddly, I felt brave pretending to be Nadezhda. But as the clock in the dining room chimed through forty-five minutes and I stayed on my knees fulfilling my look-alike's job, I became more and more worried. Then I realized she was waiting for the guards to be called to their dinner, the one time of day we could be sure of a respite from their scrutiny. When she returned her face was set, almost angry. She began to remove her clothes.

'Change back into a princess,' she ordered when I hesitated. 'That's all you can do.'

I pulled off her jacket. 'Why are you angry?'

'Your mother has given up. And your father won't force her or leave without her.'

'They'd rather die than be separated,' I said.

'And what about you, your brother, and your sisters?' she hissed. 'They sentence you to death as well. Can't they see if only one of you lives it would be a victory?'

'We're all they have left,' I pleaded as we finished our exchange. 'You must understand, it would break their hearts to lose us.'

'If you were my daughter I'd rather break my heart, I'd rather die, than take you down with me.'

'There's still time. Perhaps when Alexei is better.

He's progressing.'

'Slowly,' Nadezhda said as she took back her blue-tinted spectacles. 'Too slowly.'

'We'll have to wait and hope. Are things ready?'

'Yes.'

'Then it's all we can do.'

She sighed, giving in. We embraced and she took up her bucket.

'You did a good job on the floor,' she quipped.

'Any work is better than the boredom of this dreadful house.'

She stopped at the door, humor gone. 'My grandfather says this is a place the devil wants for his own.' We both turned to the ikon corner and crossed ourselves. And when I was alone I looked into the calm eyes of the Virgin for a long time, but no prayers came.

.   .   .

Not unlike my overwhelmed mother, I slipped into a kind of lethargy. I felt surrounded by a barrier of problems for which there were no solutions. My parents were too afraid to act, the war between the Reds and Whites encircled us, and the trials of daily living became a burden too heavy to carry. Only when Nadezhda and I were alone did the weight lift from my shoulders. Somehow, she made me smile at the cruelties of the Bolsheviks and usually brought me word of Pierre Gilliard, though she dared not communicate with him directly. He, along with Shura, was still stalling, not wanting to give up hope we might yet be reunited.

June grew hotter, and because we weren't permitted to open the windows, our rooms were stifling. We weren't allowed much time in the fresh air, and within the palisade it was almost as hot as inside the house. But we did try to get the poor dogs out every day. During these times our jailers took particular pleasure in taunting us. My sisters didn't want to subject themselves to the insults, so it was Nadezhda who walked with me.

We made sure we accentuated our differences; her dark glasses and my short hair. I also wore my one white lacy frock (Nadezhda joked it was my last royal costume, and when it was gone, I'd be a commoner like her) and she kept herself in thick coarse peasant clothes. We didn't try to fool the guards by switching. Nadezhda was superstitious, afraid our luck might not hold when it came time to deceive them in earnest. I didn't argue, but deep in my heart I was sure it didn't matter; we'd lost our chance.

But suddenly, one night—I believe it was the 4th of July—things changed. Our guards were replaced with Magyars, and though there were difficulties in communication because of language, they were kinder and much less vigilant. We were even allowed to open some windows in the evenings. And with these tiny improvements our spirits rose. We began to talk again of escape. But *Maman* worried about accommodations for Alexei and herself, as they were practically invalids.

Nadezhda devised a plan. I'd assume her persona and leave with Kuzma at the end of the day to meet with the partisans and see the arrangements for myself, so I could allay my mother's fears. Then, in the morning, we'd simply switch back.

Nadezhda was looking forward to being a princess. Though she did point out she wanted another chance to do so when she wouldn't be a prisoner, and be able to order people about and attend balls. Papa laughed and swore she'd have a ball of her very own where she'd dance with princes and wear all my jewels. 'And they'll not be sewn into a corset,' I added.

So, on the evening of 18 July, when Kuzma left his tools in the kitchen, it was I who appeared with Nadezhda's bucket and rags. Her dark glasses covered my eyes and my short hair was hidden under her scarf.

I placed my equipment where it belonged, rinsed out my

rags and brushes, and walked across to the back gate. There, with my heart pounding so loud I was sure the sentry could hear it, I presented Nadezhda's papers and was waved through the gate by a guard who couldn't have paid me less attention.

I was completely unprepared for the moment I breathed free air for the first time in sixteen months. I heard the thudding clank of the bar closing the gate behind me and wanted to leap in the air shouting for joy. In all those months I'd never thought about the depression of confinement, but when I looked up and down the street and realized I could turn either way at my own whim, I almost wept.

'Child,' Kuzma Osipov murmured, 'we can't stand here gaping about. No one is allowed to linger along the palings.' I remembered myself and took his hand. From there he led me along the streets, turning and crossing, until I was completely confused. The city of Ekaterinburg is built on a cluster of low hills along the eastern slope of the Urals, and my parents' prison stood atop one of the highest. Kuzma taught me to get my bearings by looking for the roof of the Ipatiev house.

We entered the quarters he and Nadezhda had rented when they arrived. They'd been carefully chosen and were well placed near the edge of the city center but not in an area where the coming and going of people would be something to notice. Here, in clean sparsely finished rooms, grandfather and granddaughter had been the message center for the Royalists.

It was a street of working people. The fact that Kuzma and Nadezhda were employed at the Ipatiev house had at first made them celebrities, but now that luster had faded and we got only friendly disinterested greetings as we went to the market to find food for our evening meal. Kuzma had wanted to go alone, but I reminded him he always went with Nadezhda, and we should be ourselves. Later, as I began to cook for him he became upset, saying it wasn't proper. But it did lighten his mood when he had to explain each step of the preparation; I'd never done cooking of any kind before. By the time we'd managed to get the food on the table, the tension of our status reversal had eased.

The long summer twilight set in, the hour when our visitors should have been arriving. No one came. We waited in the warm semi-darkness. A small lamp burned to signify we were there and awake.

When the church clock struck two, I said, 'They're not coming.'

'It's late, but perhaps they've been delayed.'

'It's too late... I'll not have time...'

Kuzma made tea.

We waited.

And when it was almost time for us to be at work, we walked to The House of Special Purpose just as he and his granddaughter had done every morning for almost three months.

.   .   .

We were stopped across the street by a man and his wife who also worked in the house. She cleaned the guards' quarters and he was one of the cooks. Their heads were close together as they spoke.

'They're all dead!' he gasped, his voice barely a whisper.

'No,' she insisted. 'They took them to another place. That's all.'

'But we heard the guns,' her husband reminded.

'The bloody Whites killing good Bolsheviks, his wife hissed. 'They took them away in a truck. I saw it.'

'Where did they go?' I demanded.

'Those pigs, those Magyars, say nothing. They only laugh because we're out of work.'

I lunged for the street but Kuzma pulled me back. 'Think... child.'

His grip on my arm was light. It was his eyes that held me. We walked back down the block, as if we might go home. But I stopped at the corner.

'From the first, Olga never liked Nadezhda's and my charade,' I said urgently. 'She was terrified something like this would happen, and we'd be separated. She swore to leave me a message if they were taken away! I know where to look!'

'What if the cook's right?'

'What if the wife is?'

'I'll go. You stay here.'

'You've no reason to leave the first floor where your tools are. I do.'

I felt certain I could go into the house, find Olga's note, and come back easily. And I was determined.

Kuzma relented. 'I'll go with you. We always went to work together. I'd not leave Nadezhda alone, especially when things are confused.'

'I'll tell them I left something upstairs yesterday. I must get into our room for a few moments.'

'One hiding place?'

'Three. In the back of the bureau drawer, the leg of the screen, and in the cushion of the chair, but that one's harder to get to.'

He carefully removed my dark glasses so he could see my eyes. 'We'll do everything we can. I see now you're in control. I see too you're bent on your quest. But do not tempt fate.'

'I'll not tempt fate. I promise.'

He slipped the glasses back over my eyes and we went past the couple on the corner.

I felt completely in control, that I knew exactly what to do. In Nadezhda's outspoken style I said, 'Grandfather, all my things are there. My good brushes, my feather duster, all my rags. Should we starve? And what about your tools? We must now find new work. You'll need them.'

He nodded and we walked firmly up to the gate.

'No work today,' the sentry said in broken Russian. 'No

work no more.'

'We need our things,' Kuzma appealed. 'We'll have to find other work. We need our things.'

For a moment the guard studied us, then shrugged. 'Don't be long, old man. And no stealing.' He laughed. 'Not much to take.'

We went into the kitchen and snatched up his toolbox and Nadezhda's bucket. I stuffed the rags into it and we hurried up the back stairs. Everything was in disarray. There were boxes and trunks half-packed, food still lay on the table in the dining room. We could hear some of the guards downstairs talking and joking; they sounded a little drunk.

In the doorway to the room I'd shared with my sisters, where Nadezhda had spent the night as a princess, I paused. In the half-light created by the painted windows it looked like a mist had settled around the house. It was so oddly vacant, and yet everyday things were still there. The ink-bottle where we'd hidden diamonds was neatly on the desk, the drawers of the bureau had been left open and Anastasia's nightgown trailed from one. Olga's last pair of gloves was on the floor.

'Move,' Kuzma urged me softly.

I snatched the ink-bottle and went to the bureau. On the top was a diamond-filled homemade candle, which I also stuffed in my bucket. The message drawer was in place, but when I felt behind it, there was nothing. As I knelt beside the heavy screen I heard Kuzma overturning the large chair. My fingers prized out a chip of wood and exposed a small cavity—it too was empty.

'What's this?' Kuzma asked. He held in his hand a leather box about three inches square.

'They wouldn't have gone without this,' I breathed. I stuffed it into my pocket.

'And they wouldn't have gone without leaving you a note if they could. The place behind the drawer was easy to reach and not discovered. Perhaps they just had no time.'

We both looked to the ikon corner where the lamps had guttered. The dim face of the Virgin gazed down on us.

'Mother of God,' I whispered. 'Help them. Help me find them. I've taken this man's granddaughter. We must find her. Please. Help us.'

I quickly examined the other rooms for something, anything that would tell me where they'd gone. My mother's small bible was on the table and I reached for it, but jerked my hand back at the sound of heavy footfalls in the stairs.

As we stepped into the hallway, a sweaty Magyar, uniform shirt open and bottle of vodka in his hand, reached the top step.

'You! Cleaner girl. Come. Bring the bucket.'

'We were told there was no more work here,' I said.

'One more job,' he said with a snicker. 'Get the old one to help, and lots of soapy water. Royalty! Pigs!'

Unable to do anything else, we returned to the kitchen. I filled my bucket. Kuzma hid the ink-bottle and candle in his toolbox, then filled another bucket and got a mop. The soldier pointed down the stairs to the half-basement; the house was built on a hillside. 'Clean it up. We killed a pig in there last night. It was a real celebration.'

We started down the stairs. I smelled the stench of blood before we got to the room, and when we entered I was transfixed. The whole place was saturated in gore; walls, floor, even the ceiling was spattered. On one wall the plaster had fallen as if it had been chopped off and was mixed with the blood. The floorboards had gouges in them that looked like they'd been made with an ax, and blood puddled in the grooves.

The soldier gave Kuzma a shove. 'Get to it old man. It has to be done by noon.' Then he sat on the steps sipping his vodka. Kuzma took my hand and his pale eyes found mine. There was no choice. We went to work.

It was past noon when we'd cleaned up the worst of the mess, but there was no getting the stains out of the plaster or the floor. There was now the smell of bleach and carbolic soap over the blood, but the damp odor wasn't pleasant. We stepped out into the yard to empty our buckets for the last time. Red-stained water still stood where we'd dumped several before.

The guard slouched in the doorway. 'Now go. And remember, it was pigs that were slaughtered here. Only filthy pigs.'

We stumbled away, supporting each other. I concentrated on moving my feet and keeping a grip on the smooth handle of the bucket. Kuzma had made it for Nadezhda and it was a work of art—curving handle and fine wood slats so well placed it looked like it had been carved from a single piece. I could hear the soft clink of Kuzma's tools, the tiny squeak of the bucket handle, and our ragged breathing. His hand over my fist led me onward. We crossed the wide street and made our way down the block. I know there were people we passed but I remember none of them. On we went, step after step. When we finally shut the door to our rented rooms behind us I sank onto the floor by the dead hearth. Kuzma stood, his back against the wall and his head fallen on his chest, eyes closed. It was stuffy in the small room, and very still. In the distance I could hear the faint booming of guns like distant thunder.

Kuzma sank to the floor with a sigh. Our eyes met.

'They were in that room,' I whispered. 'I know they were in that room.'

He shook his head, not wanting to believe.

I held out my clenched fist and opened my fingers to expose a ruby, large as a walnut, glowing red as blood. It caught the sunlight and a rich flash of color danced over its faceted surface.

'I covered this with leather and made it into a button for my coat,' I told him dully, my eyes on the gleaming stone, 'I thought myself a very clever little seamstress.'

'And my Nadezhda was wearing that coat.'

'I found it in the corner, between the baseboard and the wall, under a paste of plaster dust and...'

In the silence that fell between us we knew there would be no priests to chant the mass for the dead over the bodies of our loved ones, no last kiss, and we weren't qualified by love alone to speak the proper words.

The old man turned his eyes to the ikon corner and his lips began to move in a prayer I knew well. It was a simple blessing to put someone into God's protection.

I shifted until I was beside him and together we began our mourning.

'He shall give his angels charge over thee, to keep thee in all thy ways. They shall bear thee up in their hands. He shall cover thee with his feathers, and under his wings shalt thou trust.'

THREE
NADEZHDA—1918

The next thing I remember is a dream. It's one I still have, and as it still does, it woke me weeping. I'm on my hands and knees, beside me is Nadezhda's bucket, her brush is in my hand. I'm scrubbing up the blood in that room of horror. I see the striped wallpaper pocked with bullet holes, and smell the stench. But as I scrub, exhausted by my endless task, the blood keeps welling up through slashes in the floor and I can't clean it up. I scrub and scrub and weep for the people I loved.

It was evening, Kuzma was puttering around the fire. The sticks and charcoal under the pot snapped and crackled. Then I smelled a wonderful borsht, rich with the fragrance of vegetables and garlic.

I sat up and dried my eyes. In my hand was the leather box Kuzma had found hidden in the chair.

'I'm so hungry,' I said with a yawn, setting the box in a small table beside the couch where I'd been sleeping. 'Is it ready?'

Kuzma spun around, eyes wide, and the ladle clanked on the stones. Almost tiptoeing, as if he were afraid to disturb someone, he came to kneel beside me and looked so intently into my eyes I was frightened.

'What is it?' I stammered. 'I'm sorry, I fell asleep. Not the right thing to do on such a day, but... Kuzma, what is it?'

'I thought you'd never speak again,' he murmured. 'It's been three weeks.'

'Three weeks! What three weeks?'

'You remember nothing?'

'I remember praying with you...'

'That was three weeks ago. Since then you've not spoken a word, and wouldn't let that leather box out of your grasp. About ink-bottles and candles full of diamonds you didn't care, only that box. You did as I instructed like a puppet, but your eyes were vacant and you never smiled. I was afraid I'd—'

He stopped, tears filled his pale blue eyes, and he smiled through them as he patted my cheek.

'I'm sorry, Grandfather,' I said, speaking for the first time the name Nadezhda had always used. 'I wouldn't have worried you for the world.'

'I was afraid it had unhinged you, that the Virgin had taken your mind because you couldn't face the pain.'

I felt terrible. I'd caused his precious granddaughter's death, and then he'd feared that I too, her image, the only comfort he had, was also gone. I threw my arms around him and wept.

'You were just resting,' he said, patting me on the back and stroking my hair. 'Just resting.'

'Would you like to see my treasure?' I asked, putting the box into his hand.

He pressed it back into mine. 'You show me.'

'This was a gift from my father to my sisters and me the Easter before the war, the work of the master Faberge,' I explained as I opened the box to expose a green jade egg nestled in black velvet. In the smooth surface of the jade lay a tiny flower with four white petals and a jet center. I took the egg into my hand and pressed the flower catch, it opened the long way and revealed four tiny bunnies curled together sleeping in a nest. One was red, one blue, one gold, and one brown jade—all had jet eyes. I took them out and each, in a different pose, sat on the rough table by itself.

'But they don't look like they could stand alone,' Kuzma

marveled. 'When they're in the nest they seem as one.'

'He always called us his bunnies,' I murmured, swamped in the warmth of memory. 'He always said how much he loved his little bunnies.'

'And he always will,' Kuzma said gently.

I nodded and put the little rabbits back in their nest, closed the egg and set it into the safety of the box. 'It's all I have now,' I sighed, closing my hand over the scarred leather.

Kuzma put his gnarled fingers on mine. 'Things aren't memories. Those they can never take.'

For a moment I was drowned in the loss of my past, and then I looked into the clear and strong eyes of an old man who refused to give up. I got up to serve the soup, insisting he sit at the table. And when I'd set a hot fragrant bowl before him and we both had good dark bread in our hands, I asked what had passed while I'd been hiding in my mind.

'The Whites took Ekaterinburg.'

'When?'

'Eight days... after...'

'Eight days. Had the hand of fate been stayed for only another week we might all have been saved.'

Kuzma shook his head in denial. 'Both sides can call themselves what they please, but they're no more than brigands. And the little tsarevich would have paid the price of their ambition and greed.'

'That's why you didn't go to them about me.'

He looked down at his work-worn hands. 'I couldn't give up a child to strangers when she wasn't able to defend herself. But if...'

'I don't want other than what I have,' I assured him honestly.

He went back to his soup and I to mine. We'd decided. We'd take care of each other now. We'd share our past grief and whatever came of our future.

'Is it safe in Ekaterinburg now?'

He shrugged. 'Safe enough for some. But I think not for you. We have to go.'

'Where? I've been taught of all the places on the globe. But I've no idea how to find sanctuary in my own country.

'Here in the south, near the railroads, it's not safe.'

'Will I be a danger to you?'

He patted my hand and smiled. 'You're simply my grand-daughter. You always have been. You can see that by our family picture.'

I turned my eyes to fireplace mantel. There was Nadezhda's treasured photograph of herself and her grandfather. She stood at his shoulder looking straight into the camera, proud and sassy. It was my face, but I was sure I'd never had that spark of confidence in my eyes. Kuzma sat in a photographer's fancy prop chair, no pose, no pretense, simply a weathered face and a slightly mischievous gleam in his pale eyes.

He rose and took up the picture. 'She was the partisan. She was the one who had to do something,' he mused. 'I was happy to work with wood, do little jobs for money, and share her days. But she was fearless, and so determined. Since she was a child she was sure she could bend the world to her will. No one could have turned her from her purpose once she found her cause.'

'She was more an empress than I ever was. But then, I was raised to be pliable and polite.'

'Nadezhda said you were the only one who had the courage to make the plan work.'

'I don't like to dither and squabble. If there's a clear path, that's the one to take. If there's a choice, nothing will happen unless you make it. But I don't think it's courage.'

'And now you'll choose the life of an old man?'

I smiled. 'I'm in good hands.'

He nodded.

'But, where will we go?'

His face changed, his eyes grew bright, as if he had a delightful secret to tell. 'Have you ever wanted to see America?'

I'd met a few Americans. They'd seemed awed at first by the titles and formality of our little world of royalty, but when they relaxed I was taken by their confidence and self-esteem. They'd nothing but their own achievements to fall back on, and got along well without the props of title and required deference. They had the ability to laugh at themselves and at each other, to make light of foolish things but not necessarily brand a person a fool for doing them. But more than that I'd taken from them the opinion that America was a place where hard work and determination was rewarded with success. No one needed a title, the sponsorship of the tsar, or now a Bolshevik, to get ahead.

My vision was, of course, quite naïve, formed at a time when I knew nothing of the world. But when Kuzma spoke of his idea, I realized I needed to leave Russia behind if I truly wanted a new start.

'How will we get there?' I asked. 'If the trains aren't safe, how should we go? We have money. The jewels.'

'If you're willing, I'll sell one or two of them. But only small ones, such as a man like me could come by, and not all to the same person at the same time. We'll get just enough for an old man and his granddaughter to make their way north out of this war, and from there to safety. And perhaps along the way I'll teach you to cook.'

'You've been planning.'

'I'd have taken you even if you were still... We would have left as soon as the forty days were past. I couldn't go without a proper farewell.'

I felt a chill that turned to a flicker of hope. 'You know where they're buried?'

'Ekaterinburg is a small town. People talk. If a soldier did something he's proud of he'll brag about it when you give him vodka. It was an ugly story, but in the end I knew where they'd been taken.'

I sat beside him. 'Tell me.'

'Here's what I pieced together. They shot them all. In that room. No warning. They weren't easy to kill, the bullets seemed to bounce off your sisters. Some said they were protected by angels.'

'It was only the stones in their clothing. Nothing could have saved them.'

'Even your little dog, the smiling one with the ears of a bat, died there.'

'And Alexei's sweet Joy?'

'No. He was spared. The Whites found him half-starved in the house. And I saw him in the arms of the little tutor with the soft eyes when he left.'

'Monsieur. But why didn't Joy come to us?'

'He was probably hiding. The smell...'

'So there was one survivor of that charnel house. Go on.'

Kuzma squared his shoulders. 'When they were all dead, Botkin and the companion as well, they loaded them into trucks and took them out to a remote mine called the Four Brothers. There they stripped them, took the jewels the women had been hiding, and threw the bodies into the flooded mineshaft.

'But, as I said, people talk and soon it was all over town. So, with the Whites bearing down on the city they had to move them. I was there, at the Four Brothers, when they came. I hid and then followed. It's not far. The bodies were destroyed— burned, then buried. No one will find them now; unless someone again gives away the secret. And I think the Bolsheviks made sure there weren't many left who might do that.'

'Can we go there? Can we make some kind of marker?'

'There's a small stand of birches not far from where they lie,' Kuzma said. 'But I'd not like to get closer for fear of exposing them.'

We Russians have always believed, stemming from old pagan times, that our ancestors inhabit birch trees. We plant them on our graves. And I felt satisfied, as did Nadezhda's grandfather, that if we went there to pray our loved ones would hear us. There had been no funeral, but we could be there on the fortieth day to say our farewell, when their souls departed for heaven.

'You're right,' I agreed, instantly seeing the validity of his feeling. 'Let them rest. I shudder to think what kind of spectacle might be caused if they were found now.'

There was no more to tell, no more to say. I broke the ink-bottle, and after giving Kuzma some stones, re-hid the remainder—along with the great glowing ruby—in a second candle we could take on our journey without comment. And, over the next few days, Kuzma crafted me a box with a false bottom in which to hide my precious egg. I stuffed the box full of underwear and other small items.

Over those days we heard the gossip confirmed; anyone with the name Romanov was being slaughtered out of hand. Kuzma had been right to keep me hidden. We also decided there was no chance we could go west into European Russia and then on to America that way.

In the more cosmopolitan cities and towns there'd be questions, checking of papers, and people who knew my face. We decided to go east. Kuzma, who'd been born and raised in Yakutsk on the banks of the Lena River, knew how to make his way through the vast taiga across the thousands of miles that stood between us and the port city of Okhotsk, where we could cross the North Pacific to the American west coast.

By taking a northern route, using the soon-to-be-frozen Vilyuy River as our road, we could travel unmolested. We felt confident from what we'd learned that no Bolsheviks or bureaucrats would be interested in the slim pickings of the north and much less in a poor old man and his granddaughter working their way home to Yakutsk.

Plans made, we began securing our equipment for the

journey. No one was surprised we wanted to leave and no one cared where we were going—they were all too busy doing the same thing. We bought warm clothing, and I insisted on a wolf-lined cape for Kuzma against the cold weather. He was no longer young, and while we Russians are accustomed to the intense cold of our winters, I'd heard Yakutsk was the coldest place of all.

The initial overland trip from Ekaterinburg to Turukhansk was the most daunting. We'd be going on horseback and sleeping outdoors. After that, we'd get space on a winter river coach and let the ice of the frozen watercourses be our road, making the trip much easier than in summer. As the days passed and we came close to our departure date, I had a good feeling about the future. To tell the truth, I found the whole idea of trekking across Siberia exciting. It was a transition to another world, another life. And because I was in the hands of a man I trusted, I felt no fear.

· · ·

On the fortieth day, we left before dawn and made our way by a circuitous route to the wooded boggy area where my family had been buried. I wouldn't have noticed, but Kuzma pointed out the signs of activity the Bolsheviks had carefully disguised. Here a broken branch, there a scratch in the soil, that told of the passage of trucks and men. He also showed me the seemingly innocent circle of grass, fallen trees, and moss that hid what had once been charred earth.

We entered the stand of birches. The leaves were soon to turn and there was a faint kiss of fall in the air. The rising sun bathed the spot in a thin gold light. From within the shelter of the trees we could see the burial site.

Again, neither of us knew the correct words of the *panikhida*, chanted by the priests in church Slavonic no one learned anymore; so we repeated the prayer we'd said that terrible day when we first knew: 'He shall give his angels charge over thee, to keep thee in all thy ways. They shall bear thee up in their hands. He shall cover thee with his feathers, and under his wings shalt thou trust.' But this time it was said into the gentle morning wind. The rustling leaves seemed like a choir humming along with our incantation.

'Do you think I might speak directly to your parents?' Kuzma asked. 'It isn't appropriate, I'm a common man.'

'I think you're who my father would like to have been,' I told him honestly. 'A man who cared for his family and did his job.'

Kuzma walked a few paces to face the rising sun. I set my back against one of the larger birches, and as I looked up into the flickering leaves, said my farewells. With my warmest love and remembrance, I kissed them each in my heart. And then I spoke to Nadezhda. 'I can never repay what you've given,' I said. 'I can only make two promises. First, I'll never leave your grandfather as long as he lives. I'll love and care for him as I know you would.

'Second, I won't squander your sacrifice. In all my life as a grand duchess I was as much a prisoner as when you met me. The strictures of my station, and the secret of my brother's illness made of me a woman who lived her life in careful speeches and measured truth. But now I'm free, with only the name of my hero, the one I now bear, to live up to. And that, dear friend, I will do. I don't know what my life will be from this day forward, but I'll make it count.'

Kuzma and I made our way back to our rooms and shared *kutya*, a Ukrainian dish made of rice and raisins with honey, which is traditionally served after the service to commemorate the dead. Then we quietly went about our packing.

Our biggest concern would be the next two months. It was now the beginning of October and if the rains came early we'd have terrible traveling conditions—the roads would turn to viscous mud and bog down the horses completely. But we'd determined to leave Ekaterinburg. Neither of us wanted to stay a day longer than necessary. The next morning we loaded the horses and then went back into our rooms so Kuzma could remove his ikons, always the last thing to go. Before he took them down we faced them and prayed for a safe journey, then he slipped the little triptych into his saddlebag and slung it over his shoulder.

With his hand on the knob he looked at me with defiance and said, 'I'll not sit down in this place of death. I never want to return.'

I felt the same. To observe the tradition of sitting down for several moments before beginning a trip, to ensure that one day the traveler would return, was impossible. I never wanted to see Ekaterinburg again.

But when we'd ridden several *versts* into the country I did look back. Perched on its hill stood the Ipatiev house, The House of Special Purpose. Only the roof and the top of the palings were visible. Grand Duchess Tatiana Nikolaivna Romanov had died in that house as surely as had all the rest of her family.

It was Nadezhda Alexandrovna Osipov, granddaughter of Kuzma (Alexander) Osipov who rode away from Ekaterinburg that cold bright morning. I turned my back on all the world I'd known, sure I'd never hear of it again except as a footnote in history, a thing to be gossiped about as all royalty is talked of, for the rest of my life.

.   .   .

As we were clear of Ekaterinburg, a shroud lifted from our spirits. We looked forward to the next bend in the road and hill to climb. Our horses were sturdy and not without some spirit, so I was able to show Kuzma I did have some skills for the trip.

I'd never been on my own before and the simplest tasks

were new to me. Though I could now cook a bit, I'd no idea how to create a whole dinner with only one skillet. In the world of my childhood, food simply appeared, cleaned, peeled, and cooked. Every meal I'd ever had out of doors had been a picnic served by butlers and maids on fine china and snowy linens. I'd never washed a dish, carried wood, or given a thought to where the next one would come from. I'd simply known it would be there. And while I was embarrassed by my ignorance it brought Kuzma and me closer together as he taught me the ways of the road. We had money but avoided all inns and towns of any size; the inns were verminous and dirty places as well as being gathering points for soldiers and curious fellow travelers.

I came to call Kuzma *Papasha*, as he was now my father and mentor, and he called me Nadia, giving me the name he'd used when Nadezhda was small and he'd had to teach her everything. As she'd grown older she'd insisted he use her full name, but as I was now the 'child' in so many ways, we fell into the new names with ease. And I think it gave us our own identity for this new life we were living.

By the time we'd reached Turukhansk we were ready for an end to outdoor living. Winter arrived in earnest and we were glad to begin our journey along the Vilyuy by sled.

In summer the roads in Russia are dry but choked with dust. In the fall and spring, rain makes them virtually impassable. But in winter, travel is a delight. You skim over the snow on singing runners, no jolting ruts and dust, like flying. There are almost no paved roads in Russia—the climate's too hard and there are too many rivers to span. But in winter all problems are solved and the barriers created by the rivers vanish. They become the highways. Wrapped against the cold we sailed over the now frozen water, rushing toward a new life.

Little did I know, when I finally came to America, that I would be alone.

FOUR
NEDDY—1920

I pulled my cloak more securely around my shoulders and strained my eyes toward land, or where I knew it to be. Somewhere in the thick fog and drizzle Okhotsk straggled along the eastern shore of Siberia at the edge of the sea that bore the same name. I couldn't see the city I was leaving behind, nor the simple marker that showed where my last link with Russia, and my only friend, lay buried.

It had taken almost two years to make our way to the port of Okhotsk. When we arrived weary and triumphant in July of 1920 it was a simple matter to arrange our papers and purchase tickets on the trading ship *Bering Princess*. In two weeks we'd depart for Alaska and then go on down the coast to Astoria in the state of Oregon. We'd talked about staying in Alaska, but Kuzma had heard that in Oregon the weather was so warm it seldom snowed, and he'd had quite enough of the arctic.

For me, I wanted to escape the memories and constant worry that were a part of my Russia. There was no future in a country where my very name was now a crime punishable by death. I wasn't so reactionary as to think another autocracy was a good idea, but there had to be some middle ground if I were to have any hope at all here. Under the Bolsheviks the pendulum had swung too far the other way.

And I think Kuzma was ready to leave Russia behind, too, for more compelling reasons than the weather. His losses

grieved him. He was glad to leave his graves, marked and un-
marked, behind. But then, as we left the shop of a venerable
Chinese gentleman who'd bought some of our precious stones
to give us money for our trip, something caught up with us that
knew no politics, boundary lines, or emotions.

Inexorable time. Kuzma began to have difficulty breathing.
His color faded from robust to grey in a matter of moments. He
was always so knowing and competent I'd never thought about
him growing old. But as I sat beside his bed in our rented room
I saw age snatch away his dreams. And when I asked him how
old he was, he told me he'd been born in the very middle year
of the reign of Nicholas I, the tsar who'd sent the Decembrists
to Siberia. This meant he was eighty.

When he saw me realize this, he smiled. 'My time has come,
Nadia. Don't be sad.'

'No, no, we'll just postpone our sailing,' I insisted. 'And
when you've rested... then we'll go. There's no hurry. When
you've rested... then we'll go.'

He silenced me by laying his hand over mine on
the coverlet.

'This is no time to pretend, child,' he said gently. 'We've
come too far.'

'What will I do? How can I go on without you?'

'Because you were spared,' he whispered. 'You were saved.
And surely the reason for that wasn't to spend your days in this
dingy port when our dream is so near.'

'I'll go, *Papasha*,' I whispered and forced a smile. 'I'll go to
that place where it doesn't snow and the winters are warm.'

'You must live now for yourself. You must take the place you
were meant for.'

'But how will I know? How—'

'You'll feel it.' He touched my chest with one finger. 'You
will feel it here.'

I kissed him.

'Now child, while there's time, fetch that grand and wonderful cloak you gave me.'

'Are you cold?'

'Bring it. I must show you.'

I did as he asked and he fumbled with the heavy fur but couldn't handle the weight.

'In the pocket,' he said breathless from his labor. 'There on the side. I meant to give them to you on the ship. When we were free of this cursed country. I meant them for a new beginning.'

I dug in the voluminous garment and found two squares wrapped in oilskin.

'These?'

'From your father and mother,' he said, and I saw satisfaction in his eyes. 'Open them. You'll see that an old man is smarter than a Bolshevik sometimes.'

In one package was a small photo album. And I instantly knew without having to open it and see the pictures of my sisters and brother, *Maman*, my Grandmother, Monsieur Gilliard, Dr. Botkin, and Shura, and even the dogs that it was the keepsake my father had made for himself to take to the front when the war began.

'He was such a great keeper of pictures,' I said, slowly turning the pages, caught in the good memories they brought. 'He loved to sort them and make books for people. I remember him doing that in the evenings.' When I came to the end and turned the last page, I saw Kuzma had added the picture of Nadezhda and himself into the book.

'Now we'll all be with you,' he said with satisfaction, and pointed to the other package.

I knew, even before I had the wrapping completely off, what it was. I saw the lavender ribbons and knew it was my mother's bible, the one I'd been afraid to pick up from the dining room table back in Ekaterinburg. It was small and dog-eared; my mother had always kept it near—on her night table, in her sewing bag, or beside her divan in the lilac boudoir. It seemed, as I kissed the cover, that it even smelled of her favorite perfume.

Clutching my two treasures I laid my head beside Kuzma's and he stroked my hair.

'I'm tired,' he murmured. 'I'll sleep.'

In an hour he was dead.

. . .

I found him a resting place where there were some trees and fine boulders. And though his coffin was simple, I'd wrapped him in his wolf cloak to keep him warm for the forty more days his soul had to stay in Russia.

On the prescribed third day after his death I stood alone at his grave and listened to a priest who'd never known him rush through the service. The words rolled impersonally off his lips, correct in detail and inflection but without a drop of caring. He was doing a job. And as I watched him hustle away I held my mother's bible to my chest and repeated the prayer Kuzma and I had said for those we'd loved and buried together in the birch grove. Only then did I feel the service was complete.

It was a good day for this time of year. The waters of the bay were bright blue, and on the far horizon was the majestic rise of the Kamchatka Peninsula, smoke from its towering volcanoes making banners across the sunlit sky.

'I was safe under your wings,' I told Kuzma. 'And now I'm alone. You've set me a hard task.'

I stepped to a boulder and sat in the chilly sunlight. I removed from my pocket the small leather box that held my father's Easter gift, comforted by the four bunnies sleeping together, cozy and safe in their green egg, keeping each other warm. And then I took into my hand another Easter gift. I don't recall the name of the tiny village where Kuzma and I spent our first Easter together, but it was one like all the others along the Vilyuy. What I do remember is the beautiful little church, hand-built by a colony of Old Believers, where we waited in the snow holding candles for the priest to open the doors at midnight and say Christ is risen. It was the first time in my life my father and mother weren't there to give me the three-fold kiss and speak the simple phrases that marked the most important holy day in the Russian Orthodox faith. Kuzma had put his arm protectively over my shoulder as he said, 'Christ is risen, Nadia.'

'He has indeed, *Papasha*,' I replied. And then, into my hand he slipped a gift. It was a small perfect wooden egg, carved to look like tall grass, and protected within its nest slept one rabbit. The egg and its inhabitant had been cut from a single piece so the bunny was always safe inside its seamless bower.

Putting the treasures safely away, I left the hillside and forced myself to finish the preparations for my departure. And I walked firmly up the gangplank of the *Bering Princess* three days later vowing to make the best of things.

· · ·

As soon as the ship left the shores of Siberia behind, I was too busy to feel sorry for myself. The *Bering Princess* wasn't large, but she was certainly not the smallest vessel that plied a regular trade from Alaska to Siberia, Japan, and America. There were eight passengers besides myself and every one turned out to be a poor sailor.

While I was still saying a final farewell to Kuzma and we'd barely cleared the harbor, I saw one woman turn green and lose her lunch. She was followed within hours by all her fellow passengers except me. And this was while we were still in the relative shelter of the Sea of Okhotsk. When we came into the northern Pacific things got worse. The weather grew rougher and the ship wallowed in the troughs and fought its way to the crests. My nursing skills, more aptly my strong stomach, from my hospital days was all that stood between those eight people and complete chaos.

While the crew battled unending storms, the cook and I teamed up to keep the cabins clean and their occupants as comfortable as possible. But it wasn't until we'd spent almost four weeks of constant labor and made our way to the relative shelter of the Aleutian Islands that I even had time to look about me. We came into the harbor of Unalaska Island storm-battered and exhausted, but with all hands and passengers alive and relatively unhurt.

I stood on the deck in the bright cold, taking in one of the farthest reaches of my new home. A small port of low buildings hugged the shore, the only level spot in sight. Many of the buildings were stout *izbas* bearing the stamp of Russia in their brightly painted window and gable trims. Others, newer American additions, mixed companionably among them. To my right stood a small white Orthodox church with its unmistakable onion-domed spire. Directly behind the town was a dormant volcano, huge and green, yet treeless. About halfway up there was brilliant snow in the depressions. After so many days below deck in the worst of conditions, I welcomed the air and open vista of America.

From Unalaska the *Bering Princess* traded her way along the Aleutian Chain into the Gulf of Alaska and I was able to rest a bit from my duties. The passengers departed as we went along and were replaced with more seaworthy folk.

I spent as much time as I could on deck awed by the landscape that slid by day after day. I'd been in magnificent country for almost two years, but this was incredible. Huge mountains rising from the sea at their feet, clustered about small harbors with low and storm-worn houses clinging to the very rocks when the winds blew. Some days the skies were so blue they glowed against the forbidding scarps of rock that pierced them. And all this majesty was made small by the fury of the northern Pacific in a storm.

Though I was technically in America, the reminders that

sixty years ago all this had belonged to Russia were constant. The names of ports and the buildings were as if I'd never left Siberia. There were onion-domed churches and cemeteries with all the graves bearing Cyrillic characters on the crosses. I often heard Russian spoken in the streets. It gave me an odd sense of unbalance. I'd left Russia behind, but not quite. And though there were certainly more Americans than Russians to be found, they all had the same weathered look and were dressed for the elements. This was a place where only a fool allowed fashion to replace function.

Our progress was plodding, and it was the middle of October when we hove to beyond the mouth of the Columbia River. Astoria, Oregon was just ahead, but we had to wait for an experienced bar pilot to take us through the treacherous entrance to the river itself. When he finally came aboard after twenty-four hours, it seemed quite simple for him to guide us past the treacherous shoals and sandbars he knew so well, while our captain, who had bested the worst the north Pacific had to offer, was more than glad to have him in charge.

With the ship still in the hands of the local pilot we went upstream. But instead of going directly to where Astoria hugged the muddy banks and marched up the hills behind the wharves, lumber mills, and canning factories that stood on stilts over the water, we went across the river to the small port of Knappton where I was to make my official entrance into the United States of America. An officious health inspector came aboard and everyone was quick and courteous. He had the power to pass the ship immediately or decide to fumigate, which meant burning sulfur below decks to kill rats and other vermin. The captain and crew were doing his bidding as we passengers and our personal goods were herded off the ship into a building where we were to be divided by gender and examined by a doctor.

As the only woman, I had a large drafty shower room to myself. I peeled off my clothes, feeling a bit like I was shedding skin, then scrubbed down with hot water and their strong carbolic soap. This was a far cry from the bubble baths and tender washings I'd had as a child, and when I'd used the stiff brush to the satisfaction of the matron, I felt scraped and sanded. I wrapped myself in a thin scratchy towel and she marched off to get the doctor.

Away from the warm water, the room was cold and forlorn. I shivered as I waited, aware that here in this dingy place I was going to have to pass an inspection. I was going to be judged on the cleanliness and health of my body, no exceptions made for bloodline or parentage. In a cracked and darkened mirror I saw a skinny, auburn-haired woman with a very frightened pair of grey eyes in her sharp-pretty face. I ordered the cold, hunched shoulders back and made myself smile.

'Take nothing from these people, Nadezhda,' I whispered to my reflection, setting my chin as she would have done. 'You're as good as any of them.'

The doctor, when I came before him, couldn't have been less interested. He gave me a cursory glance to be sure I had no obvious sores or rashes, and checked my hair for lice. Finding none, he placed an icy stethoscope against my back and had me take several deep breaths. For his final responsibility he went down a long list of ailments and conditions asking if I suffered from them or any of my family had died from them. Hemophilia and bullets were not on the list. I passed.

I was then taken to another room, just like the other, except that my clothing and trunks, all opened and examined, waited for me there in a forlorn pile.

I quickly dressed and then began to inventory my things; making sure that my eggs, the bible, and the photo book were quite safe in the hidden part of my box. The gem-laden candle lay innocently among my underwear. Aside from a bunch of worn and crumpled clothing, and a beat-up pair of shoes, the only things of value I had to my name were Nadezhda's bucket and Kuzma's toolbox. An odd collection of things for a former grand duchess to carry. To them I added my books. Along the way I'd found copies of War and Peace, Anna Karenina, and a volume of Pushkin's poetry, and had read them to Kuzma by the fire. I restored the entire assortment to my trunk and threw my heavy cloak around my shoulders, then I dragged my unwieldy treasure chest out onto the dock where I thought to find the *Bering Princess* waiting to take me across the river to Astoria.

Instead I was shuttled to a waiting area for the ferry and watched the *Bering Princess* make her way to the other side a full seven hours before I was permitted to follow.

· · ·

A misty rain was falling from low scudding clouds when I first set foot in Astoria, Oregon. I stood on the wharf alone, looking up and down the waterfront as if I'd expected a welcoming committee. But there was only the dirty buildings and what I told myself was the smell of rotten fish, but in truth had too much of the outhouse about it to be denied.

The city that peeked in and out of the mist was smaller than I'd created it in my mind, but once it started up the hills from the water it seemed quite settled and clean. All around me men were hustling about their work, shouting and running, carrying things. I could see people walking on the streets above, cloaks pulled in tight against the rain, but had no idea how to get myself to where I needed to be and lacked the courage to demand help. I'd wasted what little I had on the doctor who didn't notice. My spirits flagged. It was just the end of the journey and there was nothing to mark it but uncertainty and trepidation.

I was on the verge of tears when someone tapped tentatively on my shoulder. It was Gustav, the cook from the *Bering Princess*.

He was a sandy-haired, weedy man with few teeth, but I'd learned he was stronger than he looked and a good worker. He stood before me, turning his hat in his hands, keeping his eyes on his boots.

'Meant to talk to you before... On the ship... Before...'

I'd been able to tell from the first that Gustav was painfully shy. While we'd been doing a job together he could forget that. But as soon as the crisis had passed he became nervous and tongue-tied around me so I let him withdraw from our former familiarity. We'd passed the second part of the voyage almost as strangers, with the exception of a shared smile when one of our former patients left the ship.

'You were a help,' he went on, speaking quickly to get it over with. 'No doubt of that. I thank you and so does the old Princess.'

'I was glad to be of use. It made the trip easier for me.'

'Easier!' His surprise brought his eyes to meet mine.

'I'd planned to travel with my grandfather, but he died before we were to leave.'

Gustav was now truly uncomfortable as he tried to think of something proper to say. He desperately scanned the wharf. 'Are your friends not here to meet you, Miss Neddy?'

On the Bearing Princess I'd gotten a new name. It was hard for all the different nationalities on the ship to get their tongues around Nadezhda, and I wasn't wiling to share Nadia, the name Kuzma alone had called me. Neddy was simple and had, in my mind, a nice American ring to it.

'I don't know a soul in Astoria.' I hated to burden poor bashful Gustav, but had little choice. 'I need a respectable place to stay. Have you any knowledge of the town?'

'If you go straight up Eighth, right over there, that's Eighth. Then turn right on Bond you'll see Larsen's. Not expensive. Clean. She's a good lady. A Finn. Goes to church regular.'

'Thank you, Gustav. I expect you'd best get back to work.' I wanted to release him from the agony of so much communicating. Gustav gave me a nod, jammed his hat on his head, and practically ran back to the sanctuary of the *Bering Princess*, his home and haven.

By the time I'd hauled my trunk to the end of the pier a burly man offered to carry it for a nickel. When I told him where I was going, he knew the way and deposited me on the front stoop with a smile. I rang the bell. In a few moments the door was opened by a worn but pleasant looking woman who took one look at me and pulled me and my trunk in out of the weather clucking like a mother hen. Not until she had my cloak off and ascertained I wasn't soaked through did she introduce herself.

'Gertrude van Dorn. I own the place. I expect you need a room?'

'I thought this was Mrs. Larsen's boarding house,' I said, feeling wary. The sign on the outside had said simply, Larsen—Rooms.

'Was. When I bought it I figured there were more Finns in town to please so I kept the name. Not so many Hollanders like me, especially ones who grew up in Batavia and never saw more than a picture of either country.'

'I'm in need of a small, reasonable room,' I said, intending to be businesslike. 'I have to find work, as my resources are quite slim.'

'You come to the right place. Clean and reasonable with simple food and no bugs. There's also a bath where you can wash off that stinky carbolic soap from Knappton and feel human again—twenty-five cents if you haul your own water.'

'I shall haul my own water,' I said firmly.

'You get cleaned up and come to the kitchen,' Gertrude instructed. 'I know they didn't give you a bite to eat over there on the other side and you spent the whole night waiting for that ferry. I've got a good chicken pie just ready to come out of the oven that'll fill you right up.'

I paid for a week in advance, as well as the bath, and was

installed in a small plain room just down the hallway from the kitchen. It was scrubbed and dusted till the quilts were faded and the floors shining. Starch put a pleat in the curtain fabric and the small wardrobe smelled nicely of lemon oil.

'I put you here on this floor for privacy,' Gertrude told me frankly. 'It's a bit small; once used it for a girl I had working for me. But then you and I are right next door. My house is full of men at present, doesn't always happen that way, but thought you'd be happier kind of separate from all that.'

I assured her the room and its location were perfect. And after I'd gotten into the hot water with a bar of mild soap, I felt much better. I had ten dollars in my purse, my treasure hidden away for an emergency. I was about to take the first step in fulfilling the dream Kuzma and I had talked of every night for two years, and felt he'd be guiding me every step of the way as he had all across Siberia. I came out of the bath confident I could find some kind of work within a week. When I was dressed I followed the delicious smell to the large scrubbed kitchen, my landlady and two other women looked up from their coffee cups in frank but friendly appraisal.

'This is Roma,' Gertrude van Dorn said, indicating a young woman about my age with a baby asleep on her lap. 'She's our resident romantic, sees a prince or a princess around every corner.'

I nodded to the pretty girl who blushed and smiled. 'This is Norm Junior. We just call him Junior.'

'I'm Evelyn,' the other older lady said. 'I work at the bakery down the street. Have a roll, right from the oven.'

'Sit,' Gertrude ordered. 'I'll get you fattened up in no time.'

I took my place and she set before me a plate of delicious steaming pie. As I ate, they asked me where I was from, was I married, why was I in Astoria. I felt alone and exposed, though that certainly wasn't their intention. I wound a little of Nadezhda and Tatiana together for my history and told them I'd been a tutor in a wealthy family in Russia. When they heard that, I had to speak some Russian for them and they applauded. Then I told them a little about my journey and they were impressed more by the distance than anything else.

But when the pie was finished and I'd entertained them with my history I thought it was my turn to ask some questions. My first was to Evelyn.

'Do they need any help at your bakery? I'll do anything. I need a job.'

'No places there. It's pretty much a family business.'

'You're a teacher,' Roma asked, 'and a nurse?'

'You need a license for anything like that in this country,' Gertrude pointed out.

'What about at the big house?' Roma went on, and then turned to me. 'Do you like children?'

Gertrude frowned. 'The poor captain.'

'But...' Evelyn said, elbowing Gertrude. 'What about... you know.'

'How do you feel about chinks?' Gertrude asked bluntly. 'And I mean working for one.'

I was confused and didn't want to put my foot wrong. 'Chinks?'

'Chinese.'

'Is it a good job?'

'The captain's ever so handsome,' Roma said with a sigh. 'And you're so pretty and then he'll fall in love with you—'

'Roma, you're the silliest thing,' said Evelyn shaking her head.

'You know,' Gertrude said, 'she might be right.'

'What? About all that romantic nonsense?'

'No, course not that. But the captain sure does have some kids who need taking care of since their folks died.'

'That poor baby,' Roma sighed. 'She's only a couple months old and no mother.'

'So this Chinese captain needs help with a baby?' I asked, trying to get to the actual job.

'Oh, dear,' Gertrude whooped. 'We sure do know how to mess up at story.' Norm Junior woke and protested the loud interruption and his mother concentrated on soothing him. 'Here's the facts,' Gertrude explained. 'Captain Tilton was a sea captain.'

'Still is,' Evelyn interjected.

'Anyways, Captain Tilton had a brother. That was Ira.'

'Younger brother,' Evelyn added and got a look from Gertrude that made her shrug and surrender the story to her friend.

'As I said,' Gertrude went on with a steely eye on Evelyn. 'Ira married young and his wife was a sweet empty-headed thing.'

'But pretty as a picture, you can see why he fell for her and all.' Roma now put in.

'But not a lick of sense,' Evelyn continued.

Gertrude sighed, arms crossed over her ample bosom. 'Here's the long and the short of it. Ira moved into his father's grand house and they were fine till he and half the maids was took with the influenza and died. His little slip of a wife went into a decline and when she was giving birth to their third child, a girl, just two months ago, she up and died.'

'The mother, not the baby,' Evelyn said quickly.

'Now, the captain, that's Henry, was living a nice bachelor life in a little establishment out at the beach. He had a China man named Chin and his wife Mai Lin to keep his house.'

'That's the Chinaman's wife,' Evelyn explained.

'I said that,' Gertrude retorted and went on. 'Well, now he's moved into that big place with Chin and Mai Lin and they're trying to make a go of it with the kids, but with all the help gone, things are a mess.'

'And since you're a nurse and a teacher and you like kids you could be his governess and baby nurse and get to live in a grand house and probably make all kinds of money,' Evelyn finished with a flourish of her coffee cup.

'And maybe marry the captain. He's ever so handsome,' Roma had to add.

They were all smiling at me in triumph as if the whole thing was settled.

'There are two other children?' I asked.

'Boys, around ten, real close in age.'

'But surely there are lots of women—'

'The China woman's in charge of the house, of everything really. Most won't stand for that,' Gertrude said.

'Is she a good housekeeper?'

'Neat as a pin,' Evelyn asserted.

'Do these Chinese people speak English? I don't speak Chinese, though I suppose in time I could learn.'

'He sounds the same as you and me,' Gertrude said. 'And she does fine too, but not so correct and some accent. Course when the three of them, the captain speaks their lingo too, talk to each other they're jabbering away nine to the dozen and no one understands a word.'

'How would I get this job?' I asked. The idea of working for a Chinese woman didn't faze me in the least, especially when coupled with the idea of a big house and lots of money.

'You'd have to live in, in the house, with a baby that small,' Roma pointed out.

'Is that a problem? Isn't this Captain Tilton a gentleman?'

'Oh, he's as kind and as fair as they come,' Evelyn said. 'My brother Burt sailed with him four years before his wife made him give it up. Said he was strict and fair and nobody cared more for his men.'

'And he has no wife?'

'Married to the sea,' Roma sighed.

'I'll go and talk to this housekeeper right away,' I said, getting to my feet.

'Chin. He probably does the hiring,' Gertrude corrected.

'Fine, then I'll talk to this Mr. Chin.'

'Best face him first thing in the morning with a good night's sleep under your belt,' Gertrude warned. 'You still look a bit peaked to me.'

And in truth she was right. I was exhausted. The morning would have to do.

. . .

However, after a good night's rest I could see my wardrobe was in desperate need of refurbishing. Four years had passed since I'd thought about presenting myself to someone for inspection, and one needed little in the way of frills wandering across the wilds of Siberia. When I truly looked at my supply of clothing, I was at first shocked and then had a good laugh. It was another of those moments when I realized how far I'd come from the palaces of my youth, but this time I found it a good thing.

Some time at the laundry tubs, an outlay of half my precious ten dollars for necessities, and a day of sewing put me sufficiently to rights to face a prospective employer with confidence. Several of Gert's good meals (she instructed me to call her Gert) had dispelled my exhausted pallor and made me feel healthy enough to manage three children. I was ready.

Three days after my decision to become a governess and baby nurse in the home of Captain Henry Tilton I set out to get the job. It was a beautiful Saturday morning, cool and clear. In addition to the work on my wardrobe it had been necessary to purchase a pair of shoes that were sensible but not quite so functional as those I'd worn to cross Siberia. I felt quite stylish as I made my way up the hill on Eighth Street and stopped where it intersected Duane.

When I saw the house I stopped across the corner to study it. It was a grand lovingly cared-for Victorian painted crisp white, the windows picked out in an elegant cherry color, and all the glass sparking. And, as Gert had informed me when she gave her directions, it did indeed sit in a spacious yard that took up an entire city block. The fancy trim and lavish detail, probably painted other colors at the height of the Victorian era, gave it character in the monochromatic color scheme. It had a hexagonal tower that rose another story above the third floor and must have afforded a magnificent view of the Columbia River.

I squared my shoulders and automatically said to myself what I always had before a state occasion. 'You're the daughter of an emperor. Queen Victoria was your great-grandmother. You are a grand duchess.'

Heartened, I marched right though the front gate and up the walk. But as I set my newly shod foot on the bottom step I stopped. I wasn't entering the house for a social call. I was seeking employment. I turned to my left and went along a wooden path that led to the back of the house, to the service areas.

I passed the bowed windows of a conservatory and came to the corner around which I saw steps leading to what I hoped was the kitchen, and as I paused I heard the distinct sound of a very small baby crying inside the house.

'She does that all the time,' a voice said.

Startled, I looked around and saw a boy crouched down beside the back steps, partly hidden among the hydrangeas. He couldn't have been more than seven or eight, had a dark shock of hair, a thin face, and a pair of smudged rimless glasses. He stood up, brushed back his hair, and pushed his glasses up his nose. He was skinny with knobby elbows and knees. His hands, made for the piano, looked large and ungainly for his frame. 'She never stops,' he murmured, and I saw there were tears in his eyes, though his voice was angry. 'I expect she'll die, too.'

I cocked my head for a moment. The baby was obviously in distress and furious, but didn't sound weak.

'I never look at her,' the boy went on, the emotion in his

tone stronger. 'I don't want to like her if she's going to die.'

'Why do you think she'll die?'

'Poppa got sick and died and then all Momma did was cry—but not so loud as that. And then she died. Joe says I'm crazy, but I can't like her if she's going to die. I just can't.'

I was drawn to the boy and for several moments didn't know why. But then realized that in his fragile courage and acceptance of a terrible fate, he reminded me of Alexei.

'Give me those glasses,' I instructed. And when he did I cleaned them with my handkerchief. 'Now,' I said as I set them back on his nose. 'Show me that baby, and let's see if we can get her to stop crying.'

He hesitated, eying me.

'I've come to apply for the job of taking care of your little sister and maybe if I can get her to stop crying I'll impress the person who might hire me,' I told him. 'I need the job. I'd get to be gov—tutor to you and your brother as well. If I'm hired. Will you help me out?'

'I won't look at her,' he warned. 'I can't like her.'

'I'll make you a bargain. I'm a nurse. And if I tell you she's all right, will you believe me?'

'I'll show her to you,' he said, unwilling to commit himself to more. We went round the corner and up the back steps. In the kitchen, in a basket, lay a tightly swaddled baby screaming her head off. I reached in and unwrapped her. Immediately her tiny knees came up to her middle. I scooped her up and put her against my shoulder. Then I began to massage her back, feeling her round gas-filled tummy against my breast.

'That's my sweet bunny,' I crooned. 'You relax and I'll help.'

After only a few minutes she let out a belch that would have done justice to a man of two hundred pounds, spit up a little on my freshly starched shoulder, and relaxed against me.

'You're a good little bunny,' I went on, still caressing her back but now cuddling her in with a blanket around her. 'Now you can sleep. Are you a sleepy bunny, are you?' I swayed side-to-side, humming an old Russian song I hadn't thought of since Alexei was a baby.

The house was quiet, still, as if it were holding its breath. I had the feeling the very air around me was waiting to see if the tiny baby cried again. But it was more than that—it was a kind of tension that surrounded me, making me think no one in this place was any happier than this mite in my arms. She let out another burp and even a little toot as some of the gas in her stomach went out the other way. Then she drifted off to sleep and sank all of what could not have been more than seven or eight pounds into me.

My eyes found the boy, who stood by the door to the mud-room, hand on the knob, every line of his body set for escape. I nodded to him and smiled.

'She has colic. She'll cry a lot, but it's not fatal. Probably because she had to drink cow's milk since her...'

He nodded once, a curt movement of understanding. Then he ventured across the room and handed me a diaper for my shoulder.

'I don't want to put her down,' I whispered. 'I think she'd rather sleep like this. But I do feel like a bit of a kid-napper. Would you go and find whomever I should talk to about this job?'

He nodded and slipped out. Alone in the kitchen I looked about and was more than pleased by what I saw. It had all the latest conveniences, including a grand gas stove and electric lights. The sink was copper and had two faucets, which meant hot and cold running water. I peeked into a well-fitted but-ler's pantry that dazzled with china and crystal. On the hutch stood a magnificent gleaming silver tea service. I also poked my head into the well-stocked storage closet and saw a big bag of rice, something that was going to make the baby's life and mine easier if I could just get the job. Not wanting to be caught snooping, I walked slowly around the center worktable. Judging by looks and the fresh smell, not one corner of this space had been neglected when it came to cleaning.

Then I heard footsteps coming up from the basement and brushed the top of the sleeping baby's head with my lips. 'Wish me luck, little bunny. Here comes the boss.'

Dressed in the traditional Chinese costume of jacket and loose pants in formal black, Mai Lin Chin was barely taller than the boy with the glasses. Her shining black hair was screwed into a no-nonsense knot at the back of her head, and she was as plain and scrubbed as her kitchen. Her jaw was set, but I saw the anxious look she cast to the baby on my shoulder.

'She's sleeping,' I assured her.

She came around and peered up at the baby's face, then laid her hand on the tiny back gently as a feather.

'Understand Captain,' she said in the short clipped English sentences I would come to know so well. 'Him I feed. Know Chin. Him I feed. Don't know babies. Chin and Captain Henry only. She cry and cry.'

'The cow's milk makes her stomach hurt. It's too rich for her. So she cries and then swallows more air, which makes it worse.'

'Not mother's milk.'

I nodded. 'If she sleeps like this, so the gas can escape, she might sleep better.'

'Until next bottle,' the little Chinese woman said flatly.

But I saw again the sadness in her eyes, and would learn it was seldom what Mai Lin said, or her expression, but the emotion in her beautiful tilted eyes that spoke her heart.

'I saw you have rice in the pantry?'

'For Chin. No potatoes for him. Not good American like me.'

'If we grind it and mix it with water she might find that, with

~ 96 ~

only a little milk, easier to digest. She'll eat more often, but she won't burn up energy crying so much. We might get some weight on her that way. Then all she has to do is get older.'

'Mr. William,' she said pointing at the dark boy with the glasses and saying it We-yum, 'say you baby nurse.'

'Yes, and a tutor for the boys.'

'Tutor? Like nanny?'

'Yes. But when boys are so grown up, they need a tutor to help them with their studies and make sure they mind their manners, not a nanny to dress them,' I said, meeting her eyes.

'Ah! Tutor.'

We all looked up, as there was a sound of doors beyond the kitchen area.

'They're back!' William said eagerly. 'Wait till I tell them she's not crying anymore.'

'Now just a minute, young man,' I said firmly. 'This little bunny is still going to cry. Until her stomach's old enough for real milk. Maybe six more months. But she won't cry so much.'

'And she won't die?'

'Not from colic, Mr. William.'

'Will,' he said with the shyest of smiles.

The door that connected the kitchen with the rest of the house burst open and a boy, followed by a Chinese man in an impeccably tailored Western suit, entered the kitchen. This boy, the one Will had called Joe, was taller and broader than his brother. His fairer, squarer features were as open and curious as Will's were introverted. He too examined the sleeping baby, but his satisfaction was clear in his blue eyes, and when his brother told him I also had a way to feed her that might make her not so sick, he grinned at me. Then they both went off to try out the new bicycle Joe and Chin had been picking up when I arrived.

'This house is full of sorrow,' Chin said as soon as they

boys were gone. 'I would guess you know some of it or you would not be here.'

'My landlady, Mrs. Van Dorn, said I might find work here.'

'She good smart lady,' Mai Lin said. ' Clean. Talks nice to Chinese.'

Chin straightened his tie and made sure his cuffs were set just right. 'The captain has set down guidelines for finding a governess for the young masters.'

'Tutor,' Mai Lin corrected.

He looked at her questioningly and she shrugged, pointing to me.

'I thought the boys looked a little old to take to the idea of a nanny or governess. Tutor is only a word. I'm sure I can handle things the way Captain Tilton wishes them done.'

Chin's face grew firm, almost angry as he said, 'It is Mai Lin who is in charge of the house,' as if he was ready for me to argue. 'Is that a problem for you?'

Not wanting to see my face when this news was imparted, Mai Lin had averted her eyes to the careful refolding of a perfectly folded dishcloth.

But my answer was easy, and Chin saw this instantly. 'From what I can see of this house, and I feel the kitchen is where the true competence of the housekeeper shows, it's obvious this home is run by an expert. I've no concerns about working under someone so good at her job.'

Chin reverted to his usual formal manner. 'You would have sole charge of the boys. Much of the time there will be no man in the house.'

'I can manage the children on my own. The boys seem respectful and bright. And I'm glad to leave the rest of the worries to you and Mai Lin. But this is a huge establishment. Does Mai Lin manage it alone?'

'She would have to hire Chinese assistants,' Chin explained flatly. 'Is that a problem?'

'I speak English, French, German, and Russian,' I said, 'but no Chinese. That's the only problem I see.'

A look flashed between the couple, and without a movement or signal I could see they'd decided. Chin frowned and produced from his pocket a piece of paper. 'Latin?' he asked.

'I'm qualified to help the boys with their studies in that as well as mathematics, geography, composition, penmanship, literature, and deportment.'

'Have you been a gov—tutor before?'

'No. But I often helped with my younger brother's studies and know the ways of boys. And as for this little bunny, I've experience with them too. I like children, Mr. Chin.'

He folded the paper carefully and I turned my attention to the sleeping baby.

There was a rapid torrent of Chinese, his tones mellifluous and hers the same staccato as her English. When it was over Mr. Chin turned to me, but then paused and said something quickly to his wife followed by a shrug from her.

He cleared his throat and squared his shoulders. 'Miss...'

'My name is Nadezhda Osipov,' I said, understanding his dilemma at once. 'I'm from Russia. I arrived in Astoria three days ago and it was in a grand home in Russia that I received my education and training. I had a fine master,' I went on, spinning the story I'd settled on when I knew I'd be alone. 'I was educated with his daughters as well as being their servant. I'm now twenty-three and left Russia because I'm not a Bolshevik and found it hard to live with that government. I hope I've not offended you with my opinion but the reason I've no references is because the family I worked for had to flee for their lives. My grandfather and I were left to fend for ourselves. There. Now you know me.'

'Your grandfather is here with you?'

'He died just before we were to leave the country.'

There was a quick comment from Mai Lin.

'And your brother?' Chin asked.

There was whoop of laughter out in the yard from Joe as he careened along the walk, past the kitchen windows, on his new bicycle.

'My brother died two years ago,' I said, keeping my eyes on the window. 'He was ill for a long time.'

'You would like to see the rest of the house,' Chin said after a silence. 'I can show you where you will sleep. If all is satisfactory I think we can make a tentative agreement; subject, of course, to Captain Tilton's approval when he returns.'

'And when will he be back, Mr. Chin?'

'Please. Just Chin. Perhaps a month, maybe longer. There are no precise schedules at sea.'

'Will I receive a salary before his return? I must admit my wardrobe is quite depleted and I don't want to appear shabby in such a fine household.'

'If you decided to stay Miss Os- Os—'

'Neddy. Please, call me Neddy. Russian is a hard language on the tongue.'

'Very well, Miss Neddy, if you decided to stay we will arrange for an advance.'

'Oh, I'll stay, Chin—if I pass Captain Tilton's inspection. I hardly think I could leave this sweet little bunny even after such a short acquaintance, and those boys look like they've had enough change in their lives.'

I actually saw Mai Lin allow a flicker of a smile, and Chin acknowledged it with a nod.

'Why do you call her Bunny?' Chin asked.

'I don't know her name,' I laughed. 'And it was a term of endearment my father used to use.'

'Her name is Emmaline. The captain called her for his grandmother.'

A grand name for such a little scrap of girl, I thought.

· · ·

Still carrying the sleeping Emmaline, whom I already called Bunny in my mind, I followed Chin on a tour of Captain Tilton's home.

From the kitchen we entered a central hallway that ran all the way to the front door. It was broad and richly carpeted in deep red, trimmed in polished wood and dustless—always ready for guests. Just to my left was a beautiful staircase to the second floor with a side door to the street beyond. Everything was of the finest finishes and the hardware expensive. To my right was the formal dining room, done in the fashionable Eastlake style with the conservatory beyond. Next on the same side was the music room. Like the dining room, it had an oriental carpet as well as a grand piano, and rich comfortable furniture. Across the hall was the formal parlor. It was closed and only used for special visitors, important occasions, and funerals. Now it stood dim, the furniture shrouded in dustsheets, the light from the lowest level of the hexagonal tower muted with lowered blinds. I thought I caught the scent of flowers as the door was opened.

It had been a long time, and many miles in both distance and emotion, since I'd been in such a lovely place. And had I not been holding a baby I know I would have run my fingers over the fine woods and touched the expensive fabrics with pleasure. The smells of beeswax and lemon oil were a delicate perfume I'd only just remembered, and I felt more at home in this house than I had felt anywhere in a long time.

Chin led me then to the room beside the formal parlor. This was the library, and obviously the domain of the man of the house. The chairs and overstuffed sofa were scarred leather. There was a table made for working, and the massive desk that commanded the back corner wasn't for show. It smelled of books and a sharp spicy scent that made me think of faraway places. I had a good feeling about the man who worked here, that he was honest and strong and very sure of himself.

'This is Captain Tilton's room,' Chin said as if introducing me to the captain himself. 'It is exactly as it was when old Captain William who built the house used it.'

I'd have liked to linger there, but Chin led me on up the grand staircase. The moment we reached the top of the stairs, the furnishings and woodwork became less ornate. This was the private part of the house. And just as in Russia, the rooms the family shared with only each other were more comfortable and relaxed than those used for entertaining.

There was a rather opulent guest room at the head of the stairs, and on the same side two rooms that adjoined. It was easy to see this pair of rooms belonged to the boys. The one that overlooked the street had two beds with matching dressers. The other directly behind it contained desks, a small red upright piano, and a large train table. A baseball bat stood in one corner and books were spread over a good-sized worktable.

At the front of the house to the left of the hall, over the formal parlor, was a lady's bedroom that had part of the tower in the corner. It too was closed up, the ornate French furniture swathed in dustsheets.

Next to this room was another bedroom, obviously occupied by Captain Tilton. Like the boys' rooms, it had life in it. It wasn't covered despite the fact the captain was away, but simply maintained with regular cleaning. It was ready for his return at any time. As Chin led me back down the hallway, I found myself comforted by the fact the return of my employer was looked forward to every day. Rather than being daunted at the thought of facing him, I was eager to meet him and know I was secure in my job.

I was shown a magnificently fitted bathroom, and though Chin told me one had been installed when the house was built in the 1880s, this was a total refurbishment of that former space and completely up-to-date.

Tucked in across from the bathroom was a sewing room that had been converted to a nursery by simply adding a crib, but I got the impression the baby wasn't here much, and was probably kept with Mai Lin wherever she was. There was a simple white-painted metal bed on one wall and a sewing machine under the window. It was light and airy with informal curtains and an old worn Aubusson on the floor.

'May I share this with Bunny for now?' I asked. 'I'd like to be close to the children.' But then I realized servants didn't usually sleep on the same level with their employers. I'd just allowed myself to feel too much at home. 'If it's all right,' I added hastily, hoping to cover my faux pas.

'That was my plan,' Chin said casually, much to my relief.

'All the planning in the world will be for naught if Captain Tilton doesn't find me suitable.'

'Would you like to see the third floor? Mai Lin and I live there. The tower room where the captain used to watch for ships when he was a boy is up there. But there is a small ladder.'

I patted the baby's back gently. 'We'll see that another time.'

'There is furniture stored up there. If you are looking for things for your room, that is the place to start.'

'I'll keep that in mind. Thank you.'

As we descended the servants' stair to return to the kitchen, Chin asked politely, 'When can you begin your duties?'

'Today, if you like. All I need is my things and that will take no time at all. There isn't much.'

'Excellent,' he said, unable to hide his relief.

'If I can hand this little one back to Mai Lin, I'll go and fetch my trunk.'

Chin looked warily at the sleeping baby. 'Perhaps it would be wise for you to remain here and assist my wife in the preparation of the next bottle,' he said in his formal speech that didn't hide his nervousness at the thought of being left with the baby.

'I shall send for your things. If that would be acceptable.'

I nodded and tried not to smile. 'That would be more than acceptable.'

'Good,' he said, relief evident. 'Welcome to Captain Tilton's employ, Miss Neddy. I think you will find him fair and generous as long as you do your job.'

'I'll do my best not to disappoint, Chin,' I assured him. 'And I hope you'll be able to give me a good recommendation when the captain returns.'

.   .   .

And so began my employment, my first post. The job itself wasn't difficult, but it was little Bunny who cemented my success. The rice flour worked and she was much happier. It was only a simple thing, but it won Mai Lin's respect, and lifted everyone's spirits.

The first afternoon, when the new diet had wrought a second nap, I found myself unpacking with special care. I wanted to find just the right spot in my small room for each of my treasures. And when I realized I was truly settling in, making the space my own, it frightened me. It had been so long since I'd belonged somewhere I'd become inured to the lack of a real home. But as I felt the cozy sewing room becoming more and more my own nest, and watched the baby sleep as I worked, I knew I wanted to stay; and the specter of the unknown Captain Tilton, now the master of my fate, became almost sinister.

I went down to dinner with a sense of foreboding and was conducted to a table set in grand style with Joe, Will and myself separated into fortresses of china and crystal that made communication impossible and put any kind of companionability out of the question. Never had I seen such formality except at a state dinner.

'Do you always dine like this?' I whispered when Chin had left the soup.

Joe looked at the closed kitchen door and then whispered, 'When Uncle Henry was here we sat around the end together, you know, closer.'

'When Uncle Henry went to sea,' Will added, also in a whisper, 'Chin said young gentlemen must learn proper manners.'

'So you've been having your meals like this for more than a month?'

Both boys nodded glumly.

I was sure Chin had been trying, in the only way he knew how, to be sure the boys learned proper social behavior. He wouldn't have thought it proper to eat with them or correct their manners, but by making things so formal he was at least showing them what needed to be learned.

'Well, then, I expect you've learned a great deal about silverware and napery in that amount of time,' I assured them confidently as I got up and began moving their place settings to the end of the table where I'd been installed. 'And when the King of England comes to dinner you shall remember it all.'

The boys eagerly brought their chairs closer and began their soup—but not before I'd taken the first spoonful as the lady at the head of the table.

When Chin returned to clear the plates the boys looked a bit apprehensive, but didn't move.

'I understand Captain Tilton preferred to dine with the family in this manner,' I said, trying to sound calm and brave, pretending I was at a court function. 'So I should like, when we are only family, to follow his wishes. However, if there's company the settings will be proper, and I assure you, Chin, I'll not allow any laxity in manners despite the informal arrangement here. And please tell Mai Lin the soup was delicious.'

Chin regarded us all impassively for several moments and then carefully removed the soup plates. We remained silent until he'd brought the salad and then dissolved in giggles as soon as the door closed in his wake.

But while the boys had kept their eyes on their lettuce so as not to laugh, I'd seen what they had not. As the door swished silently closed Chin gave me a small nod.

. . .

After almost a month in the house, Thanksgiving Day approached without a sign of Captain Tilton. He was the only real constant in the boys' lives and even I had taken to climbing to the tower to look for his ship, though I wouldn't have recognized the captain's *Raven* had she been lifted from the water and tied up to our front hitching post. Nor, to be honest, would I have recognized Captain Tilton. I'd seen one photograph taken when he was only sixteen that showed no more than a nice-looking young man without distinguishing features. He was now thirty-five and probably quite different from the boy he'd been.

So when I went out onto the front steps with Bunny (everyone called her that now) to wait for the boys' return from school, I was only mildly interested in the man who trudged up the hill with a stout basket in each hand. But when he stopped across the corner and gazed for a moment over the house, his eyes wandering slowly to the top of the tower, I suddenly knew who he was.

My heart jumped and my first reaction of joy for Joe and Will was swiftly replaced with fear. His look was stern as he crossed the street, but it turned to puzzlement when he came to a stop at the bottom of the steps.

'I'm Miss Osipov,' I said quickly. 'Neddy. Chin hired me to be the boys' tutor and to care for Bunny.'

He came slowly up the steps and peered into the bright blue eyes of the baby in my arms. 'I thought not to see you again, little Emmaline,' he murmured and then smiled at me. 'Thank you, Miss...'

'Neddy,' I said. 'I'm Neddy.'

'Thank you, Miss Neddy, for taking care of my niece.'

He was a handsome man with darkish hair, no beard, and a strong face. He was deeply tanned and his hair curled about his collar and forehead, giving him a charmingly unkempt look. His eyes were warm, his words for the baby soft. And I admit that while I usually didn't like to be so close to men, he didn't intimidate me in any way and in fact I was taken with him. And that was certainly not like me.

I heard a small scraping sound and looked down. One of the baskets he'd been carrying tipped precariously toward the steps.

'Oh, Captain! Your parcel!'

He bent to retrieve it and I heard scuffling and complaint.

'Aren't the boys due any minute?' he asked as he turned to scan the street. 'Ah! Here they come now.' He opened the lids, and from the wicker kennels tumbled two of the largest black puppies I'd ever seen.

'Newfoundlands!' I gasped as they bumbled down the steps. The boys met them halfway, discarding their books and lunch pails without a second thought. There was a huge rollicking greeting between the ecstatic nephews and their uncle, and the dogs showed complete delight. In the midst of this chaos Chin appeared. He stood in his spotless black suit, old-fashioned collar, and black tie, and he gaped—but only for a moment. Then his face resumed it usual blank mask.

'Dogs,' he said flatly. 'I thought it was bear cubs on my front porch.'

'Not just dogs,' Captain Tilton almost shouted, extricating himself from the pile of pups and children. 'They're Newfoundlands.'

'Courage without ferocity,' I recited from childhood memory. 'And all the virtues of man without his vices.'

'There,' the captain said pointing at me. 'She's quoting Lord Byron. That's what he said about them.'

Chin's dryly disapproving look didn't alter.

'He'll love them soon,' the captain assured me with a wink.

'I suppose they won't be living in the carriage house,' Chin asked, grasping at a last straw.

'With Joe and Will,' Captain Tilton said firmly. 'These dogs need people, and the boys should learn responsibility.'

Chin passively regarded the rollicking dogs and boys before him. 'I hope they keep better track of them than of their bicycles and rain boots.'

Captain Tilton ignored him. He was watching Joe and Will with their new puppies.

. . .

The rest of the day was filled with riotous fun. And while I watched every minute with happiness, I felt outside the circle. I didn't belong in this family. And while the boys had always been kind and accepting of me, I now saw how they adored their Uncle Henry and blossomed in his presence. The connection between them was deep and historic, but I was the outsider, not even sure I'd be allowed to stay another day. I was afraid of losing my job and realized it had become much more than that to me. I cared more than an employee should for my three charges.

Joe named his dog Pete because he liked the name, and Will called his Tar for the obvious reason. They showed their pups all over the house and yard, only taking a break for supper, which they gobbled down and fled back to their new best friends. All four of them were sound asleep as soon as they crawled into bed, each pup at his master's feet.

I waited until I heard Chin and Mai Lin climb to the third floor. Then, sure Bunny was sound asleep, made my way to the captain's library. It was time for me to tell him a little more about myself. If he was going to take me into his employ he had a right to know some of the truth. Marshaling my courage, I tapped at the door and entered, but realized the captain hadn't heard me. He stared at a painting over the fireplace, hands deep in his pockets, lost in thought.

'Captain Tilton?'

He turned, surprised, and seemed embarrassed I'd caught him woolgathering.

'It wasn't an easy decision for you, was it? Giving up the sea, I mean.'

'And I thought I hid it well,' he said, sinking into a chair with a sigh.

'The boys were so glad to know they'd have you around all the time they didn't notice. They've missed you. Will it have to be permanent?'

'Someone has to run the business,' he said darkly. 'Since the war ended Astoria's gone into a real slump. There was a time,' he went on tiredly, 'when fur and lumber and salmon seemed a well that would never run dry. And if you were in on the ground floor, there was lots of money to be made.'

'But now it looks as if the bonanza they started predicting way back in old John Jacob Astor's day isn't going to happen,' I said.

He focused on me. 'How did you know about Astor?'

'I read Washington Irving's "Astoria" several years ago. And a sailor like yourself should remember it was we Russians who sheltered some of Mr. Astor's employees when the British took over Astoria in 1812.'

The captain smiled. 'I think that book is right here in this library and I too read it years ago. How could I have forgotten?'

'I know my history,' I said. 'But why are things so difficult now?'

I had his interest. He sat forward in his chair and motioned me to another. 'Do you really want to know all this?'

'I do,' I replied as I sat.

'Our port's now passed by as ships go direct to Portland.

And that bar, the treachery in those waters, holds smaller shipping at bay. There are times, especially in winter, when the fog and storms can keep ships waiting out there for a week or more.'

'And I thought it was bad enough we had to wait twenty-four hours.'

'What ship did you come in on?'

'The *Bering Princess*.'

'A good old girl.'

'But, tell me, why is the bar so dangerous? Can you explain it so a non-sailor can understand?'

He thought for a moment. 'Untold amounts of water, millions and millions of gallons, spill from the Columbia out into the Pacific. Sometimes you can see the plume of fresh water as far south as San Francisco or north to the Strait of Juan de Fuca. When the tide comes in it collides with the outflow with such force it's like two freight trains running into each other. That makes for extremely rough seas, especially where sand collects on the bar.'

'I've heard people call it the Graveyard of the Pacific.'

'That bar has been the demise of more than two thousand vessels, particularly during winter storms when the wind-driven swells can reach twenty to thirty feet.'

'I'd imagine you've crossed it many times without incident,' I said.

'A man has only so much luck, Miss Neddy. And right now I need to save mine up a bit for the sake of Joe and Will.'

'And Miss Bunny,' I reminded him.

He shook his head and smiled. 'When I left I was so sure she wouldn't be here I closed my mind to her. She was such a little bit of life.'

'But a very tenacious one,' I said, laughing softly. 'And since I know she'll soon want her late snack, I'd best talk to you about my employment.'

'I hope you mean to stay. Despite his fury with me, Chin was quite effusive in his praise of your abilities with the boys.'

'Effusive? Chin?' I said, raising my eyebrows skeptically.

Captain Tilton smiled. 'Mai Lin made it clear she wasn't letting you go. She isn't geared for children.'

'But she does have infinite patience,' I observed.

'She's been married to Chin since she was sixteen.'

Now I had to smile.

'And thank you for accepting that she's more at ease with Chinese assistants. When my brother and his wife ran this establishment there were no Chinese in their employ. They weren't...'

Appropriate?'

'Exactly. Now, what is it we need to discuss? If it's more money I'm willing to accommodate you.'

'Oh, no,' I assured him. 'My salary is very adequate. But...'

He waited politely but I could see he wanted to get on with business.

I'd come to do exactly that, but had been distracted. It had been a very long time since that had happened to me. Usually, I was very careful with men, always being sure to keep my distance and not let my guard down. But I'd forgotten to protect myself with Captain Tilton, a man I didn't know at all.

I took a deep breath. 'I left Russia; more aptly escaped from Russia, because I couldn't in any way conform to the Bolshevik regime. And in order to do so I've changed my name and covered my past identity.'

'Have you done anything illegal?'

'No.'

'Have you lied about your skills in regard to your job?'

'No.'

He rose and once again faced the picture over the mantel. When he turned to me his eyes were candid, his expression honest. 'Your past is your past. As long as you're happy in your job, and feel you can completely commit to my nephews and my niece, I see no need to pry. You've begun to bring the boys through a difficult time. In only one day I can see that. And I'm not sure our little Bunny would be here at all without you. And, finally, I don't like Bolsheviks much myself—they don't pay their bills. Will you stay on with us?'

'Yes, yes, I'd like to stay,' I told him.

We said good night and he returned to his desk as I headed for the kitchen to make Bunny's bottle. But as I snuggled her against me, filled with happiness because my place was secure, I couldn't help but think that Captain Tilton wasn't cut out to be a businessman. The way he'd looked at that painting over the fireplace with pure longing, and faced the pile of ledgers on his desk with such obvious distaste, told me it was going to be a heavy burden for him to keep his family afloat.

. . .

My first Thanksgiving was one I shall never forget because it was the worst ever, and the best ever.

It began with Joe and Will's astonishment that I'd never celebrated Thanksgiving. This was their favorite holiday, after Christmas. They said they would give me a real American Thanksgiving—but beyond that, they would say no more about it. From the conferences with Captain Tilton in the kitchen and some kind of secret work going on out in the carriage house, it was obvious that an extravaganza was in the works. The boys were running around in the attic and poking in the basement every day. And when they had to carry their secret treasures though the house I was sent to my room until they'd hidden everything. Even Chin and Mai Lin fell in with the plans. This was the first holiday in a string they'd be facing without their parents, and I was a distraction.

On the Wednesday before the great event, I was completely barred from the downstairs without an escort and Chin was looking particularly pained. So, I found a patch of sun by the big front windows of the upper hallway to play with Bunny. As she gurgled and squeaked over a wooden spoon, I absently watched a huge motorcar come slowly up the street. Then, to my surprise, it stopped before the house and a tall, broadshouldered, large-bosomed woman in deep mourning was assisted from the back seat by a uniformed chauffer.

When the doorbell rang I made my way toward the stairs with Bunny in my arms to see who this majestically overwhelming and completely unexpected personage could be.

'My lord Henry, what a nightmare of a trip I've had,' came an imperious complaint. 'Why you must keep the boys here in the wilderness when they'd be so much better off in San Francisco, I do not know.'

'Aunt Hester,' Captain Tilton said. 'What a surprise.'

His tone made me hesitate at the top of the steps.

'When I didn't hear from you I knew your provincial mail service had made some sort of mistake and kept right on with my plans. You know I came to Ira and poor dear Annabelle for Thanksgiving every year. Though this year it's almost more than I can bear to set foot in this house of tragedy when the funeral of my poor darling girl was almost the death of me. But I knew I simply had to come for the sake of those two poor, sad, little orphan waifs.'

'You shouldn't have put yourself out so, Aunt Hester,' the captain said, with the same polite reluctance in his voice.

'Oh, sacrifice is nothing new to me,' she assured him. 'And I know my darling Annabelle, may she rest in peace, would've wanted me to be here to condole with her precious boys and help them bear up on this sad, sad, day.'

Suddenly, I realized this unexpected arrival was going to be staying in the house. I ran to the nursery and dumped Bunny into her crib with a pile of toys, then dashed across the hallway to the guest room where I began pulling dust sheets off the furniture.

Only a moment behind me Mai Lin appeared, duster and rags in hand. Between us we had the room presentable in only a few moments. I was sneaking out, the dust sheets under my arm, when I almost collided with the colossus in black I'd seen come up the walk.

'Well! And who might you be?' she demanded, lifting her veils and peering at me through a lorgnette that hung on a gold chain from her massive bosom.

'I'm the nanny, ma'am,' I said as I dropped a curtsy and tried to conceal the dust sheets, 'and the tutor to Master Joseph and Master William.' I'd never called either one of them that, but somehow it seemed the right thing to say to this hard-eyed inquisitor.

For several moments she continued to examine me. 'Did you say nanny?'

'Yes, ma'am, for our Miss... Emmaline.'

'My God! Do you mean my little girl, that precious baby of my precious baby has survived?'

'Oh, yes, ma'am. She's doing very well. Would you like to see her?'

'You're far too young to be trusted with Annabelle's baby,' she declared.

There was no reply to the comment, but fortunately at that moment Harris the chauffer, Chin, and Captain Tilton appeared with an assortment of suitcases, trunks, and hatboxes.

'Henry!'

The captain set down the three hatboxes he'd been juggling. 'Yes, Hester?'

'I thought that baby died!'

'If she'd died I'd have informed you immediately,' Captain Tilton said flatly. 'I know you wouldn't have wanted to miss a funeral.'

'To do one's duty is so often a terrible burden. But as you dashed off to sea almost before the lid was down on my darling

Annabelle's coffin, I assumed I'd hear nothing.'

I saw Captain Tilton clench one fist in the small of his back, but his expression was politely bland.

'And why was she not sent to me immediately? How do you expect her to live in a house full of men and savages? And who's this girl you've gotten to take care of my precious darling?'

'This is Miss Neddy, Miss Osipovna,' he said applying the correct Russian form of my name.

'Neddy? What kind of a name is Neddy?'

'Short for Nadezhda,' I said.

'And where are you from? Surely with a name like that you're no American.'

'I'm from Russia, ma'am.'

'Rubbish! Henry, this girl's lying to you. She's no more Russian than I. Her accent's English if anything. Heaven only knows what else she's hoodwinked you over. I hope you keep a close eye on the silver.'

I told her politely and with a smile, in Russian, she was a meddling busybody and it was lucky there was a double door on her room, which I gestured to as I spoke, because if there hadn't been she could never have gotten into it.

'What was that gibberish?'

'Russian,' the captain said, trying not to laugh. 'Shall I send up tea?'

'And be sure it's hot,' Aunt Hester ordered. Then pausing at the door she added, 'And not served by one of your savages. I'll not have slant-eyed savages in my room!' The door closed behind her.

'Oh dear,' I said. 'You understand Russian.'

'Enough to know she got what she deserved.'

I blushed. 'She made me angry.'

'Yes. I could see that,' he chuckled.

'But why didn't she want to see Bunny? I offered, but she was more concerned with my provenance than the baby.'

'That's Annabelle's Great-aunt Hester Barnstable. Correctness before sentiment in all things—except her Annabelle and the shortcomings of the Tiltons. Besides which, she doesn't really like children much—unless they're completely biddable, like Annabelle.'

'I'll get her tea myself,' I said as I turned to rescue Bunny, who was beginning to protest her incarceration. 'You count the silver.'

. . .

I was busy making tea when the captain came into the kitchen and scooped Bunny from the floor. 'What am I going to tell Will and Joe,' he sighed. 'They'll be so disappointed. That old bat will be weeping crocodile tears and dropping a pall over the entire holiday.'

'She sounds as if she means to take Bunny,' I said.

'Nonsense. I told you she doesn't like children. She gave up saying she wanted to take the boys as soon as I pretended I might consider it.'

'But Bunny's Annabelle's daughter,' I pointed out. 'That might make a difference.'

'Annabelle was the blandest, quietest girl on the face of the earth and catered to Hester night and day. No one with our Bunny's spirit is going to be to her liking.'

I set up the tea tray without further comment, but couldn't quiet my concerns.

'Hester Barnstable,' the captain growled, as he kissed the top of Bunny's head, 'my children stay with me.'

At that moment Joe and Will burst into the kitchen. They'd been working out in the carriage house.

'Is she here? Is she staying?' they demanded in turn.

'Afraid so,' Captain Tilton said.

'It all has to go,' Joe said, hands deep in his pockets. 'We have to take it all down.'

'She'd never think it was right,' Will went on glumly. 'It would be fun and nice and no one would be crying. She wouldn't like that one little bit would she, Uncle Henry?'

Before he could answer I said, 'Captain, could we afford another turkey?'

'Another turkey? Yes. But—'

'Good. Then I have to ask you boys a favor.' I had their attention, and the plan came together as I spoke. 'I want you to go into that dining room and take down every scrap of the special things you've made for my first Thanksgiving. And tomorrow you and your uncle will have turkey, and cranberry sauce, and yams, and pumpkin pie with your great aunt. You'll mind your manners and she'd never know it isn't really Thanksgiving at all. And as soon as she leaves you're going to set everything right back up and then we'll have my real first Thanksgiving dinner.'

For a moment there was complete silence in the kitchen and then Joe said, 'We could do it! Sure we could. We could have all that stuff down in the basement in no time!'

'And she'd never know,' Will murmured with a small smile.

They ran off to begin their work, and I saw Chin raise his eyes to the ceiling, though whether he was praying or casting a look toward the room where the author of all his problems was waiting for her tea, I didn't know.

I kissed Bunny and started up the stairs with the tea tray, but Captain Tilton gave the baby to Mai Lin and took it from me. 'The least I can do after you've saved the boys from a terrible disappointment. Now they'll have something to look forward to.'

'So will I,' I told him wryly.

'I don't know how she does it,' he went on as we climbed, 'but she can always poke someone where it most hurts.'

'You mean the comment about your rushing off to sea?' I asked, remembering the clenched fist.

'There was a deadline on that cargo. And a severe penalty, not to mention the bad feeling, if it was late. Ira made the contract before he died. He never understood how perilous it is to make promises where the sea is concerned.'

'And he always had his big brother to save him.'

'I couldn't save him from the influenza. But I can't help wondering if I didn't do enough to save Annabelle.'

'Annabelle, what could you have done?'

'When Ira died she quit, she just gave up. Nothing I said about the boys needing her penetrated. I thought when the baby actually arrived it would wake her up to all she had to live for.'

'Do you believe she died because she wanted to?'

'I don't know. There was so little to her, as if she was made of cobwebs. And she never had any kind of passion I could see, just kind of a translucent beauty.'

The cup clinked against the creamer and I remembered my duty. Taking the tray I whispered for him to escape down the stairs before I knocked.

'Enter!'

I set the things on the table.

'Shall I pour, ma'am?' I asked, cringing inside when she motioned for me to proceed.

Great-aunt Hester Barnstable, divested of her voluminous mourning garments, was less massive, but her hard face and penetrating eyes made her seem more threatening when not veiled. She watched me pour like a cat watching a bird.

'Sugar?'

'One lump.'

'Lemon?'

'Heavens no!'

'Cream?'

'Just bring the pitcher.'

I set the cup on the small table at her elbow and brought a little selection of delicate sandwiches Mai Lin had whipped up in moments.

'Now watch me carefully and perhaps you can get it right next time and do your job properly,' she said harshly, as if she'd already told me over and over exactly how she wanted it done.

Clasping the creamer in her fat ostentatiously ringed fingers she looked up at me to be sure I was paying attention before she poured a hearty amount of the thick liquid into the tea, almost overflowing the rim of the cup. Then she wiped the drip from the spout of the creamer and licked her finger.

Her bad manners almost made me giggle, and I wanted to ask, was I to wipe the spout or allow her to do it?

She saw my mirth and her eyebrows drew down. 'And I do not like tea in the saucer, missy. 'Do you think you can manage that?

I was becoming angry again. I didn't mind serving the tea, but didn't care to be treated poorly. My mother and father had raised me to be polite to servants. Even a grand duchess, my mother always said, had no right to treat another human being poorly, particularly one who can't speak up for themselves because of disparity in rank.

I took back the creamer and started for the door.

'Oh, Miss— What's your name again?'

'Neddy,' I said, facing her, hands behind my back.

'And do you live in? Neddy?'

'Yes, ma'am.'

'So you sleep here with Captain Tilton?'

Her rude phraseology and insinuating tone shocked me. I made no reply.

'In my day, a young lady would have guarded her reputation more closely. But I suppose wherever it was you were brought up such things weren't important.'

My momentary astonishment vanished. In the back of my mind I heard the real Nadezhda urging me on. Assuming my most patrician manner, I fixed Hester Barnstable with a coldly superior look I'd seen my mother employ. 'Captain Tilton is a true gentleman. If I had any doubts about the safety of my reputation under his roof I should not be here. Your implication is unseemly. Ma'am. Now, if that is all, I have duties to attend to.'

'Perhaps not for long, miss. Don't think you can get above yourself with me and not suffer the consequences.'

'When Captain Tilton is unhappy with my work, ma'am, I'm sure he'll tell me. And now, you'll excuse me, unless I can pour you another cup of tea? Ma'am?'

She dismissed me with a wave of her hand. And I was hard pressed not to slam the door as I left.

. . .

When the boys came up to bed they were glum and near tears. Tar and Pete too seemed as blue as their masters.

Will was angry. 'She cries, but all she did at the funeral was carry on about how bad Poppa was to take her darling away from her and now she was dead; as if it was Poppa's fault.'

'And tonight she was blaming Uncle Henry,' Joe said, puzzled. 'But I don't know how he had anything to do with it.'

I heard footsteps on the stairs and shepherded them to their room.

'I thought it would be kind of fun to have a secret from her,' Joe said as he sank down on his bed. 'But she, well, she just makes a guy feel so bad because he's trying to be a man.'

'Some people,' I said, putting my arm around him, 'need someone to blame when things go wrong. It helps them to be angry with someone.'

'Oh. Yeah. Like Uncle Henry told us.'

'What did he say?'

'I was kind of mad at Bunny, you know, because of Momma. And Uncle Henry said it wasn't her fault, and I could see that but it didn't really make me feel any better. Then he said

I could blame God. The idea scared me, but he said God had broad shoulders and he'd understand me being angry. And then when I wasn't so angry anymore, I could say sorry to him and it would be alright.'

'Your Uncle Henry is a wise man,' I said. 'Now you two get ready for bed, and I'll read to you from *Robinson Crusoe* for a while.'

When I closed the book they were both asleep in Joe's bed with the pups at their feet. As I bent to move Will, the door opened and Captain Tilton came in with Bunny asleep in his arms. He passed me the baby and gently scooped up Will. Tar followed and they were both snuggled down in a moment.

Out in the corridor he murmured, 'I gave her a bottle. Those boys were real troopers tonight.'

'Despite that nasty old lady, they're going to be all right.'

'I know, I know.'

'I wonder she's willing to besmirch her reputation by staying in the house with a hussy like me.'

'And a dirty depraved old sailor like me. But she's a truly dedicated woman. No sacrifice too great to make children miserable.'

'Good night, Captain.'

. . .

The next day began quietly and stayed that way. I was permitted into the music room to assist the boys at the piano, and they did admirably. Joe played his usual little collection of ballads and simple pieces, accepting his praise from his great aunt with a smile. Will, who was showing real signs of becoming a fine musician, played beautifully and as I stood behind him turning pages I had a real sense of pride in his performance and could see that Captain Tilton, who held the fascinated Bunny on his lap, was pleased as well.

And then Great-aunt Hester said, 'Goodness William, such

a grim piece of music. But then I suppose a melancholy child like yourself would chose something sad. It made me think of your dear mother.' And she dabbed at her eyes with her black-edged handkerchief.

Will said nothing and kept his eyes on the floor.

Aunt Hester then took Bunny from the captain and started hugging and kissing her. Bunny, frightened by a stranger, immediately started squalling. When Chin appeared to announce dinner I folded her into my arms and she stopped crying.

'Can't Bunny and Miss Neddy come and have dinner with us?' Will asked, eyes round and innocent behind his glasses.

'Now William,' Hester admonished, 'this is a family dinner. I'm sure Emmaline's nanny would feel out-of-place in such a gathering. You mustn't embarrass her by putting her into such a difficult social situation.'

I could see Joe, who always wanted to please, was nervous. Captain Tilton too seemed a little worried about where this was going to go. And Will, by the set of his chin, looked like he was ready to press the point.

'Don't you worry about Miss Emmaline and me,' I said to him. We'll be having our own supper in the kitchen and I'll let her have some mashed potatoes and gravy. Now you go in there and do justice to that wonderful meal Mai Lin prepared. Remember,' I said with a wink, 'Thanksgiving comes but once a year.'

. . .

After dinner when I came into the corridor from tucking Bunny in I was surprised to see Hester's door open. I paused, not wanting her to see me and send me on some useless errand. But then I realized the captain was with her and I admit I simply decided to eavesdrop.

She was complaining that the boys ate like birds and how did the captain expect to keep them healthy if they only picked at their food. Then she observed that since the meal had been pre-pared by a savage, it might have been a little off. She'd thought it was, but didn't like to complain. The captain returned that it had been downright kind of her to have put away three helpings of everything to make the woman feel good about her labors. Then I heard him rise from his chair.

'Well, good night, Hester. Shall I tell Mai Lin you'll be here for dinner tomorrow night, or did you want to hurry back?'

'I'll be visiting friends tomorrow during the day and depart for San Francisco on Saturday. But I might stay another day or two. Would that be an inconvenience?'

'I only hope this storm that's coming on doesn't hold you up.'

'Such a dark and gloomy place, no wonder the boys are such silent waifs.'

'Well, they do miss their mother. Though no one misses her as much as you, I'm sure.'

'And now, Henry, what's to become of my little Emmaline?'

'She's fine, Hester. Good night. You'll have to excuse me. I have bookwork to do.'

He carefully closed the guest room door and then saw me.

'Everyone in bed?' he asked.

'Mmm. The boys are fine and Bunny's an expert with mashed potatoes.'

'Did you hear? She's staying for a while.'

'We'll manage. At least you can hide out in the library.'

'The first time I can find something good about that bloody bookwork,' he sighed. 'I don't know how Ira did it. He always seemed so interested in it all, and I guess I thought I'd find that same pleasure when I got going.'

'Perhaps it will come with time,' I said.

He gave me a dry look, and with a small gesture of farewell, went down the stairs.

On Friday, Hester spent the morning out and then stayed in her room most of the afternoon claiming fatigue. But I had to deliver a lot of sandwiches and tea, and she sent her chauffer out with several letters she insisted couldn't wait. When I took up the third pot of tea she announced she'd not be leaving until Monday. We were in for a long dull weekend.

On Saturday she was again out for a while, and when she returned spent most of the afternoon bustling about in her room. But there were no requests for tea. The boys and I spent the afternoon doing their lessons, not something they ordinarily would have been keen on, but it served, like the captain's bookwork, to keep them away from Great-aunt Hester. They manfully assisted their uncle with the duty of dining with her. They even played the piano after the meal, and Will selected only silly simple pieces while Joe reprised his former performance to the delight of his great-aunt, who again insisted on holding Bunny with the same tearful result.

Next morning, as breakfast was being served Hester sent down for a tray as she was feeling a little poorly. She then added she'd keep to her bed and forgo the pleasure of attending services with Captain Tilton and the boys. So they set off for the Presbyterian church with a sense of escape at the same time Chin and Mai Lin departed for the Methodist service.

I put Bunny down for her morning nap and went into the boys' rooms to check their homework for Monday, thinking I might be busy in the afternoon and evening waiting on the invalid in the guest room. And it was from this vantage point I saw Hester's motorcar round the corner from town and pull up in front of the house. Harris came smartly up the steps and I watched as her luggage was toted down and stowed in the boot.

As I continued to stare, puzzled but delighted, a plump red-haired woman emerged from the car. At the same moment

Bunny wailed from her room, so I gave up my watch to go to her. The distasteful visit would soon be over; I didn't have to see the actual departure. Though I did feel, superstitiously, that if I didn't witness the event, she might not actually leave. I shook my head at my own silliness as I went down the upper hall, but stopped when I saw Aunt Hester disappear down the stairs, the protesting Bunny in her arms.

'Stop!' I shouted.

The old woman glared up at me.

'What do you think you're doing?' I demanded, flying down to block her passage on the landing.

'Out of my way.'

'You're taking Bunny,' I accused. 'You're stealing her.'

'I'm saving her. I'm taking her to a home were she can become a proper lady. I'll not allow her to be subjected to the goings-on in this house, to be raised by floozies and savages.'

'There are no "goings on" in this house,' I snapped. 'Give her to me.'

'I'm not blind, young lady. I see they way you cozy up to those poor boys, using them as your pawns. And Henry Tilton's no better, making such a fuss over you, turning a blind eye to your lies. I don't doubt you and that lecherous sailor cooked up the whole nanny scheme to lend respectability to your lascivious pursuits. I'll not have this baby living in a brothel in the care of a whoremonger and his trollop!'

I stared. Her righteous certainty and the look of pure loathing in her eyes were like blows. She threw her considerable weight against me, knocking the air from my lungs, and I fell into the corner as she scuttled past, a look of triumph in her eyes. But Bunny's wail brought me scrambling to my feet in only a moment, and I raced down the steps.

Near the front door I was confronted by three people. Hester Barnstable was being assisted into her traveling cloak by the chauffer, and the red-haired woman was struggling with the now completely frantic Bunny. The baby lunged toward me, arms out, and the red-haired woman almost dropped her.

I snatched Bunny away, clutching her hard against my body. But now I was between Hester and the chauffer.

'Harris. Take my niece away from that tramp. You may use force.'

I could see there was no determination in the chauffeur's eyes, and he made no move toward me as I spun to the side and slipped past him.

With a grunting shriek, Hester swung her umbrella at me. And then my body was pressed against the doorjamb, protecting Bunny from the blows with my arm. I saw stars. The hallway was before me, an escape route, and I moved into it.

A pair of arms closed powerfully around my torso.

'No!' I screamed, fighting the confining embrace. 'No, you can't have her!'

'Neddy!' Captain Tilton's voice came firmly through my panic. 'Neddy! It's me!'

I stopped resisting. 'She's trying to take Bunny,' I gasped. 'She's trying to steal Bunny.'

He pushed me behind him and turned to face Hester. 'Get out of my house,' he said, menace in every measured word. 'Now.'

'I shall summon my attorney,' she snarled. 'You'll not keep me from doing my duty to poor dead Annabelle. You beast.'

'Do that, Hester. I'll fight you with every ounce of my strength and dollar to my name. These children where left in my care—by both their parents. Leave. Now. Or I'll call the police.'

'You wouldn't dare,' Hester gasped, drawing her cloak around her as majestically as she could.

'There are no shortage of witnesses to what you tried to do. Attempted kidnapping, like kidnapping, is a crime. Or didn't you know that? And that would include Harris here and this woman.'

He rounded on Hester's accomplices. 'Does she pay you enough to go to jail for her?'

The red-haired woman turned on her heel and was off down the steps instantly.

Captain Tilton then fixed his hard gaze on Harris the chauffer.

'Miz Barnstable?' the terrified Harris said. 'Best we go?'

Hester Barnstable knew she was beaten, but wasn't about to leave without a parting shot. 'I wash my hands of you all,' she informed us imperiously. 'And that means completely. These children will never see me again, nor one penny of my fortune.'

'We don't want your old money,' Will shouted. 'You hurt Miss Neddy. She loves us and we love her, not you!'

'You tried to steal my sister,' Joe said. 'Gosh, she's just a little baby.'

'Go, Hester,' Henry Tilton said tiredly.

'Not one penny, Henry Tilton. Not one. You and those ungrateful boys can stay here in this decaying town and starve for all I care. And that goes for that Bolshevik you call a nanny as well!'

With those parting words she swept out the door.

'Gee, Miss Neddy,' Joe said. 'I thought you were a Russian.'

.   .   .

Following on the heels of our disastrous visit from Great-aunt Hester my first Thanksgiving Day in America was an unforgettable and hilarious event the shades of which are still with us.

Joe and Will were gotten up as Indians, but of the Great Plains variety if my history studies were correct. They wore improvised buckskins made of old clothes from the attic, and their headdresses were a bizarre collection of what must have once been the trimmings of some of the finest ladies' hats in

Astoria. They'd constructed a teepee at the edge of the conservatory windows painted with buffalo, horses, and deer, which looked quite authentic and became a fixture in their schoolroom for years.

Bunny, the captain, and I were to play the pilgrims and were provided with hats and large white collars to give us a sense of participation. The hats were made of felt and paper and the captain's was a little small, which lent to the hilarity. We were instructed (in a note pinned to the dining room doors) to enter and beg the Indians we found there to help us, as we were starving.

This we managed to do with straight faces as Joe and Will, now called Red Deer and Big Buffalo, complete with war paint, pronounced Bunny a 'cute papoose' and consulted with each other on whether they should help us or not.

Red Deer announced, 'We help. You not starve.'

The captain and I possibly overacted a little in our effusive gratitude, but I don't think the boys thought so. Big Buffalo rose and, clapping his hands like a sultan calling up the dancing girls, summoned the feast from the kitchen.

And here was where the day became truly memorable, for the boys had somehow persuaded Chin and Mai Lin to wear Indian costumes. The captain and I were speechless. It was a never to be forgotten image. Chin and his wife looked completely the part with their dark hair and a little face paint. Mai Lin, long braids over her shoulders, brought turkey, corn, and sweet potatoes to put before us. Chin assisted her with a fierce, chief-like frown.

The captain carved the turkey, but all the rest of the serving was done by the boys, trying to stay in character, as Bunny crowed with delight from her high-chair and banged her spoon, making us all laugh.

It was a grand event and did much to wipe out the bad days we'd just come through. When it was over, Red Deer and Big

Buffalo carted their tent upstairs with plans to sleep in it, and I took Bunny off for a bath and her evening bottle.

But when I put her into the bathtub and looked into her bright happy face, the bruises on my arm and the tender scrape on my temple reminded me of the close call we'd had just the day before. And I knew I'd come to love Joe and Will and this baby. It was no longer just a job—it was a home, something I never thought I'd find again when I left Ekaterinburg behind.

· · ·

I felt we'd recovered our balance, bruises not withstanding, but was soon to find that the captain hadn't. At the end of the week he took the boys into his study after dinner and they stayed for over an hour as I tried to busy myself in the schoolroom and not watch the clock. But when they came in I saw serious faces.

'Something wrong?' I asked, trying not to sound as if I was prying.

But they said nothing and went right to their homework.

I squared the books in the bookcase, and set the baseball bats right where they'd been before as I pretended to organize them. I wanted to help, but in my position as governess I had no right to question them about the business of their family.

Finally, Will sighed and put down his pencil, closing his book with a thump. 'Uncle Henry wants to 'dopt us.'

'Adopt,' Joe corrected, also putting aside his books.

'But he said at Momma's funeral that we were a family,' Will was close to tears. 'Why does he want to have some judge tell him he's our father?'

'Do you think your Great-aunt Hester trying to take Bunny away might have something to do with it?' I asked carefully.

'Then he could 'dopt Bunny,' Will said sensibly. 'She doesn't even remember Momma and Poppa.'

Now I was on firm ground. 'Do you think if your Uncle Henry adopts you it'll mean you have to give up thinking of your parents as your parents?'

Joe got up from is desk and went to the dark window, his serious face reflected dimly in the glass. 'I can't see their faces,' he said softly. 'I try and try but I can't remember what they look like, so I go and get the photograph of them, but it's just a picture of some nice strangers.'

'I remember them,' Will said darkly. 'I remember them dead and pale-looking there in the parlor, where I listened to people say they looked so peaceful, and both times I wanted to jump up and shout, no they don't—they look dead! But I never did.'

'Three years ago my parents died,' I said, making them come to the bench under the window, where I sat them down so they could both see my face. 'And for a long time it was as if they'd vanished in a fog, as if they'd never been. But I had my *Papasha*, just as you have your Uncle Henry, to remind me every day that we were still a family and I was loved very, very much.'

'*Papasha*?' Joe asked. 'What's a *Papasha*?'

'It's a name in Russian for father, but not what I'd called my papa. And as time went on I began to remember my parents, how they looked and the sound of their voices. I still love them just as much as I ever did, but I loved my *Papasha*, my second father, too. And now I miss him just as much.'

'So then, Uncle Henry could become our *Papasha*, and it would be all right?' Joe asked.

'I should think so. Your parents could have made Great-aunt Hester your guardian, but they chose him. Now he wants to be sure he can say to the Great-aunt Hesters of this world that no one can break up his family, the family your parents wanted you to have.'

'I guess he really wants to be our father,' Joe said reflectively, 'else he would have let that mean old lady take Bunny.'

'Of course he does! Why wouldn't he want two such fine sons?'

'And now that Bunny doesn't cry all the time she's kind of fun,' Will added.

'Maybe we should go and tell him,' Joe said. 'He told us we should think about it, but he was kind of sad when we didn't say yes right away.'

'He's had all week to work this out,' I reminded them. 'I expect he didn't realize it was a whole new idea for you.'

'That's just what he said!' Joe marveled. 'How did you know that?'

'Because Miss Neddy understands people better than anyone else,' Will replied matter-of-factly. 'Haven't you figured that out yet?'

Joe smiled and took my hand. 'You come, too. In case we need help?'

·   ·   ·

When we entered the library the captain looked up from a pile of ledgers.

'We want you to be our *Papasha*,' Joe and Will almost shouted. Then Joe went on, 'We talked to Miss Neddy about it and she said we could still love Momma and Poppa even if you were our new one, our *Papasha*. Because she had one, too.'

The captain came around the desk. 'You sure? You don't need to think about it?'

Both boys shook their heads. 'Nope,' Joe added, grinning up into his uncle's eyes.

Captain Tilton closed them into an embrace and kissed the tops of their heads. 'Now you two get back to your books. I've kept you long enough.'

'Yes, *Papasha*,' the chorused and dashed out.

'Thank you, Miss Neddy. Once again you've rescued us.'

'They're having a hard time picturing their parents' faces,' I explained. 'And were afraid if you 'dopted them, as Will says, they'd forget them altogether.'

'I can see Ira all the time, recall whole conversations we've had about one thing and another. But Annabelle... She was like a cobweb spun in the sun. I always thought she'd drift away if the breeze came up.'

'And so she did,' I observed more to myself. 'Such an easy way out.'

He looked up at me sharply. 'Not something you'd do, I'd guess.'

I was embarrassed and I blushed. 'It's not—'

'What?'

'It's not something I could do, if I had three such fine healthy children,' I admitted, perhaps speaking ill of a dead woman I'd never known. 'But there was a time when I came very close, so I'd best not judge.'

'I wasn't much better. After the funeral I was grateful to go. I needed to spend my emotion on the water, so I could come home to the boys and not tarnish their memories.'

'And now?'

'What do you mean?'

'Where do you go now when you need to think?'

He pointed to the picture of the ship over the fireplace. 'I hitch a ride on the *Denali Princess* with Grandfather William, and we fight the storm in the painting together. I never actually knew him, but right now he's where I turn for strength. Then I do battle with these ledgers, bills of sale, cargo manifests, and captain's reports.'

'Not as magnificent as a storm at sea.'

'But just as dangerous,' he said with a wry expression. 'Just as many snares and pitfalls for the inexperienced as the Bering Sea.'

'You've sailed the northern oceans?'

'Since I was a boy. I've even been to your homeland, though some don't call Siberia Russia.'

'I do. Sometimes I think it's the very heart of Russia, the

~ 132 ~

part that stands for her vastness and strength, for the multitude of cultures and expanse of possibilities she offers. Dangerous like the ocean but beautiful, and limitless.'

'You speak of it with so much love.'

'There's nothing for me there now,' I said, deflated by the realization of all I'd lost.

'I, for one, am glad you found your way here, Miss Neddy,' he said with genuine interest in his eyes, even curiosity.

'I am too, Captain,' I replied, turning away from his invitation to talk about the world I'd left behind. 'Now I'd best see to my students before I'm out of a job.'

'*Papasha*?' he asked as I reached the door. 'Papa in Russian? Right?'

'I didn't mean they had to call you that.'

'I like it. All my own. Not Ira. Me. A new name for a new beginning. If you don't mind?'

'You're welcome to it,' I said. 'It suits you.'

.   .   .

Christmas came and went along with the New Year. And in the middle of January a huge storm roared in from the north seas, raging around the house, buffeting the trees, and howling in the chimneys as it lashed the windows with rain. I'd been checking on the boys, who were sleeping soundly while I worried they'd be frightened, and decided I needed a cup of tea. I slipped down the back stairs and found Captain Tilton engaged in heating water.

'Oh. Captain. Did the storm wake you?'

'No, this is pretty much a standard winter blow in these parts. I was up working on the damn books. Beg your pardon for the language.'

'No need,' I said as I got out the mugs and began measuring tea into the strainer.

The captain went to the stove and watched the pot, but

when it boiled he didn't notice, though the marbles Mai Lin had put in it to sing when it was ready were clinking away quite musically.

I stepped in to take it off the heat and as I closed my hand over the handle, made a decision. I took a deep breath, poured the water over the strainer and said, 'Captain, may I ask a question?'

He nodded.

'You spend most of the day down at the wharves, what goes on there?'

'Ships coming in, going out, cargo to distribute, schedules to plan,' he said with a tired sigh. 'Every day's different because the sea isn't like a road or a train track, you can't depend on good weather or fair wind. So each day decisions have to be made about how to get your cargo to where it's going efficiently; which ship, which captain, a route and ports of call.'

'Do you have many ships?'

'Four. But I also buy and sell cargos, fill orders, and use other ships to carry my goods.'

'And they sail to Alaska and Siberia?'

'As well as Hawaii, Canton, Singapore, Batavia, South America; any part of the Pacific.'

'Then you come home and do all the bookwork each day's changes bring about?'

'Exactly. If things don't get entered properly the first time, a real mess can ensue when plans have to alter. And since no insurance company's going to pay for losses that can't be documented, the paperwork becomes very important.'

'It was Ira who used to do that?'

'He was a genius and he created a good system. But I'm not like him. I need to get my hands on things, do something, not spend my days keeping track of where things go and how much they cost.'

I poured the fragrant China tea and handed him a thick

white mug as I tried to find just the right words to broach a difficult subject.

'Captain Tilton?'

He smiled. 'More questions, Miss Neddy? I'm bored with all this talk of numbers and schedules already.'

'I'm very good with numbers,' I said rapidly, determined to speak my piece now that I'd begun, 'and as the boys are in school all day I've time on my hands. Bunny's very little work. All the household chores are done by Mai Lin and her girls. Could I possibly be of help to you with your books?'

He stood very still, the untouched mug in his hand, and stared at me.

Under his gaze I felt I needed to say more, say something, say anything. 'I know it may not be my place, and I don't want to cause embarrassment, or pry into your business, or lose my job. I hope you'll consider my offer in the spirit of a business proposition and not think I'm prying. Oh dear, I already said that, didn't I?'

'Are you telling me you'd consider doing the bookwork for me?'

I nodded. 'Yes, Captain. If I could be of help. If I wouldn't be overstepping my place.'

'You like working with numbers?' he asked skeptically.

'It's fairly easy for me. Numbers. I like keeping track of things. Not the most ladylike trait I'll grant you, but there it is. I like to be the person in control.'

He grinned. 'Miss Neddy, if this isn't a dream, I'd consider it a huge favor if you wanted to take a hand in the bookwork.'

'When shall we start?' I demanded, relieved and eager.

'This storm will stop shipping for days. No one will be able to cross the bar in or out. If we begin in the morning I should be able to explain how things work by the time I have to go back down to the wharves and unsnarl the tangles this storm's going to cause.'

'Grand! I'll be in your study as soon as I have our Bunny up and fed. She can play in there, if you don't mind, while I work.'

'Aren't you afraid of exposing her to your "un-lady-like" talents?'

'I have the feeling that our lionhearted Miss Bunny won't worry about such things.'

. . .

My taking over the bookwork settled the family into a solid routine. The captain wasn't distracted by the pressure of work and so had more time and energy for the children. And I was happier too, being mentally challenged every day and knowing I was helping out.

The boys loved the extra attention and called the captain *Papasha* easily. Even Bunny knew the word and would turn her brilliant blue eyes on him when it was said. That the legal adoption went along without a hitch didn't matter much to the Tiltons; it was the closeness and security they'd found that mattered. Nineteen-twenty-one was sailing along smoothly into spring. And I was looking forward to my first summer in America.

I was in the kitchen alone when there was a knock at the door and I found my former landlady Gertrude van Dorn on the back step.

'Gert! How good to see you. Come in out of the rain this minute. What are you doing out on a day like this?'

'They're all like this around here till June, think I'm growing webs between my toes,' she grumbled.

'Come in, get that slicker off. I'll make us some tea.'

'Got no time for that,' she said harshly. 'Just thought you should know something.'

'Oh? What?'

'Man came to my place asking about you. Didn't start out

that way, thought he was pretty slick, but I saw where he was headed soon enough.'

My heart jumped into my throat. 'What do you mean?' I said, forcing down the panic and keeping my voice calm.

'He was a sweaty little man. Had dark hair, what there was of it, and he needed a wash something fierce. Smelled of dirty linen. Know what I mean?'

An image of Rasputin leaped into my mind and I felt a chill at the back of my neck. But it also served to clamp an iron hold on my fears. I needed to know what I was up against. 'What did he want?'

'Came down to, with all the slimy charming comments and sleazy talk taken out, he wanted to know where you were from and if you were who you said you were.'

Now I was truly afraid and straightened some jars on the table so I didn't have to look Gert in the eye. 'What did you tell him?'

'To mind his own business and get out of my house. That's what I told him.'

'Thank you.'

'But then, well, he said he was trying to make sure who you were and where you were from because you'd come into some money—if you were really who you said you were. Now, at the time I didn't believe him, but then I got to thinking maybe I was too hasty and maybe he was for real. He said it was a bunch of money. An inheritance. And just because a guy smells bad don't necessarily mean he's lying. I'd hate to have done you out of a good thing. You know?'

'No one's left me any money,' I said, keeping my voice firm and calm. 'If he was legitimate, it's not me he's looking for. You did the right thing sending him away.'

Relief flooded Gert's homely face. 'Wouldn't like to have done you a bad turn. You know?'

'You didn't,' I smiled, determined to make light of the

whole thing and send her on her way without worries—or sus-picions. 'I'm a nanny, Gert. No one's left me a fortune, even though Roma might want to believe it could be so.'

'That girl is the silliest thing,' Gert chuckled. 'But she's got a heart big as all outdoors. Having another baby in the fall.'

'Now, how about that tea?' I offered, hoping she'd not stay.

'No, no, got to get back. Have a house full. You come down and see me soon,' she said as she tied her hat back on and went down the steps.

'Yes. Soon,' I replied.

I watched her make her way back to the street and kept my eyes on her until she vanished in the rain. Then I literally ran up the back stairs to my room and locked myself in—the first time I'd turned the key on my door since I'd arrived.

Tears welled in my eyes and I couldn't catch my breath. One word hammered in my brain to the rhythm of my heart. Run! Run! Run!

Frantically, I collected my treasures on the bed, *Maman's* bible and Papa's photo album, the egg with the bunnies and the one Kuzma had made. From my desk I grabbed the collection of newspaper articles I'd gathered about the Russian expatri-ates who represented the last threads of my family now living in Europe, and shredded them with shaking hands. I was desper-ate to hide any tie to Russia.

Then I snatched up Papa's album, thinking to destroy that as well, to completely erase the telltale connection. But when faced with the trusting happy eyes of my family I couldn't bring myself to tear them apart, to deny them yet another time, and collapsed on the bed, hunched over their images. I could pre-tend I was someone else but these people were who I belonged to, they represented the root of my being. And when the cha-rade of my life brought me down I needed to have this proof that I was real, that I'd been loved and cherished even if those days were long gone.

I dropped the album on the bed and brought the box Kuzma had made, the one with the secret compartment, from the closet. As I laid my memories in their hiding place, I felt a terrible weariness, an emptiness, a foreshadowing of the rest of my life. Tears slipped down my cheeks. Once again I must flee for my life, but this time I was completely alone.

And in this grey and lonely place I heard a laughing gurgle and spun around to see Bunny watching me from her crib where she'd been napping. She was seven months old now; I'd been caring for her almost five months. She grinned, delighted I was there, safe and secure in my caring and devotion.

I looked at the small bedside clock. The boys would be home in an hour. What would they do if I disappeared without even a goodbye? How could I do that to them?

I found the photo of Pierre Gilliard in my father's little album. Then of Nadezhda and her bold smile. And after that, the faces of my father and Kuzma, two men who'd loved their children more than anything else. I dried my eyes and carefully put away my little trove of memories. Then I took Bunny into my arms, holding her bed-warm baby body against my heart, smelling her skin, feeling the connection between us.

'I can't leave you, little bunny,' I whispered. 'I'll not give you and your brothers up without a fight. Not this time. Not again.'

. . .

One day, almost a month after Gert's alarming visit, I walked into the school room carrying Bunny to tell the boys it was almost time for dinner and was met by a sudden silence. The boys looked guilty and embarrassed. I'd intruded on something.

Since I'd found out someone had been inquiring about me, I'd felt the need to protect myself, and only within the walls of the house, in the circle created for me by the people in that house, did I feel safe. But the way the boys were watching me, wary and unsure, separated me from the comfort of belonging I usually found in their company.

Stepping back toward the door I said, 'I'm sorry, don't let me interrupt.'

'No. Wait,' Joe said. Then he turned to Will. 'Maybe Miss Neddy can talk to him.'

Will's eyes, always hidden slightly by his glasses, studied me for a moment. 'Maybe.'

I waited for them to decided whether to include me or not.

'We need you to talk to *Papasha*,' Will finally said.

'About what?'

'Ecola,' they murmured. 'About going to Ecola.'

'It's a place?'

They nodded solemnly.

'And you want to go there? Why?'

'It's the best place ever!' Joe exclaimed.

'But we didn't go last summer,' Will said glumly. 'And maybe because of Poppa, *Papasha* won't want to go this summer. Things are all different now.'

Joe gave this some thought and then his optimistic nature came to the fore. 'But now that Miss Neddy's here maybe it would be all right again. And we could show Bunny everything. She's never been. Maybe *Papasha* wants to go, too—just like us. Maybe, maybe it could be that way...'

I put Bunny down and went to sit on the window bench. 'Tell me about Ecola.'

'When *Papasha* was Uncle Henry he used to live there. And we'd go out and stay in his house every summer—for the whole summer. There's this giant rock to climb on and the lighthouse, all the tide pools and the dunes and the mountains and the creeks. Just everything. We always have the best time at Ecola.'

'But things are different now,' Will reminded him. 'He doesn't even sail on the *Raven* now.'

'The one I keep the books for?'

'But now someone else sails it because he has to stay here all the time to do the business,' Joe said. 'And when I grow up I'm going to become his wharf-master so he can go back to sea and be happy.'

'And I'm going to keep the books,' Will added. 'I'm good at my sums.'

'And then what shall I do?' I asked, touched by their understanding of the captain's sacrifices.

'Oh, you'll have to give all your time to raising Bunny and finding her a husband,' Joe told me seriously. 'And it won't be easy, especially if she stays bald forever and it looks like she will.'

I laughed aloud as I caressed the baby's head. 'She will not stay bald,' I told them as we made our way down to dinner. 'She has fuzz now and it'll turn into lovely hair before she'll need to worry about finding a husband. If she wants one.'

'That's what all girls want,' Joe assured me.

'I don't know that I want one,' I said.

'Want one what?' asked the captain as we met him at the dining room door.

'A husband,' the boys informed him. 'All girls want a husband.'

The captain took Bunny who was demanding his attention. 'I hope Miss Neddy doesn't want a husband too soon. What would we do without her?'

There were more questions from the boys about exactly how old I was and did I mind being a spinster and didn't I really want a husband. I was getting thoroughly embarrassed, so I took the bull by the horns and told the captain the boys had been talking about going to Ecola this summer.

'You want to go?' he asked, his tone light, but he was guardedly studying their faces.

They were all eagerness, and he smiled at their plans to show me and Bunny around, and the chatter about working on their canoe, which had been waiting in the shed for three years now. And then they told me they'd take me clamming.

I knew nothing about clamming and the topic filled the rest of the dinner hour. I gained little from the boys' attempts to explain it to me other than that there was digging and lots of fun. There was also a great dinner at the end—chowder with corn and bacon and biscuits.

I was squarely behind the plan. First, because the boys and even the captain were so excited about it. But also because the idea of getting out of Astoria, putting some distance between myself and anyone who might be looking for me, appealed greatly.

The captain, being the voice of reason, informed me it wasn't a fancy place and there was no room for extra servants—Mai Lin and I would be doing all the work. He and Chin would come out at the weekends, and the trip wasn't for the faint-hearted. But he also assured me he knew I wasn't the faint-hearted sort and would do fine.

I was caught by the boys' eagerness. It took me back to my own childhood when we'd spent the warm months on our yacht in the fjords of Finland with our toes in the water enjoying the sunshine. So as soon as school was out it was with wholehearted anticipation I started on the train journey to the little town of Seaside. All our bundles, trunks, boxes, and paraphernalia were piled into the baggage car. Once there we'd have to depend on what we'd brought. The captain and I took our seats with a pair of giant black dogs, one baby, and two small boys who were practically popping out of their skin. Chin and Mai Lin were stoic throughout the ride, passing out food when needed.

I finally succeeded in keeping my effervescing charges in their seats by telling them about my own adventures living the rustic life. I'd certainly gone without the amenities of town living on the road with Kuzma and was able to inform the boys I was a good marksman, excellent horsewoman, and strong swimmer. And I think Captain Tilton was glad to hear of my woodsman's skills as well, since he'd have to leave me to work in Astoria and come out on what the boys called the 'daddy train' on the weekends.

We spent the night in Seaside as the trip to Ecola the next day would take more than seven hours and an early morning start was best. So after only a few hours of much interrupted sleep because the boys knew it would be dark when we rose and kept asking was it time to get up yet, I was ready to begin the last leg of our odyssey.

The boys tore down the stairs of the old hotel and out to the wagon the moment it pulled up, and began carrying their equipment and bags to help. Mai Lin checked her food supplies for the day while the captain and Chin focused on the business of loading and getting underway. I had to keep the boys in check, but found their excitement too delightful to deserve harsh words. Bunny, who knew nothing of what was going on, simply basked in the happiness that surrounded her and the dogs looked worried until we actually got underway and they were riding with us.

In the dark and salt-smelling predawn, we left Seaside behind and took to the Ecola Toll Road for a day of adventure. The boys, grizzled veterans of the trail, joyously informed me there were one hundred and eleven turns on the road and it was much better now than it had been long ago. And I could see, though he tried to hide it, that Captain Tilton was as excited as the boys to be returning to his former home.

As the sun rose I was enchanted by the towering pines the road wound through, warmed by good memories of trekking the *taiga* with Kuzma. The silence of the great woods and the morning light that filtered through the leaves wrapped me in a sense of peace, and the slight salt tang in the air made me eager to see the ocean again.

. . .

I've spoken of seminal moments, those things that change one forever. I'd survived some of those formative events, all negative and all costing me dearly. But I'd no idea my arrival in the small beach community of Ecola, Oregon would so completely transform my world, and my future. I'd expected no more than a fun summer and reprieve from the worry about possibly being discovered.

As noon passed we came down from the last turn and crossed Ecola Creek, finally at sea level. To my right, the fresh water of the creek curved out to meet the salt and seagulls soared through the blue sky. We entered the main street and the boys eagerly pointed out the Lanphere Co. general store and post office. There was also Himes' store, which sold groceries and beach supplies. There were little restaurants, and pointing to the trees the boys showed me roads that went off to some of the resorts where people from Portland and Astoria, and even as far away as California, came to stay. I saw a fish market and meat market as well as a real estate office. Little cabins clad with weathered silver shingles and white trim were tucked in under the pines, ready for the summer's visitors. On some porches, early comers and the few permanent residents waved a gay welcome as we passed.

At the south edge of downtown we turned up a rise, and the horses were going slowly after a long day. The boys, followed by their dogs, jumped out and dashed ahead.

'I bought the house from a man who loved it here,' the captain told me as he watched them run up the steps of a substantial porch. 'But his wife wouldn't make the trip—she hated the rough road. It wasn't even completely finished inside when I took it over in 1912.'

'Will and Joe told me this is your bachelor house.'

Henry Tilton smiled. 'That's what their mother called it.

But to me it was a refuge where I could still be close to the ocean. Not that Astoria doesn't have good vistas of the water, but it's not open, not the panorama from horizon to horizon. You should see it here in winter when the storms come raging against Haystack Rock. Magnificent.'

The big wagon came to a stop and the captain helped me down. Bunny was in my arms; she'd been caught up in the boys' excitement and only fallen asleep half an hour before. Chin and the captain began unloading while I went round the outside of the house for some quiet.

I came to the edge of the rise on which the house stood. Wind-sculpted pines framed a vista that brought tears to my eyes. The beach grass whispered in the soft wind and swept away down the steep dune to the beach. Huge pieces of driftwood cast onto the beach by winter storms—some of them whole, massive trees complete with their roots—littered the sand. Brown pelicans skimmed the waves, seeming to never flap their wings as they scouted for fish. And to the south around the rampart of Haystack Rock, nesting seagulls screamed and laughed. The water was translucent blue-green, nothing like the sky and yet perfectly matched. Out to sea toward the north stood a lighthouse perched on a huge rock, its white paint bright in the sun. I was completely bewitched by the view and the reassuring roar of the surf.

I wanted to take off my shoes to feel the warm sand between my toes, and had it not been for Bunny, would have been hard pressed not to dash down and put my bare feet into the waves. But as it was, I was grateful she provided my excuse to stand and admire, to marvel in the magic of the ocean. It was open, vast, with the huge rock and the smaller congregation around it to make the waves dance and break in an ever-changing flow. When the gulls laughed, the sound threaded in with the boys' joyous shouts from the yard.

I felt a rush of well-being, a sense of belonging I'd not had since Rasputin. The house behind me was shingled, and like most others in town, weathered to a silver grey. It was square, stout, and strong. The house of a man who knew the power of wind and sea, and had chosen it to withstand anything.

Captain Tilton appeared, already stripped of his coat, and began unfastening the shutters that protected the downstairs windows. The boys called from the large porch that jutted out from the second floor toward the ocean, urging me to come up and see the room where Bunny and I would sleep. I promised to be right there, but lingered, unable to give up the contentment of the view.

'Peaceful today,' Captain Tilton said, coming to stand beside me. 'Tide's almost high. Will start to turn in a couple hours, then we can see the tide pools at the base of the rock.'

I felt tears burning in my eyes though my mood was fantastically light. 'Your home is beautiful,' I murmured, unable to express my feelings, afraid to say too much and unleash a flood of emotions I'd kept in check for so many years. 'I feel protected here.'

'Mmm,' he agreed with a nod. And thus we stood, side by side, watching the Pacific.

. . .

The house was simple. When you entered the front door you were immediately in a long sitting room. A fireplace of round river-stone loomed on one wall, and at the room's rear was a kitchen. A dining table divided the space between the kitchen and sitting area. All the life of the house took place in this one space.

Just to the left of the front door was a den tucked under the stairs. It had bookshelves, a desk, and one old leather chair with an ottoman. I knew at a glance this was Captain Tilton's refuge.

There was a small bathroom on the first floor, too, and a

utility room off the kitchen with laundry sinks and a hand-cranked wringer washer. The kitchen looked quite well equipped and efficient, but the best thing about it was that it faced a flagged patio and the water.

Upstairs there were three bedrooms and the grand covered porch that surveyed the ocean—and luxury of luxuries, a second bathroom with a claw-foot tub built by the first owner when he'd still hoped to lure his city wife to his beach house.

Nothing was showy or expensive. All the beds had bright Hudson's Bay blankets and the furniture upstairs and down was simple, serviceable, and sturdy. There were books, chairs to curl up in and read them, and not a single frill. Comfort would never be lacking with the fire roaring in the grand fireplace on cold nights, which I had been assured were common even through the summer. Old William Tilton's house in Astoria, the monument to his hard work and prosperity, clearly stated that the homeowner was to be admired and treated with respect. His grandson's chosen home, however, spoke of strength and the integrity of simple things.

Chin and Mai Lin had quarters over the garage that housed a Ford that would serve as transportation for the captain and Chin on the weekends. During the week it would sit with all the other 'daddy cars' at the station in Seaside.

By dark we were settled in. I was impressed by how the boys, eager as they were to be playing on the beach and rediscovering their old haunts, pitched in to get the work done. By the time we sat down to devour a supper of chicken and potato salad, we were ready to begin our summer. We watched the sun set over the water with hushed awe. I was a little embarrassed to be so transfixed by it until I realized even Bunny was entranced as the orangey globe disappeared below the waterline. She waved to it.

'Makes you feel the earth turning,' Henry Tilton said, 'when you realize we're moving fast enough for the sun to disappear so quickly.'

And I thought, 'No wonder it's impossible to gain control of our lives: We're stationary and the world around us is spinning at such great speed.'

As the sky grew dark and the rhythmic circling beacon of the Tillamook Rock Lighthouse to the north swept comfortingly over the ocean, Joe and Will were drooping. I took them up and read to them from *Treasure Island* until they dozed off. I thought as I laid the book down that we'd have to start all over the next night, because they'd fallen asleep so quickly they'd not heard a word. Then I went down to beg a book from the captain.

'May I borrow from your library?' I asked, peeking around the door.

'Please, anything,' he said, rising from his desk. 'Bunny asleep?'

'And the boys.'

He yawned discreetly.

I found an edition of *The Count of Monte Cristo*. 'This will do for a good summer read,' I declared. 'Nothing like revenge.'

The captain smiled and nodded as he consulted his pocket watch. 'I like that one too. The boys will be up at dawn, so maybe best we turn in.'

He snuffed his lamp and handing me a candle for the stairs made sure I had matches for the kerosene lamp beside my bed.

I didn't read one word. I opened the window and got into bed, cuddled down and listened to the surf. I don't think the glow of the Tillamook Lighthouse swept over me more than twice before I was fast asleep.

. . .

The feeling I'd had of profound belonging and safety didn't fade as the summer days went on. Bunny and I wandered the little town together and joined the boys on the beach. We explored the tide pools and I was educated about sea stars, sea urchins, and sea anemones. We collected limpet and razor clam shells and sand dollars as well as pretty pieces of wood. Mai Lin had her hands full with the house and laundry so I took over most of the cooking. I shopped at the little fish market and learned to prepare whatever was fresh that day. Crab and salmon were becoming specialties and the boys loved my biscuits. We'd arrived early enough to set out a small garden and eagerly awaited beans and tomatoes of our own. It was a peaceful respite and I forgot about the man who'd questioned Gert. I also took full advantage of the opportunity to devote all my time to the children and play with the boys instead of being their taskmaster about their studies. It wasn't until the middle of July that Captain Tilton and Chin arrived to stay for a whole week.

'All my cargoes are at sea,' the captain announced, 'and left to my care I'm sure the books are in such a muddle they can't be sorted out in under a week—not with me being out on the beach every day!'

When Sunday came around and he didn't have to leave, a change came over Henry Tilton, and as the days passed I became more clearly aware of the strain he'd been under since I met him.

At the time I'd taken over the books he'd explained that the Jones Act of 1920 had thrown a substantial monkey wrench into the business. The act stated that no ships of non-American registry could trade in American ports without paying high fees and tariffs, and then to make it more damaging, the act also stipulated that ships not built in America were subject to the same rules.

Four of the ships in the Tilton fleet were subject to the tariff. Two were Dutch and the two small inland waterways traders had been built in England. Only Captain Tilton's precious *Ra-*

ven had the proper credentials, and because she'd come from a shipyard in Alaska there'd been some question about her rights as she had been launched when that great northern region wasn't officially a territory of the United States.

For all the months I'd worked for him Captain Tilton had been trying to move his operations to other countries without giving up his base in Astoria. That's why he'd begun the complex and logistically demanding game of buying and selling cargo, but only if he could also count on a ship with the proper registry to carry it. With only the *Raven* to travel freely in and out of the ports from Alaska to Mexico, he was forced to expend vast amounts of time in making the unwieldy process turn a profit. As I saw him shed his cares playing in the sun with Joe and Will, I vowed to sort out the books on my own. I wanted his respite from the rigors of work to be complete.

On Wednesday, in the middle of his stay, a perfect day came to the North Pacific Coast. The wind shifted and came out of the east, dropping to a breeze as the sun danced on an almost-flat ocean. It must have been on such a day that Balboa had misnamed it Pacific.

The boys were cavorting in the shallows with Tar and Pete while Bunny, sand on her toes and chubby legs, slept under a vast umbrella at my side. Some amber-reddish hair had begun appearing on her scalp, and the breeze ruffled it delicately.

Captain Tilton flopped down beside her, white shirt spattered with seawater and baggy white pants wet to the knees. 'Those dogs were a wonderful gift for the boys,' I said, handing him an iced-tea. 'I love dogs. Though we seldom had the big ones indoors as they were reserved for hunting. But I had a little French bulldog, a gift from a soldier I'd nursed during the war. I named him *Tortino*; sort of means cupcake or sweetie pie.'

Unguarded thoughts of the little brindle dog with his funny always-smiling face became suddenly an image of him dead in the grisly half-basement of the Ipatiev House. Instantly I was on the verge of tears. I shaded my eyes, keeping my gaze on the boys, and asked, 'Was your grandfather really a pirate?'

'Not really. I suppose you'd say he was more of an entrepreneur with a very flexible code of business.'

'Was he a smuggler then?'

'Oh, sort of. He was born in New Bedford in 1815 and went to sea, whaling, when he was fifteen. Then he jumped ship in Sitka, which was called New Archangel back in 1835 and still belonged to your country. He fell in love with Alaska and the whole Northern Pacific; Siberia, the Bering Sea, even Barrow, where he'd wintered once.'

'It's a magnificent if daunting world,' I mused. 'What did he do there?'

'Exactly how he got his first ship is a little clouded. I know he knocked around sailing for the Russians. He had a good ear for language and was quick with numbers. But when he was about twenty or so I think he managed to get his hands on a cargo of sea otter pelts by hook, crook, or maybe a card game. He came back from Canton with his own ship in the early 1840s. That was the *Denali Princess*.'

'The painting in your study.'

'Exactly. Then he traded in Hawaii and California hauling supplies to the Russians in Russian America and selling their furs in Canton. He also got involved in a scheme where tons of ice was cut from Alaskan lakes, brought to the harbor, and stored in holds of ships where it was so closely packed it was virtually airtight—it didn't melt. Then it was taken down to California during the gold rush so the saloons could have ice. He made a fortune!'

'They do that in Petersburg,' I said. 'They cut the ice from the Neva River and store it in the basements where it lasts all through the hot summer when everyone craves ices and sherbets.'

'Well it sure worked for Grandfather William. He always had his finger in a pie or two up and down the coast. But when he fell in love in 1840, the lady, a San Francisco beauty, didn't want to live in Alaska. So he settled in Astoria where she could visit her family when he was at sea. My father was born in 1845, just before the ice project.

'In 1878 he decided to retire, leaving the business to my father, Joseph. Then old William decided to build himself a house and get involved in the business of making Astoria into a great city. The shipping, logging, canneries, breweries, and hotels made and lost money, but he and my father always got in at the beginning and out before things slipped. After old William died, my father went into the first pulp mill and the Astoria and Coast Railway that brought us to Seaside.

'I was born the same year my grandfather died, 1885. And while I was growing up it was his widow, my grandmother Emmaline, who told me all about him. She was sixteen when she married him, almost twenty years his junior, and was still very spry when I was a child. I loved her stories, the more outrageous the better. But my parents were terribly respectable and my mother in particular found his slightly shady dealings, which had set her up with the fortune she was happy to spend like water, something to be hushed up.'

'And did your grandmother admire him for his... clever ways?'

'She did. And she loved to tweak my mother's nose by mentioning some scandalous thing Grandfather William had done when my mother was trying to impress the local matrons. Poor woman, she was at the top of the heap in Astoria, but it might not have been worth the effort of living with Grandmother Emmaline.'

'The top of the heap's a precarious place,' I mused, thinking of my father. 'And somehow from up there your view is refracted so those who are most eager to bring you down appear to want only that you remain there safely. My father always said it was a cold, lonely, and dangerous place to have to live.'

The captain looked at me expectantly, waiting for me to go on. But then saw I'd said too much and, respecting my privacy as he always did, went on with his own story.

'I was twenty when my father died. I was at sea. Ira had only just gotten started at university. My mother thought she could manage things but took the advice of the wrong people. Not really her fault. I didn't want to be responsible for the business end of things and convinced her I had to stay afloat. By the time Ira got his hands on the reins we had to seriously buckle down. Funny, he did such a good job we were beginning to come out of it, beginning to see some prosperity again, when he died.'

'That stupid Jones Act would have made a right mess of things even if he'd lived,' I said sharply, angry he was thinking about business again. 'There's surely nothing you could have done about that.'

'I don't need my life to be easy,' he said, sitting up, his eyes serious, wanting me to understand something important. 'I don't expect to have good things handed to me. And I don't need to be at the top of that heap you know something about. But explain this, Neddy, why does it have to be so complicated? Why can't an honest man do honest work and provide for his family without all the maneuvering and chicanery, the flirting and self-prostitution, that somehow always gets in the way of a straightforward idea?'

Again I thought of my father and realized he'd been confounded by the same question all his life. And I knew too that he'd never been as strong, independent, or free as the man who sat beside me, and who was still trapped in the same conundrum.

'*Papasha! Papasha!*' Joe shouted from the water's edge, holding up a mammoth orange sea star. 'Look what I've found.'

'And then,' Henry Tilton said as he jumped to his feet,

'some things are so simple, aren't they?'

As I watched him run down to examine the huge tide pool creature and make sure Joe put it carefully back in the water, I realized I was completely in love with Captain Henry Tilton, and would love him with all my heart until the day I died. It was simply a fact.

Rasputin had taught me to distrust men, and I'd always kept my emotions carefully under control when around them. Even during the war, when there were all manner of innocent romantic opportunities with soldiers who were hampered by crutches and slings or confined to a wheelchair, I was always too cautious to go beyond the light bantering of the flirtatious stage. But as I watched Henry Tilton, his hair shot with sunlight, the waves sparkling around his feet, and two small boys listening adoringly to his every word, I knew I was in love. And though I was sure there was no future for my newly discovered feelings, I thanked all the gods of romance that I'd been given this perfect moment of discovery, a memory to cherish all my days. I'd been on the ugly end of passion and power, and I knew how precious this gift was.

At that moment he waved to me, grinning, as boyish as his two companions.

I waved back.

He turned to replace the sea star.

My eyes traveled to the sleeping baby girl beside me. Surely I'd be needed to care for her for many years. And if all I could do for him, should he marry, was become a trusted employee of his shipping business, then that would suffice. I was oddly calm, and felt a completeness envelop me as it had when I'd seen the vista before me for the first time.

'It all goes together,' I murmured. 'Him. Me. This place.' At that moment I didn't expect or hope for more.

. . .

There are those who believe being the daughter of a tsar would be paradise. But in truth, one had to learn early to manage one's hopes and follow rules. I, from childhood, was expected to adhere to a rigid code of behavior.

My own father was coached before every court event, meeting with foreign ministers, or conversation with an ambassador from another country, on how to act correctly. He lived in a world of secrets where the object was to learn about the other person but not reveal anything that might expose him to ridicule or put him in a position where he had to give ground.

I'd been trained to this kind of behavior all my life and knew well how to guard the secret of my love for Captain Tilton. And when I thought about the alternatives; loss of my job and the children, loss of the captain's respect, and worst of all his pity, it was easy to keep silent. I chose to make the best of what I had. He found me valuable, and respected my opinion and judgment. This relationship put me in a stronger position than many wives I'd observed.

Also, I was shy of a real relationship. The story of my past was a secret I needed to keep. I might be living far from Russia but wasn't ignorant of what was happening in the world I'd left behind. And it was much closer than I liked, as I'd learned from Gert.

Now that the government had passed completely into the hands of the Bolsheviks, leaving no space for royalty within the borders of Russia, I knew there was a large community of expatriate monarchists who plotted and planned for the future return of the emperor. The fact that I had no desire to play at pretend court in Paris and Berlin didn't change the truth. Were I discovered, I'd be by default the strongest candidate to rally the cause of restoring the throne. But this was a chimera I couldn't in conscience espouse.

Russia had changed, had needed to change. There was no going back. After being forced to plumb the depths of my own being and learning to make my way on my own, I was sure I couldn't participate in the delusions of those who chose to pretend some new Camelot or Xanadu might still be found in Russia.

Whomever it was who was prying into my world, whether from the Bolsheviks or the Monarchists, I wanted no part of them. The former because it could mean my death, and the latter because it would mean giving up my self for a fantasy. And so, as we left the beach behind at the end of August, I decided I'd care for those I loved and try to protect myself from trouble. This was what my life had come down to since I was a child.

. . .

One afternoon just after Joe and Will returned to school I was working in the study. When I checked the clock I was glad to see I'd be finished before Bunny woke from her nap and the boys came home. But I was surprised when Chin entered— surprised, because he hadn't knocked.

'Miss Neddy,' he said, straightening his tie and coming to stand almost at attention before me.

'Chin, what is it?'

'Are you seeking other employment?'

'What are you talking about?' Fear filled my chest, taking the air and gripping my heart.

'Today, at the butcher shop I was accosted by a person I did not know.'

Chin referred to anyone above him in station as gentleman or lady, and those he felt to be equals as man or woman. When he used person, he meant someone completely inappropriate such as a drunk or a bum, though he'd never stoop to such common terms.

I dropped my pen, blotting the page of the ledger without noticing. 'What did this person want from you?'

'He wanted to know what exactly your duties were in this

house, where exactly you had come from, and how you had come to us—meaning on whose recommendation.'

I waited for the rest, afraid to speak, feeling the foundations of my works tottering.

'He knew my name, Miss Neddy. And he knew far too much about the goings on in this family to be a stranger and yet I know I'd never seen him before.'

'What did he look like?' I already dreaded the answer.

Chin raised one eyebrow in distaste. 'He was dirty, smelled. His hair was thin and dark and though it is not warm, he was sweating.'

'Why did he tell you he was asking about me?'

'He said he was the agent of someone who had left you a large inheritance.'

'But you didn't believe that?'

'He said he was trying to verify your identity, but his questions did not fit this story. And why should he be sneaking about if he was a legitimate agent of a reputable person?'

'I'm not looking for another job Chin,' I murmured, close to breaking down.

'Then he was some sort of miscreant,' Chin said with satisfaction. 'I told him as much to his face.'

'I don't want to leave Captain Tilton's employ,' I whispered. 'But I don't wish to make trouble for him.'

Chin made derisive gesture. 'I've dealt with his kind before,' he said harshly. 'They think that because you are foreign, not born in this country, they can treat you badly. Well, I was born here, in San Francisco. And I am an American, as American as they are, those narrow-minded bigots!'

'You know that man?' I asked, still too afraid to do more than whisper.

'No. I know his kind. They call themselves the Ku Klux Klan and want to rid their world of anyone who is different from them. They say we take their jobs, but it always seems to me they are stupid lazy men who have only been educated to be prejudiced.'

I felt a small glimmer of hope. 'And you think, because I'm Russian, they're interested in me? But why ask you questions?'

'If they could find out something scandalous about you, or even thought they could get away with saying you had done something incorrect, they could perhaps get you fired. If they can't find something to besmirch you with, they will make it up and start whispering it about.'

'Would they go to Captain Tilton?'

Chin now actually smiled. 'If they do, they will be sorry. This was already tried—with reference to my wife and me. They told it around that we were not married. Captain Tilton put a stop to such talk. Do not forget, he made his way to his captaincy by the legitimate path—from the bottom up. He knows how to deal with scum... with undesirable persons.'

'Thank you Chin. For all your help.'

'And I can rest assured you will not leave us, Miss Neddy?' he asked returning to his usual formal manner.

'You can rest assured I would never leave this family by choice. Never, Chin. Never.'

'Yes. That is what Mai Lin said. 'But I had to be sure. Now I am.'

.   .   .

In November 1922 I celebrated my third Thanksgiving at the corner of Duane and Eighth Streets. The boys, now very grown up at ten and nine, were beginning to leave such childish things as costumes and tents behind. But Bunny insisted the tattered tent be set up and the captain wear his Pilgrim hat. We had our traditions remembered, if not completely intact.

Bunny had been moved into the guest room and now had her own sumptuous bed and place to play. This relieved the boys, who often spent hours with her at a time, but had been forced to ban her from their rooms because there were too many ship models, delicate constructions, and train tracks for her to touch.

I kept the small former nursery for my own and had made quite a nice nest of it, setting the Easter egg from my father on the desk along with the one carved by Kuzma. After Chin had dispelled my fears of discovery, I again put my mother's bible on the bookcase. I kept my father's album hidden in a drawer, though. It was something I couldn't let others see; the pictures could generate too many questions and too many lies. But I'd shared the significance of Easter time and the giving of eggs with the children and they respected my treasures, being very careful when they handled them.

Even curious Bunny clasped her hands in her lap as I took the tiny jade bunnies from their nest for her to see. She always insisted they be placed in a close circle around the bunny in his grass nest so it wouldn't be lonely. There was an endless game where she then named the little rabbits, different names each time, and made me tell her stories about them.

The boys were doing well in school and I took great pride in that. Will was becoming more and more of a pianist and had branched out with a concertina he liked to take to the beach. Along with a balalaika Captain Tilton had given me the previous Christmas, we now had summer concerts.

However, our summer haven was no longer Ecola. The location of the house hadn't changed. But locals, after much aggravation over lost mail that was misdirected to a southern Oregon city called Eola, petitioned to change the name of the town to Cannon Beach. This resurrected some local history— a ship called the *Shark* had foundered trying to cross the bar in 1846, and one of its cannons had been washed up on our beachfront. Naming the town for that put an end to the confusion. Everyone was pleased.

In short, our lives were good. But in the early morning of

8 December 1922 we were wakened by what I was sure was cannon fire. I pulled on my robe and grabbed the terrified Bunny from her bed. When I ran to get the boys I almost collided with Captain Tilton, Joe and Will right behind him. He dashed for the stairs in only his nightshirt and trousers, and climbed the tower and see what was happening. We all trundled up behind him, Tar and Pete as well, but Chin was already coming down from the vantage point.

'Fire,' he announced grimly.

Captain Tilton made his own visual survey. 'This one's going to be bad, Chin. Worse than 1883. Not so many gas lines back then.'

'How bad?' I demanded, my initial panic under control. 'Do we need to leave?'

We followed him down the stairs and right into his bedroom. 'I'm going to see what needs to be done,' he told us as he finished dressing. 'Though I doubt there's anything that can stop it. The buildings are wood, the streets are wood. The gas and water lines run under the streets.'

'And they'll rupture as the streets burn,' I said, showing him I'd grasped the situation. 'The gas will ignite and there'll be no water to put out the fires.'

He nodded curtly. 'Get everyone dressed. Each of you collect a small bag of clothes, only what you can carry, what's important to you so you'll be ready. Chin, keep watch. If the fire gets too close, get them to Youngs Bay and across the river. I'll find you there.'

'What do you want me to save for you?' I demanded, grabbing his arm.

For an intense moment his eyes probed deep into mine, then he pulled me into his arms, Bunny and all, and kissed me.

No man had given me more than a chaste peck in my life except Rasputin. But that ugly night vanished completely when Henry's lips met mine. I wasn't afraid and didn't shrink from his ardor. I kissed him back.

'You save the children,' he ordered, eyes warm with knowing I returned his love. 'And while you're at it don't let one hair on your head be lost until I can come back and ask you to marry me.'

Then he kissed me again.

'Yes, Henry,' I said, wanting to hear the name out loud I'd only said in my mind.

Then he embraced the boys and murmured words of courage and love to each, and his last kiss was for Bunny. Finally, with only a meaningful look, he was gone down the front steps to where the flames roared into the dark sky.

Chin's eyes found mine. The proper servant was gone. We were going fight a battle together. 'I'll dress the children and get them packed,' I said briskly. 'Then I'll move the important papers and books down to the root cellar. Will Mai Lin need help with the food?'

'No,' he said shortly, and vanished up the stairs to his watching post.

Poor Bunny was terrified. The screaming sirens, roar of the fire, explosions, and crashing of buildings gave her no respite and she wouldn't let me put her down for a moment. In the dark house the light of the fires cast lurid and frightening shadows through the rooms, and this scared her even more.

I was never more proud of the boys. I knew they were as afraid as their sister, perhaps more so because they understood what she didn't—that their beloved *Papasha* was out in that nightmare of thunder and flame.

In the flickering darkness I became the commander, Will and Joe my lieutenants. When we'd packed their things and some for their *Papasha*, we went on to my room. I was touched to see each of them snatch one of the garments I tossed on the bed and wrap my eggs and bible safely before they were stuffed into a canvas bag. I dug out my father's little photo album and my diamond filled candle myself, but left the wooden bucket, toolbox, and traveling box Kuzma had made behind; they were too clumsy to carry. I was fleeing for my life. But this time I was the adult, the one in charge of saving my children's lives. I knew what needed to be taken and what left behind.

As the hours passed the fire consumed all in its path, coming closer and closer. Chin was within an inch of shoving us all into the car when Captain Tilton appeared.

'They're going to dynamite some of the buildings to make a firebreak,' he told us, wiping soot from his face and gulping down the water Mai Lin handed him. 'Get into the basement. I don't want you on the streets when the detonations start, despite how close the fire is. We might lose every window in the place, so you need to be away from the flying glass.'

'The foundation is of stone,' I said. 'We should be safe, and in the root cellar there's earth over the ceiling. If the house doesn't survive, you'll find us there.'

He left as Mai Lin and I took the children downstairs. Right behind us came Chin carrying the painting of the *Denali Princess*. Again I was proud of Will and Joe, who grabbed two old shovels as we passed the disused coal room.

'Can dig out as well as dig in,' Joe said, his voice firm as he laid his shovel by the doorway.

'Plenty to eat,' practical Mai Lin observed setting down her bag of food and eyeing the shelves of canned goods.

There in the chilly dark we huddled together around the single lamp Chin allowed and waited. Tar and Pete curled up with the boys and Bunny clutched me for dear life.

I began humming songs to her, and didn't realize until I felt the boys' gazes that I was singing in Russian. The poor little mite seemed comforted, and though she didn't sleep she relaxed.

Below ground the roar of the fire was subdued. We heard and felt only the shuddering crash of the explosions. Chin, despite the captain's orders, remained on the first floor, afraid to give up his watch on the encroaching flames.

After what seemed an eternity, the explosions stopped and Chin appeared beckoning us upstairs. We all climbed to the attic windows. The entire business district, from the wharves to within only a few blocks of the house, was gone. Nothing remained but the shattered shells of buildings and lone chimneys. Their silhouettes drifted in and out of the smoke like ghosts wandering in the dying flames. We could also see people running aimlessly through the charred and dangerous streets with armfuls of goods. As I watched their seemingly random movement a small warning bell went off in my head. There was a furtiveness about some of the men, something that didn't speak of helping.

'Chin. Does Captain Tilton have a gun in the house?'

'A gun?'

'Look at those people in the streets. I've seen that kind of behavior before in devastated towns. Some of those people are looters.'

Chin vanished down the stairs and returned with a small pistol, a large revolver, and some kind of cutlass. 'Can you fire this?' he asked bluntly.

'Give me the smaller pistol,' I said, extending one hand as the other held the clutching Bunny. 'I can't fire the bigger one with only one hand.'

He passed me the gun, but when he wanted me to take some cartridges I couldn't and Joe took them.

'Stay at the top of the stairs,' Chin ordered. 'I will walk downstairs. Master William, lock the door to the back stairs. Put the key in your pocket. Then go from room to room and watch out the windows. Even into the room of your revered mother. Can you do that?'

Will nodded, one curt bob of the head. He and Chin departed.

'Do you know how to load this gun?' I asked Joe.

He shook his head.

'I'll show you.'

I took a position at the top of the main staircase and Mai Lin brought blankets and pillows to make us a resting place. When she wrapped Bunny in the quilt from my bed, the little girl relaxed slightly against me as it enfolded her. Miraculously, after about an hour, she fell asleep.

We waited as the afternoon passed and night came on. Pete lay across the top of the stairs, his huge body a black bulwark. Tar followed Will on his rounds. As night fell in earnest and Will came to tell me it was too dark to see anyone in the street, I heard the front door open.

I pushed the boys behind me and handed Will his little sister. Then I took my place at the top of the stairs. Mai Lin stayed at my side, holding the cutlass. I knew, if it meant protecting the children, I'd shoot whomever was coming up the steps. For the first time in her life, I heard Tar growl, a low menacing rumble deep in her chest. She too was ready to do whatever it took for her children.

A light flared in the darkness and I heard a murmuring voice. But not even when I saw Henry Tilton's broad form on the landing did I lower the pistol.

'Don't shoot,' he begged, raising his hands in surrender, a grin splitting his grimy face.

My hand dropped to my side and my shoulders sagged with relief. He looked like a tattered scarecrow. 'Pop-sha!' Bunny shouted, fears forgotten because we were all smiling and laughing. Henry took her into his arms and the boys threw themselves at him as well. He sat down on the steps with them and listened to their tales of the excitement, praised them for their courage, and assured us all by his relaxed presence that the worst was over.

'Did the school burn down?' Joe asked hopefully.

'You don't have to worry about that,' Henry assured them. 'With Miss Neddy here as your tutor you won't miss a day.'

'But if you're gonna marry her, then she won't be our tutor anymore,' Joe said.

'But mothers make you do that kind of thing too,' Will pointed out.

'She hasn't said yes yet,' Henry whispered theatrically.

Both boys, Chin and Mai Lin as well, turned their eyes to me.

'So is it yes?' Henry asked, and I heard a tentative note in his voice.

They were all so happy, smiling up at me, the boys giggling. And suddenly I felt like a stranger among them.

'You don't know me,' I said.

'You love the children,' he replied, his eyes never wavering. 'And you love me. Nothing else really matters, does it?'

I wanted to believe him. 'I'm not who you think I am.'

'Are you married already?'

I shook my head no.

'Are you running from the law?' Joe asked, the hopeful note still in his voice.

'Or,' Will added, 'a bank robber?'

'No, no, nothing like that.'

'Then what?' Henry said. 'Tell me your dark secret, Neddy.'

I had to say something; there was so much to tell him. But now wasn't the time for the story of my life. 'I... I can't have children,' I whispered.

He continued to smile up at me, Joe, Will, and Bunny in his arms. 'I think we have enough of those to do us just fine, don't you? Anything else we can talk about later.'

I nodded, my eyes filling with tears.

'Then say yes,' he urged. 'Marry me, Neddy, be my wife. Will you?'

'Yes,' I sobbed, laughing and crying at the same time. 'Yes,

Henry Tilton, I'll marry you.'

'I told you they would figure it out sooner or later,' Chin said derisively to Mai Lin. 'And you said we needed to do something.'

Mai Lin shook her head. 'Never think to burn down half of city.'

. . .

The boys insisted in restoring our treasures to their proper places and while Mai Lin and I handed out sandwiches for dinner, I was constantly aware of Henry as he passed me carrying bundles, bags, and the *Denali Princess* from the basement. I could feel his exhaustion in my bones, and see the happiness in his eyes. He could walk right by me, only brushing my shoulder with his fingers, and tell me all about his love in that simple gesture. I felt strong and open, complete and free. And when I saw him with the canvas bag holding my treasures in his hand, I felt as if they were finally and truly safe.

Mai Lin stood firmly by as the boys ate, making them stop their chatter about how brave they were and what a grand adventure they'd had to keep putting food in their mouths. And when they'd finished, she presented them with ice cream.

I gave her a look of surprise.

'No power. All melt.' And then, when they dug in and wouldn't notice, she let her fingers brush each of the boys' backs. But I'd noticed.

And I saw too that Chin took her hand as they started up the stairs to their own rooms, something I'd never seen him do before.

I had to rock Bunny to sleep, and as she drifted off I looked up to see Henry in the doorway watching us. He'd cleaned up and changed out of his grimy clothes. In the light of the lantern he held in his hand I saw a dark bruise on his cheekbone that wrung my heart. I slipped the girl under her covers and rubbed her back, making sure she was well and truly settled.

'She'll get over it sooner than we will,' Henry whispered coming to my side.

'You read my mind. Poor little mite, I couldn't explain it to her.'

'But you were there for her the whole time.'

'I need to talk to you. Are the boys asleep?'

'Out like lights. I didn't even make them brush their teeth. They're curled up with Pete and Tar just like any other night.'

'Can we go down to your study?'

'Neddy. It can wait; forever if you want. It's still the same. I love who you are, not who you were.'

'There are things you must know. Things I must tell you.'

He laid his arm around my shoulders and we walked down to the study. He went to the cabinet and poured two brandies for us and then sank into one of the old leather chairs and put his feet up on the ottoman. I stood before him glass in hand, not knowing what to do, how to begin.

He took my hand and pulled me gently into his arms so we were both on the big chair and I was curled against him just as Bunny liked to be.

'Shall I tell you what I've guessed?' he asked. 'You're not such an enigma as you think, Miss Osipov. But we already know that's not your real name. You told me that when you came to work. Which, of course, made me curious.'

'I can't tell you my real name. Nadezhda is who I am now.'

'That's fine. Now, should I go on with what I think I know?'

I nodded and he stroked my hair.

'You're a highborn lady from Russia. A name can be changed with ease, but how we were raised and educated are ingrained in us, second nature. We can assume a costume or a pose, but there's no hiding who we were brought up to be. You were a lady, perhaps even a princess, or whatever it's correctly called in Russia. But when the Bolsheviks had their revolution they wanted to stamp out the aristocracy. You became someone whose life was in jeopardy. How'm I doin' so far?'

'Amazing,' I replied, sitting so I could see his face. 'Tell me more.'

'I think someone, a man, took advantage of you in a way that makes you very cautious of sharing yourself. There's a wall around you, Neddy, that has nothing to do with your identity, it protects and separates you from men.'

I dropped my gaze. The guessing game had come too close.

'But despite hard knocks,' he went on, allowing me my privacy, 'you decided to make a life for yourself and you've succeeded.'

Now I could once again look into his eyes.

'And,' he went on, the smile in his eyes warm, his hand on my hair gentle, 'I'm the luckiest man in the world because you love me.' He kissed me. 'What else do I need to know?'

'I have diamonds. Jewels. Old family pieces taken apart. I smuggled them out. If we're to be married they belong to you.'

'What did you plan to do with them?'

'They were for security, so I'd know I had something to count on. But now I'll have you, so I won't need to hoard them against a rainy day.'

''You keep them,' he said easily. 'Since I won't have to pay you that vast salary, I'll be rich. Give them to the children someday.'

'But if we need them...'

'If we need them you'll be the first to know. Being my wife will not spare you from keeping the books.'

'One last thing,' I said, watching the brandy swirl in my snifter as I turned it in my hands.

But he made me look into his eyes. 'There's nothing you can say that will change my mind. Nothing, Neddy. You can trust me.'

I told him about Rasputin and at first I was as frightened

as if it had just happened. But then as I spoke about it, trying to find the words to describe that moment in my life when I'd lost the security I'd childishly thought would always be mine, trying to explain to him and to myself the lonely place the rape had put me in, I realized I was no longer in that place. It had been ten years since that dark and ugly moment had stopped my world. And now, it was turning again and I could see I'd be able to leave that night behind.

I stumbled and cried through the expression of all this but with Henry's arms around me I managed to finally understand who I was then and who I'd become. I came to see on the night after that terrible fire who Neddy Osipov really was, and I liked her. I respected her, and that was what I'd lost to that filthy monk: my self-respect. And I'll never forget what Henry said to me at the end of it all.

'That you trust me, know me as someone who'd never hurt you like that, I take as the greatest compliment you can give.'

I kissed him, a deep and giving kiss that held all the passion I felt for him. 'I fell in love with you that perfect day on the beach the first summer in Ecola, when you were playing with Joe and Will. That day I saw who you were before you'd taken up the burden of a business. I promise to always be there to shoulder it with you.'

'Would tomorrow be too soon for the wedding?' he asked. 'Or do you need to plan fancy things?'

'I think tomorrow would be grand. But...'

He questioned me with his eyes.

'I wish we could be married there, at the beach house.' Then I kissed him with a laugh as he grew pensive. 'But I most surely don't want to wait until June!'

'There's a perfectly good road there,' he said softly.

'In December?'

'If we go carefully.'

I jumped to my feet. 'Oh, Henry! That would be the very

best wedding I could wish for!' And I danced around the quiet study joining him in his delighted laughter.

. . .

As responsible citizens of the devastated Astoria we couldn't run off to Cannon Beach the very next day. Henry had to help organize the repairs along the ruined wharves and we ended up taking in two burned-out families for several weeks.

Somewhere in those first days after the fire I did tell him about the sweaty man who'd asked about me. He agreed with Chin: There was no way for the man to confirm my identity, and the Bolsheviks were probably not interested in me anymore, anyway. There were many of the former Russian nobility living all over Europe in plain sight, and no one cared about them except when they got into the social pages or another pretender to the throne showed up. And as nothing more had happened on that score since Chin's interview in the butcher shop, I decided he was right.

Henry gave me his grandmother's diamond, the one his somewhat piratical grandfather had given her, and it suited me well. I like to think the old gentleman would have approved of a former princess who'd given the Bolsheviks the slip and trekked her way across Siberia.

Will and Joe were all for the marriage, especially when they found out we were going to make a winter trip to Cannon Beach, something they'd never done. And I was touched and honored they were so willing to let me into their family.

Then one afternoon, just a few days before we were due to leave for the beach, they led me across the hallway from the schoolroom into what had once been their mother's bedroom with an air of ceremony. I was surprised to see that all the dustsheets had been removed and the room cleaned. The furnishings were very French and very feminine. Laces and satins dressed the bed and the curtains were of the softest rose pink, completely fitting for their mother as she'd been described to me.

Joe escorted me to a delicate chair and announced, 'This room is for you now.'

Henry had offered me the room already and I'd said I hoped to share his room, as my parents had always shared theirs. We'd instantly agreed this was what we both wanted. But I couldn't hurt the boys' feelings and knew they were completely accepting me as their mother with this gesture. I was in a quandary.

As I tried to think of the right thing to say, Bunny toddled in trailing her blanket. She looked about the lacy magnificence and her eyes glowed. 'Pitty,' she breathed. 'Oh, so pitty.'

I watched her looking at the space as if she'd entered some kind of fairy castle. And though they were determined to do the right thing, I could see the boys were less than comfortable in their mother's former room.

'I think this furniture should be Bunny's,' I said firmly. 'It was her mother's and will be all she has to remember her by. If we put these things into her room, then this could become an upstairs sitting parlor. A special place for me, with my desk and my things, but attached to *Papasha's*. My mother had just such a room and called it her boudoir. It was a private little parlor just for us, just for our family.'

I held my breath.

And after a moment's thought, the boys looked hugely relieved.

'So it would look different, but still be for you, for our new mother?' Will asked.

'Would you want me to be that? I'd be happy to be your Aunt Neddy if...'

'No, no,' they both said.

'We want you to be our mother,' Joe added.

Will nodded emphatically. 'But...'

'But?'

'What did your call your mother?' Will asked bravely.

'*Maman*. It's French. Do you like that?'

'*Maman*,' Will said reflectively.

'We call *Papasha* a Russian name,' Joe said, making things simple with his easy and eager way. 'Now we'll call you a French one. That kind of makes them go together.'

They gave me a hug and Bunny clapped her hands. Though she'd no idea what had happened she was simply glad to see us all happy.

'Let's go get Chin and Mai Lin and start moving things,' Joe said eagerly. 'This is going to be fun. They're going to be excited.'

I had my doubts about that, but as I retrieved Bunny, I heard Will say. 'Ned—*Maman* always makes it easy.'

'It'll be better her way, and just as nice,' Joe said. 'And now we have a *Papasha* and a *Maman*.'

'And I have the precious children I never thought I would,' I whispered into Bunny's amber curls.

. . .

The drive to Cannon Beach wasn't difficult. There'd been several clear days before we left, an unusual occurrence for that time of year, which I put down to luck of the bride. We arrived clean, dry, and in good spirits.

The Pacific was dark slate, and its surf pounded much higher up the beach, flying up from Haystack Rock and sending huge logs and tree stumps onto the sand one day and taking them back the next. The town itself looked a little forlorn, but the locals were glad to see us and it was fun to have more time to visit with the hotel and restaurant owners than in summer.

A minister had agreed to come over from Seaside to perform the ceremony. I became Mrs. Henry Tilton on a silver-misted New Year's Eve afternoon with a brisk wind singing through the trees and the surf crashing upon the sand. But the weather I found so beautiful meant the barometer was falling and the poor man who'd come to pronounce us man and wife raced through the ceremony at record speed. As soon as he said you may kiss the bride, he rushed out the door and back to his fireside ahead of the rain.

We toasted the day, even allowing Will and Joe a sip of bootlegged champagne, and then sat down to the bridal dinner of chicken and potato salad as the boys had requested. And they were right: It was perfect. Bunny's favorite part of the event was the cake, though at just a little over two she was disappointed until we found her a candle to blow out. Then, after we'd gotten the children to bed, we curled up on the leather sofa to savor the last of the illegal champagne.

'I can't think of a better way to get married,' I said in complete contentment. Rain slapped at the windows and the wind moaned in the chimney, making the dying fire flare behind the sturdy screen.

'When you were a girl, did you ever think you'd be married in a cottage surrounded by children and dogs?'

'Kuzma always said that only God knows why things happen, and he does not see fit to enlighten us as to his plans.'

'He was a wise man.'

A gust buffeted the house. 'It's going to be a big storm isn't it?' I asked.

Henry smiled a lazy smile and kissed me. He tasted of champagne and I found it delicious on his lips. 'Could be we'll be stuck here for a while,' he murmured.

I took his hand and led him toward the stairs. 'The road could be impassible for days?' I asked with a smile.

He kissed me again, curving my body into his, enfolding me in his scent, that mixture of leather and spice I always associated with him. 'Could be washed out completely,' he whispered in my ear. 'In more than one place.'

'Completely?'

'Trees down.' He kissed me. 'Gullies.' Again. 'Washouts.'

I kissed the corners of his eyes where the sun and sea had set their marks. 'We could be stuck here for days...'

'And nights,' he replied his hand caressing my neck as he kissed me more ardently.

'Probably safer upstairs,' I breathed.

'Mmm, and warmer in bed,' he added.

I spun out of his arms and raced up the steps but stopped at the door to our room. He picked me up. His lips were hot and urgent.

'Go ahead and blow, wind!' I whispered as he closed the door. 'Do your worst! I want to stay here forever.'

. . .

And I almost got my wish. The storm raged for three more days, and when it cleared, the damage to the road was sufficient to give me a two-week honeymoon spent with wet dogs, wet children, and an endless pile of boots drying by the fire. We brought home treasure from the beaches every day and I discovered a glass net float from a Japanese fishing boat; the find of the whole trip. I added it to the three on the mantel Henry had collected over the years and felt yet another connection between us.

But on our last morning I woke just before dawn. As I watched my husband sleep, a profound sense of sadness swept through my heart in an unexpected wave. Tears filled my eyes and a sob escaped my lips.

Henry was instantly awake, taking me into his arms, murmuring comfort.

'Sorry,' I blubbered. 'I didn't mean to wake you.'

'I've spent my life under sail,' he said gently. 'I'm always aware when the wind shifts or the sea changes.'

And when his strength and kindness had brought back my balance he wiped the tears from my cheeks with his fingers.

'Second thoughts?'

I had to smile as I shook my head. 'Just the opposite.'

'Then why the tears?'

'Since I was fourteen, since...'

'Mmm. Yes. Him.'

'Since that terrible night when I lost my security, when all my world turned upside-down, I've been in a battle. For many different reasons and though terrible losses it's been seven years since I've been secure.'

'Long time to be at war.'

'And now, here with you, I'm safe. I'm home. I'm not afraid anymore.'

'Can you tell me?'

'It's my grandmother,' I snuffled. 'My father's mother.'

'Is she still living?'

'She was seventy-six on Thanksgiving. And she's all that's left. She's alone, just as I was. And I thought I was all right that way. But now I see what a lonely place I was in and it hurts me to think of her there. But I can't contact her without exposing myself. And that I can't do.'

'Would a letter be enough? She couldn't answer you, unless you wanted to take a fairly large risk, but you could write to her.'

'Without being exposed?' I asked, sitting up. 'What do you mean?'

'Sailors have been sending letters home from far away places for centuries by passing them on to a ship going that way. Sometimes they didn't arrive for years. Sometimes they never arrived at all. Sometimes the sailor got home before the letter.'

'But how could that help me?'

'Do you know where she is?'

I nodded.

'Do you know someone close to her you can trust?'

My mind flashed on a news photo of my grandmother, Maria Fedorovna, sitting on the terrace at Villa Hvidore in Denmark. I knew exactly where she was. And I knew from the article she wouldn't go to memorial services for her family or allow their deaths to be talked about in her presence. She didn't know for certain they were all dead and wouldn't permit speculation. And I knew too that Molly Troop, her English companion and secretary, was still with her. If I communicated with Molly, she'd faithfully pass the letter on to my grandmother.

'Yes.'

'So if you wrote to this person, put that name on the envelope, then that person would pass it on? In confidence?'

'Yes.'

But then I was torn. I couldn't tell her about myself without telling her what actually happened. Was it kinder to let her live in ignorance rather than with the awful truth, even if there was a tiny fragment of good in it?

'Think about it,' he said. 'There's no hurry.'

I kissed him.

'Let me always, for all the years of our marriage, be able to bring smiles from your tears so easily,' he whispered.

. . .

When we got back to Astoria I wrote my letter and Henry sent it off with a trusted captain to be posted from Chile. And from that day forward I felt I'd completely come into my new life. It was as if by communicating the truth to my grandmother I'd fulfilled my last responsibility to the past, to the family I'd had to leave behind. The suspended quality of my world ended. Time moved forward again. Years slipped by, our children grew, and the two towns that represented our world changed as well.

Astoria began to rebuild itself, and this caused a slight upturn in the economy. But John Jacob Astor's investment in the Pacific Fur Company back in 1811 was never destined to become the trade and business mecca the dreamers had hoped. As the 1920s progressed it continued to optimistically improve itself by changing the trolleys to buses and opening the Liberty Theatre. In 1926 the magnificent Astoria Column that commanded a breathtaking view of the city, the Columbia, and the Youngs River valley was completed, and when my boys reached the top they declared our own tower, which once they'd considered the very eagle's nest of Astoria, to be no more than an upstairs window. But by then they were great boys of thirteen and fourteen, beginning to find their entire world small and confining.

They were both doing well in school, and my Joe who'd suffered through every day of elementary school had come into a love of numbers and now talked about nothing but engineering. Not that this was strange; his father had been the same way.

Will was more and more the musician, but as was always true with him, he saw more than one facet of life and did well in all his studies. He just seemed to like school in general, and his teachers doted on him.

Our Miss Bunny, despite her brother's dire predictions, had come into a glorious head of auburn curls—which she said were just like mine. She was the darling of the family. And somehow, despite the thorough spoiling she got from all of us, remained generous to a fault and laughed every day. At six she was just beginning school and demanded the boys help her learn to write her name and do simple sums so she could be as smart as they. She showed some of the ethereal beauty of her mother and looked very much the girl well-suited to French furniture and lacy trimmings. But Henry declared her personality was like that of the spunky Emmaline she'd been named for—as evidenced by her refusal to answer her teachers when they called her by that name, insisting she was Bunny.

While the 1920s didn't do much for Astoria, Cannon Beach was booming. People from Portland had money to spend and with the road improving every year, more and more of them wanted to vacation at the beach. An indoor roller-skating rink, a moving picture show, and a grand indoor heated sea-water swimming pool (called magnificently the Natatorium but referred to as just 'The Nat') competed with each other for tourist dollars. There was as well a riding stable providing very popular horseback picnics and sunset suppers. I loved to watch the horses on the beach, and the children made full use of the new entertainments.

By 1925 we had electricity of sorts. This was provided by a diesel generator at the home of Mr. and Mrs. Lynes. The power ran from 6 a.m. to 11 p.m. and Mrs. Lynes would very kindly flick the lights three times to warn us before she turned it off and went to bed. By 1928 Pacific Power and Light took over and Cannon Beach was quite up-to-date with piped water, telephones, and that ever-improving road.

Though I admit, while we loved the piped water and were thankful for heat in the upstairs rooms on cold rainy mornings, we were never sorry when the power went out and we returned to our kerosene lamps and candles. In my mind's eye, whenever we were in Astoria, I always saw the beach house lit by candles and warmed by the huge fireplace, just as it had been through the first days of my marriage.

Nineteen-twenty-eight was also the year my grandmother died and when I heard about it I was glad I'd written to her. Though she'd heeded my caution and never answered, I somehow felt when I saw a news photo of her or magazine picture I could discern a difference, a calm in her expression and firmness of eye that hadn't been there before. She knew where I was, and as the years spun on I liked to think she heard Astoria mentioned from time to time—such as when the Column was dedicated—and could think of me here and safe. And I was also glad she never knew of the disastrous financial events shortly after her death that might have caused her worry.

The stock market crash of 1929 ended the growth and future of pretty much everything and everyone. Astoria began to shrink in population and my beloved Cannon Beach, abandoned by people no longer able to maintain second homes, grew shabby and forlorn. Everyone, including the Tiltons, were facing hard times. With Joe going off to college and Will to follow right behind, Henry resumed the captaincy of the *Raven* and went back to sea. He'd cut his employees to nothing—I ran the business on land—and with only one other ship, he had to get back under sail to make ends meet.

We put in a huge garden and all pitched in to make it a success. But we were without the aid of the dry-humored Mai Lin, who had died suddenly as she was climbing the stairs one afternoon in May. Poor Chin was desolate without her but kept at his post, doing all the jobs that were too much for me alone and putting in long hours in the garden. He'd never have done this had Mai Lin been alive, but I think it filled his days and left him tired enough to sleep.

Bunny was the joyous and bright spirit she'd seemed from birth, and became a real friend to Chin, combating his lonesomeness with her love of life. At almost ten she was still a child, but beginning to peep into the world of young womanhood, to talk about boys, and giggle behind her hand at her brothers' silly jokes.

Suddenly, it was important to be starched and clean with the right hair ribbons and shoes. Her brothers, accustomed to treating her like a little brother, were confused when she put on what they thought at first were only airs and then realized were the first steps into the next stage of her life. But they too were growing, and watching tough times cause their town and home to change. And both of them began to think seriously about how to make the most of their futures rather than seeing their coming higher education as fun.

My stash of treasure still remained despite the hard times. Henry and I wanted to keep it intact for possible worse days ahead. But we did use a little of it to assure the boys' education. I reasoned if we couldn't continue to provide the lifestyle they'd grown up with, we could give them the tools to make their own way. He went to a broker in San Francisco to trade a few stones.

Joe was off to engineering school at Oregon State. Will, though I hated to see him give up a music career, pointed out it was no way to make a living and chose teaching. He did, however, make me promise never to get rid of his old red piano, which, for all its scars and loud paint, had a marvelous tone.

As 1931 began, we were hanging on, though Henry and I agreed it would be better if we could get Captain William Tilton's grand monument to success off our hands and settle in smaller quarters. With the boys away in Corvallis and Henry at sea, it was only Chin, Bunny, and myself, along with the doddering old Tar, rattling about in the huge place.

I'd been through a reduction in circumstances before and this time found it liberating rather than terrifying. The fear and uncertainty of imprisonment were no part of this situation. Those days when we were at the mercy of politics, spurned and abused for having been born into a certain world, seemed far away. It was Henry and I who made the decisions and faced the consequences together.

I'd come to the grand house at the corner of Duane and Eighth Streets running scared. And within the walls of the gracious and beautiful old home had found not only sanctuary, but peace and love. So as we drew in our world, closing unused rooms and covering the antiques old William and his bride had selected with care, I wasn't sorry we'd decided to let the place go. And until someone came along to fill the rooms with a family again, Chin and I would mind them and let them sleep.

So Bunny moved into my old quarters, her baby nursery, and the only room we kept heated downstairs was Henry's study. Chin and I chopped wood for the library fireplace and that one space became the center of the house. We ate casually in the kitchen and didn't much feel the lack of the grand Eastlake dining room.

And one day as Chin weeded and I chopped kindling he said, 'You are good with an ax, Mrs. Captain.'

'All Russians are good with an ax,' I replied.

He moved his weed bucket down the row and gave me a dry half-smile.

'My father loved to chop wood,' I told him. 'He said it was a great job because after you finished you had a lovely pile of logs to keep you warm. In Russia keeping warm was always a very important thing.'

He turned his eyes to the house. 'Looks cold and empty already,' he said, and turned his back on the curtained windows as he worked his way down a row of carrots.

. . .

In the middle of August I was in the kitchen finishing the dishes when the front doorbell rang. Knowing Chin was out in the garden, I grabbed a towel and answered the door still drying my hands.

'Telegram for Mrs. Tilton,' the young man said, holding out the yellow envelope.

'Thank you,' I replied mechanically as I gave him a few pennies and closed the door.

It wasn't chilly in the main corridor but I felt a shiver run down my spine as I stared at the envelope, superstitiously hesitant to know whatever news it contained. But when I'd called myself a fool and tore it open, the cryptic words struck me like blows:

'*RAVEN* AND ALL HANDS MISSING IN BERING SEA.

HUGE SUMMER STORM. 2 SHIPS KNOWN LOST.'

The message had been sent from Sitka.

Henry had left in May, planning to follow right on the heels of the thaw to gain cargos in Siberia where things would be piled up at the ice-bound ports. Then he'd spend the rest of the summer in northern waters picking up what he could. He also had one contract to deliver a large cargo of reindeer, what Alaskans called caribou. They were being shipped from Anadyrsk near the Chukchi Peninsula in Siberia to Nome. The animals were destined for refurbishing the herds started there long ago as a means for the natives, who'd lost so much of the sea life that they could no longer rely on the ocean to support them with commercial hunting and fishing. I hadn't expected to hear from him at all, and knew he wasn't due to return before the fall storms closed the northern ports.

I read the words over and over, denying them, willing them to be different. But each time they were the same and I was swamped by sharp flashing images of the grisly room where my family had died. Overwhelmed by creeping panic, the terror rising through me, I sought the dim almost comatose state I'd retreated into then to protect me from the pain. I felt myself shutting down, turning inward, and ran into Henry's study, throwing myself into his favorite chair.

My eyes darted and careened around the room, clutching visually at all the things I associated with him. Then my vision came to rest on the painting of the *Denali Princess* commanding a turbulent sea.

'He shall give his angels charge over thee,' I whispered desperately, 'to keep thee in all thy ways. They shall bear thee up in their hands. He shall cover thee with his feathers, and under his wings shalt thou trust.'

I'd said that prayer over and over for those I'd loved and lost. It was my private way to say goodbye. To my family, to Nadezhda, to Kuzma, to my grandmother, and then most recently for Mai Lin. But this time, as I murmured it and watched the old *Denali Princess* fight the tempestuous waves I realized it wasn't a farewell, but a plea.

Despite the ominous words of the telegram, I couldn't believe Henry was dead. Deep down in my heart I was certain I'd have felt it if his life had ended.

'*Maman! Maman!* Where are you? I'm home,' came the sound of Bunny's voice.

I jumped up and thrust the telegram into my pocket, crushing it into a tiny ball. But there on the floor lay the envelope, mocking me for my foolish and desperately stupid idea that I could hide the truth from my little girl.

I ran out into the hallway but made myself stop and tried to gain some control.

'*Maman?*'

The voice came from the kitchen.

'I was at the door,' I called. 'I'll be right there.'

Bunny stood with an apple in her hand. Chin, pulling off his gardening gloves, stood behind her. He knew instantly, though it took my baby girl a few moments.

I pulled the crumpled bit of paper from my pocket.

'What is it?' she whispered pointing at the telltale yellow of the telegram. 'What's happened?'

I tried to frame the right words but found none in the face of Bunny's round frightened eyes.

Chin took the paper. 'The *Raven* is missing at sea,' he said calmly. 'Now we wait.'

For the rest of my life I will bless him for those simple words. The telegram had stabbed me to the heart in only three short sentences, but he'd given Bunny hope without lies in less. And he'd shown me what to do.

Bunny stared at me, looking for comfort, seeking answers to unanswerable questions from the person who'd always fixed things, always made the hurt go away. I took her into my arms, holding her against my heart.

'We'll need more information,' I said, calm now that I didn't have to face head-on the hurt in her eyes. 'I'll look in the account books and see whom we can contact in Sitka to get more facts.'

'Will you telephone Master Joseph and Master William, or shall I go to the telegraph office?' Chin asked, helping me think.

I looked at my watch. Henry had given it to me and I felt another barb rip into my heart. 'I'll call them later. They're both working now. And I think we've had enough telegrams for one day.' A stillness was coming over me and I felt apart from the situation, as if I were watching myself in a play. '*Papasha* left here in May. He wasn't to be in Anadyrsk until mid-July. He can hardly be overdue in Nome.'

Bunny closed her mind to any talk of her *Papasha* never coming back. And when her more pragmatic brothers tried to get her to at least consider the idea, she cited examples of why she need not entertain their negative suggestions. Ernest Shackleton, the Antarctic explorer whose miraculous tale was absolutely true and documented, was her favorite of the men who'd survived terrible ordeals and come home right as rain.

But as the months slipped away and there was nothing further I could learn, I knew, no matter what my heart said, that it was time to think about what I was to do without Henry. We couldn't stay in limbo. Then I received a low but solid offer for the house. It was the signal for me to make a move, to step forward. Henry and I had already decided on this; I'd be doing as he'd wished.

My path became clear. I'd accept the offer of Mr. Bertram Holden-Peters of London and Canton for the house. Then I'd sell the rest of the gems to the broker in San Francisco. And when I knew exactly what we had, I'd make my plans. I was only thirty-four years old and my children were strong, and healthy.

We'd make our future, and when Henry came back we'd be waiting—no matter how long it took.

.   .   .

When I returned from San Francisco I finally felt in control of my world. I was ready if not eager to face the future on my own. I stepped off the train and as I hugged Bunny I met Chin's eyes.

He nodded, glad to see me looking strong.

There was no hurry. Mr. Holden-Peters wouldn't take possession of the house until after the first of the year, but I wanted to have our plans set. That night I slept well for the first time since the arrival of that terrible telegram and it gave me confidence in my decision. So when we gathered in Henry's study a week later, I felt good about my plans, confident Henry would have agreed with me completely.

Bunny, now twelve, looked quite grown-up. Joe and Will lounged casually in the old chairs they'd once been so lost in as children. Chin took a place on the window seat, a completely blank expression on his always-youthful face. All of them knew of the chance to sell, just not what we'd do about it.

'I've decided we need to take Mr. Holden-Peters's offer for the house and most of the furnishings. It may seem low, but it's fair in these times, and it's cash. I don't want to sit here and watch this grand old place fall apart around us, when it was *Papasha's* plan to sell it if we could.'

I could see they weren't going to dispute me and felt a rush of relief.

'Where will you and Bunny go?' Joe asked.

All his life he'd been the one to face things head on. He was better at accepting failures, and enjoying successes than the more introspective Will.

'It's not much money for the two of you,' Will observed.

'I see my boys have been doing some talking,' I said.

'We can manage,' Joe told me.

Will nodded. 'How will you get by?'

'I've a nest egg,' I said. '*Papasha* always told me to save it for a rainy day. If we, and I mean all of us, live simply, we'll be fine.'

'A nest egg?' Joe questioned. 'What kind of nest egg?'

'Nothing's worth much these days,' Will added. 'Except maybe what Mr. Bertram Holden-Peters has.'

'He was quite vague about his business,' I told them with a smile for the brash but gentlemanly buyer. 'But I suspect he likes this place because he's a bit of a pirate like Great-grandfather William.'

'But you're not a pirate,' Bunny said.

'No. I'm not.'

They all waited.

There was no point in telling a fib. 'Diamonds. Gems,' I said flatly. 'I brought them from Russia. And I sold them all when I told you I went to San Francisco on shipping business.'

Will, always perceptive, asked, 'Did you and *Papasha* already use some of them for our schooling?'

'Yes.'

'One mystery solved,' Joe said with a wink to his brother. 'And the rest of the family business? May as well get all the cards on the table.'

'There's no rest of the business,' I said honestly. 'The costal trader *Heron* is managing to keep shipshape by barter with the shipyards and chandlers. What little cash comes in has to go to the captain and the crew. We haven't seen a penny from her since 1930, but her captain hasn't asked for any money, either.'

'I hate business,' Bunny declared, frowning and crossing her arms over her chest. 'It's so cold-hearted.'

'I have money,' Chin said evenly. 'I can go. It will make things easier for you.'

'I won't hear of that, Chin,' I insisted. 'I asked you to attend this meeting because you're family. And we're keeping this family together.'

'You can't go, Chin,' Bunny said, alarmed. 'When *Papasha* comes home he'll expect to find you here. You must stay with us.'

The boys looked away from their sister's trusting eyes, but were sincere when they insisted Chin stay. They made it clear that they depended on him to keep an eye on Bunny and me while they were gone.

I could see Chin was pleased by their affection and trust, but didn't want to be a burden. 'I won't lie,' I told him with a dry smile, 'if you can pay your own way it'll make things easier.'

'I can pay my own way, Mrs. Captain,' he said crisply, calling me by the appellation he'd given me on the day of my marriage.

'Good. Then that's settled,' I said, maintaining a brisk tone to keep from embarrassing him.

'But where shall we go?' Bunny asked as she looked into each of our faces in turn, waiting for her *Maman* or big brothers to come to her rescue as they always had. And I was swept back to the day Pete had died as he slept by the hearth in this very room just 2 years ago when she'd looked at me with those same little girl-eyes and asked why he wouldn't wake up. Sometimes I saw the strong sense of self she was beginning to develop; other times, like now, she was still my baby.

For the first time in over three months I managed a genuine smile. This time I knew the answer. 'I was thinking a nice quiet place to live inexpensively might be Cannon Beach.'

FIVE
NEDDY—1932

We were allowed to take some things from the house. Will claimed only the scarred red piano; Bunny turned her back on the fancy French furniture of her mother's and took the shabby old white iron bedstead that had once been mine. Joe saved the books of his childhood and a big box of trains. All the children would have taken their *Papasha's* study intact, as would I, but the buyer wanted that. And when I pointed out the snug office at the beach house had been his retreat long before he'd taken over the one in this house they settled for Great-grandfather William's sextant, always Henry's treasure.

I boxed up the old ledgers and papers of the Tiltons for Henry. And then carefully packed my Russian language classics, Turgenev, Tolstoy, Pushkin and Dostoyevsky as well as a collection of old fairy tales and folk tales. The library at the beach was already filled with Henry's American classics so I'd not lack for reading material when I left the remaining books for Mr. Holden-Peters.

We were also allowed to take the family pictures. I was collecting them from Henry's study when Chin marched in carrying a painting of a clipper ship, which he switched for the one of the *Denali Princess*.

'This is a family picture,' he said, as if daring me to argue. 'Mr. Holden-Peters will like this other better; it's bigger and the frame is more showy.'

'Mmm, quite gaudy,' I agreed with a grin of satisfaction. 'Perfect for our esteemed buyer.'

. . .

But on the grey and gusty January day we moved out, just after my ninth wedding anniversary, there was little to make me smile. And as I saw Chin slip the painting into the boot of our car, I felt a pang of shame. The *Denali Princess* had been named for the Alaskan mountain the mapmakers called McKinley, but the natives referred to as Denali—father of mountains. It had been one of Henry's treasures, but I'd been afraid to take it.

'Captain Tilton will be glad you saved it. Thank you, Chin. It seems I'm always in your debt.'

'We'll put it in his study at the beach. He'll like seeing it there when he comes home.'

Neither of us had ever said a word to each other about the possibility of Henry's coming back. But in that moment when we'd both spoken about him in the future, we shared the small flicker of hope that couldn't be extinguished no matter how pragmatic we were about the business of getting on with our lives.

I looked back up at the façade of the old house where I'd found my life again. From the day I'd helped a tiny baby with colic and gotten a job, to the night of the fire when Henry had asked me to marry him, and on through the years as I'd learned I was stronger than the demons of my former life, it had been my shelter. I'd left finer places in the past without a qualm and knew well it was the people in those grand structures that made them special. All that was important was coming with me—my children and the love of Henry Tilton.

Chin settled Bunny and me in the car and got behind the wheel. He'd drive us to the beach and then return this last item to Bertram Holden-Peters. After, I would meet him at the train in Seaside, and we'd manage nicely with the old Ford. But as we were departing the old house in Astoria, and rounded the back corner of the property, the week-old grave of the ancient Tar caught my eye. The new mound of dirt caught Bunny's, too.

'Better they be together,' she sniffed. She couldn't remember a world without a huge black dog trailing after her, making a convenient pillow, or dozing on the hearth.

'Maybe when we get settled we can find another dog.'

'Maybe,' she murmured and snuggled against me.

I don't remember the drive. My mind was so filled with memories that I was genuinely surprised when we pulled up to the beach house with the van right behind. There wasn't much to unload apart from the piano and Bunny's bed.

I started a fire and Chin got the stove going. As the house warmed I had a powerful sense of my husband surrounding me. I felt stronger in this stout little house by the ocean than I had since that terrible day the telegram came.

'I'll be right here,' I whispered. 'I'll wait right here.'

. . .

A week later the Christmas holidays came to an end and Bunny faced her first day in a new school. I'd expected her to be timid about starting over, but she was full of enthusiasm and ate breakfast with relish. She went bouncing out the door and within a block we met a talkative girl named Viola Schmitz, who insisted we call her Vi and was delighted to be the first one to meet the 'new girl' Miss Radford had told them about. In the course of the rest of the short walk she also informed us that Miss Radford was 'divine' and warned my daughter to stay away from Gabriel Melder because he always wiped his nose with his hand. They entered the schoolyard arm in arm and Bunny fell in with the crowd of girls as if she'd been going there all year.

I went into the one-room schoolhouse on my own and handed her papers to the Miss Radford, who smiled warmly as she introduced herself. She was a plump pretty young woman with deep brown eyes and dark silky curls. After a quick examination of the Astoria records, she said she was confident Bunny would do just fine and apologized about there being no French offered. I assured her I could keep Bunny up as I'd done so for her brothers.

Then there was nothing more to say. I crossed the schoolyard and Bunny waved me off with a jaunty salute. Now, it seemed, the last of my chicks was settled and the only one with nothing to do was me. Resisting a last glance, I started home.

As I walked, collar up, hands driven deep into my pockets, and feeling quite at loose ends, I passed the small Cannon Lunch Café with its faded Weatherly Ice Cream ad, and the announcement on the side of the building that it had homemade pies. I was remembering all the melting ice cream cones Bunny had messily consumed in our early summers, when I saw a furry bundle dash around the corner of the building and pause. It was a bright-eyed terrier. When he saw me looking at him, he tore across the muddy street and jumped right into my arms.

'Where's that dern thief,' an angry voice rang out. 'I'll teach you ta try and sneak inta my kitchen.'

The bundle in my arms, scruffy with reddish-brindle fur and decidedly in need of a bath, buried his lopsided ears against my shoulder and peeped up at me with pleading brown eyes.

Just then a large man in a white apron brandishing a rolling pin came around the corner of the café. 'Gimme that mutt,' he grumbled. 'I'm gonna fix him good.'

'Is he your dog?'

'Hell no, he's a dirty stray. Seen some lumberjack dump him off a truck where he'd been hidin' in the logs 'bout five days ago. Been hangin' round town gettin' inta people's garbage an makin' a damn nuisance a himself. Good knock on the head's what he needs.'

The dog, with impeccable timing, licked my chin.

'Looks like what you need is a bath and meal,' I said to

him, ignoring the man with the rolling pin, 'not a knock on the head.'

I felt his short tail smack against my coat.

'Best you get rid a him now,' the man warned. 'I been runnin' him off with rocks and bottles fer days and he don't go. Likes everybody, even when they don't like him.'

'I suspect it's the untidy state of your garbage cans he likes,' I observed a little tartly.

'Dern stray,' the man grumbled with a sidelong look at his overflowing trash.

'I think I'll just keep him,' I said, scratching his ears. 'He's cute.'

'Wimmin,' the man retorted with a shake of his head. 'Soft as butter the lot a 'em.'

I laughed and the little dog gave a sharp bark to the cook's retreating back.

I set him down. 'I'm not as soft as all that,' I warned as I tried futilely to wipe the mud off my coat. 'If you stay with me there's going to be a bath, and you'd better do your business outside. What do you say?'

The dog cocked his head, one ear up and one down, and gave me a sharp bark as his tail flashed from side to side like an over-wound metronome.

'All right then, come on,' I said starting up the street. I passed the roller rink and turned up the hill with my scruffy new friend right on my heels. 'Oh dear,' I murmured as we went the last block. 'What's Chin going to say about you?'

But Chin said nothing and set to work cleaning my coat while I gave the dog a bath. Then the little guy had some bread and leftover chicken. But after he gobbled down a tidy amount, his head drooped. He was warm, dry, and fed; a nap was in order. I put down a blanket near the fire and he sat on it watching me.

As soon as I settled into my chair he popped up on my lap

and made himself at home, going to sleep instantly.

'Shall I serve your lunch here, Mrs. Captain, or at the table?' Chin asked dryly, and not waiting for an answer brought me a plate by the fire.

When Bunny got home I was a little worried she'd find it disloyal to old Tar to take on a dog so soon. But she pronounced him just the kind of pal I'd need to keep me company when she was in school. So I called him Pal, and his devotion as well as comic sense of humor and uncanny ability to read my mind made him indeed just the friend I'd needed.

.   .   .

We settled into the snug house easily. Henry had outfitted it to be lived in year-round, and as Bunny and I found our daily rhythm, we were much pleased with our new home. I'd not been to Cannon Beach in the winter since my wedding, and because Bunny had already found good friends at school, I discovered a whole community of locals ready to embrace someone who'd come to share their beloved rainy weather. They were a devoted group who'd managed to withstand the first crushing blow of the depression and developed ways to stay in their beach community. The grand lodges were closed, their legions of summer help gone, but if you went around to the kitchen there was usually a chowder on the stove and good coffee in the pot.

And there was time. Time to get to know the people who never had a spare moment to talk in the summer but now could spend hours in their toasty kitchens telling tales of the old days and teaching the lore of the area to a newcomer like me. Henry had always been part of the local group, and now they embraced me with a rapidity and generosity that warmed my heart.

After only a few weeks I too had become a devotee of the huge storms that tore down from the Aleutians and rolled in off the Pacific. The winter surf crashed to the very edges of the beach and the rollers in the sun were an incredible shade of sea-glass greenish-blue not seen in the warm months. I came to love my seclusion and the storm-swept coast. There was a magnificence about it that held me completely in thrall. Oddly, it took me back to my times with Kuzma and our travels through the vast and endless *taiga*. There was a pure elementalism about both places that so clearly displayed the power and beauty of nature. And when I thought how temperate the climate was here, compared to that of northern Russia, I felt myself getting the best of both worlds.

That being said, Bunny and I lived much of our lives by the great fireplace and made sure to warm our bedrooms with the space heaters before we dashed off to bed and had to turn them off. I'd had concerns about Chin in his loft over the garage, but he'd pointed out with his usual formal candor that the captain had always intended him live to there and, of course, had provided all the weatherproofing and heat he could require.

If one had a good mackintosh and a stout pair of Wellingtons, getting about in all weathers was quite simple. It never froze and snow on the beach was something to delight rather than aggravate. Daily trips to the post office tucked into Lanphere's, where all the news was gathered, became like a walk in the park on a sunny afternoon. And there were many days Pal and I braved the winds to scavenge for shells and driftwood along the beach. Unlike summer, when there were so many others doing the same thing, we often found treasures.

I was acquiring a very respectable collection of the beautiful glass balls Japanese fishermen used to float their nets. Each time I found one it gave me a good feeling to think something seemingly so fragile had come so far through the winter ocean. Surely a stout ship like the *Raven* had brought my Henry to shore somewhere.

. . .

The weather in March was fierce, and as we came to the ides

I was thinking the old Shakespearian adage was correct. But it was a good time to clean and I decided to take on the boys' room, as they'd hopefully be home for Easter. With my supplies in Kuzma's toolbox and a rag around my hair, I was just starting up the stairs when the front bell rang.

I hesitated. I wasn't dressed for callers and Chin had gone to the market. But then I reasoned it must be some stranger, for no one who knew us used the front door in winter; they all wanted to leave their boots in the utility room. I went to answer, shushing the ever-vigilant Pal.

A massive witch-like apparition, black-clad, dark veils swirling in the heavy sea-mist, stood scowling at my door. Great-aunt Hester Barnstable.

Pal renewed his barking in the face of this sinister intruder.

Ten years before, she'd been broad. Now she was corpulent and her once strong features had become distinctly porcine. I was so taken aback I simply stared. And after a moment only gathered my wits enough to pull the rag from my head and quiet Pal.

'Took you long enough,' she declared as she marched in and stationed herself near the fireplace.

I closed the door.

'But then I can see,' she added, eyeing my old dress disapprovingly, 'you've found your level.'

I stood, twisting the rag in my fingers like a guilty child, still barely believing she was real.

A dark and cruel smile of triumph spread over her face.

The marine layer that pressed against the windows, cutting off all view of the outside lost, its comforting anonymity and took me back to the Ipatiev house and its painted windows. As I had then, I felt trapped and in the hands of an enemy.

'This day's a long time coming,' Hester said, enjoying her power and my obvious fear. 'But this time no one will come to your rescue. I've won. It's over.'

'Over?' I managed, completely cowed.

'I move in circles you cannot imagine. I know things about you now, things you don't want exposed.' She extended her gloved hand and when her fingers opened the huge ruby she held looked like pooled blood on the black material. 'Did you think no one would know where this came from? It was the centerpiece of the empress's tiara. Or perhaps by the time you got your filthy hands on it you didn't know that.'

I stared at the ruby. Only a few months before I'd handed it to a gem merchant in San Francisco.

'Stop gawping,' Hester said sharply. 'Pack Emmaline's things. I'll take her with me today.'

'Take my daughter?' I stammered.

'You can't stop me. If you try, I'll expose you. There are those who have questions, who want to know what you know.'

'Emmaline, as well as Joe and Will, are my legally adopted children,' I said, more to reassure myself than discourage Hester.

'Under what name is your so-called legal adoption?'

'What do you know?' I gasped.

'You've the tools of a peasant and,' she gestured at Kuzma's box, 'you know how to use them. But you also have a priceless Faberge egg and the treasured bible of an empress, the Empress Alexandra herself!'

'You searched my room!' I accused, breathlessly. 'Ten years ago. You went through my things.'

'Of course I did! You were patently lying about who you were and had your hands on my precious Annabelle's daughter.'

'You can't have Bunny,' I managed.

'I know it all,' she said, viciously confident. 'All, I tell you. And I'll tell the world if you don't give me that child.'

Blind panic swept me. She knew who I was! I'd lost Henry and now I was going to lose Bunny. I was trapped in the maze of my own deception.

A wheezing guttural chortle erupted through Hester as she enjoyed the glee of anticipated victory. 'I have friends among the Russian Monarchists,' she bragged with a self-satisfied smirk.

I marshaled my careening emotions. I couldn't fight her without information.

'Some of them are genuine Russian Aristocrats,' she affirmed, nodding her head and setting her chins wobbling.

I waited, forcing myself to concentrate on what she said.

'I've read everything,' she went on, eager now to impress me. 'I know all about the tragedy in Ekaterinburg. And when I expose you, they'll thank me. Yes they will. They'll know I'm not just someone with a silly story like that Anna Anderson woman, but that I've the Russian Monarchy at my very heart. They'll see how valuable I can be to them. And my Annabelle's daughter will be the playmate of princesses. She'll marry a Russian prince some day! Yes! Yes she will!'

My fear evaporated. Hester was simply one of those Americans who are captivated by royalty, because a hereditary title is something all the money in the world can't buy.

'What will you tell them about me?' I asked, now calm. 'What do you think you know?'

'You were there!' she accused, coming toward me as she spoke. 'You know what happened to them! How else could you have those things, those treasures? The Empress Alexandra's bible with its lavender ribbons. An Easter gift given by Tsar Nicholas to his daughters.' Once again she extended her hand with the ruby. 'And this stone, this stone that even has a name, the Princess of Peking!'

'Gems, named or not, can tell no tales,' I observed flatly.

She ignored me, triumph driving her words, 'Did you lead them to their deaths? Did you push them down those stairs? Perhaps you only robbed them after they were slaughtered? What will I tell them? I'll tell them you're a murdering, thieving Bolshevik!'

I slapped her.

The stone flew from her hand and Pal tore after it as the flashing red object skittered over the rug and rattled across the floor.

Hester shrieked and dropped to her knees trying to grab him. But he'd played this game too often and she was much slower and clumsier than Bunny or the boys. She scrabbled after him breathlessly snorting for him to stop.

He growled fiercely, staying just beyond her reach reveling in his favorite game.

Struck by the ludicrousness of the situation, I started to laugh. I was the epitome of the kind of person she wanted to know, to dazzle. But rather than fulfilling her fantasy, she was crawling around on the floor in front of a Russian grand duchess, following a dog.

'Pal,' I commanded, through my undisguised mirth. 'Drop it.'

He did as he was told and stood, bright eyes fixed on Hester, waiting for her to throw the toy again.

But she, of course, snatched it up and began clambering to her feet as he barked and jumped against her. I sagged back against the piano laughing, and the cacophonous clash of the keys intensified my amusement.

'Don't you laugh at me, you low-born tramp!' Hester bellowed, her face red with fury. 'How dare you mock me?'

'Because you're a fool,' I said, controlling my mirth. 'Go ahead and tell your little stories and see where it gets you.'

'You'll see,' she threatened. 'You'll be sorry—'

The front door burst open and Chin appeared, towing a smallish man with thinning dark hair by the collar. As we all gaped at each other I caught the distinct odor of stale clothes. I was facing the man who'd been inquiring about me. He was Hester's agent.

'He was not from the Ku Klux Klan,' Chin said matter-of-factly, releasing his prisoner.

'I know,' Hester insisted. 'I know who you are! You'll be sorry. You'll be sorry when I tell them.'

'No, I won't. But you will. You've invented a fanciful tale around some unrelated baubles to get you into the good graces of a stratum of society you can never enter. Go ahead, tell them your story. But I warn you, though I can't imagine why I should, that if you do they'll brand you for the inane social climber you are.'

'I saw the bible...'

'And every woman who admired the empress put lavender ribbons in her bible,' I explained easily. 'My mother among them. If you could read Russian you'd have known whose bible it was.'

'But this ruby. I paid—'

'A dealer? A man who collects such things to sell to foolish status-seeking women like you?'

'It's real! I know it's a real ruby!'

'How nice for you. Why don't you have it set into a tiara?'

She stood there, her mouth opening and closing like a hooked fish.

'Get out of my house,' I said firmly. 'And take your smelly little agent with you. The two of you deserve each other.'

Hester, bested again and furious, stuffed the ruby into her bag, and with a parting attempt to kick Pal, disappeared down the front steps followed by the sweaty little spy.

. . .

By April the weather was beginning to turn—spring was coming. The garden boxes were ready along the south side of the house and Chin had been gathering seeds and starter sets from other locals. Downtown bustled with the hope of tourists soon to come and we often got out without our slickers and boots.

Bunny had become a complete coast dweller. She spoke of logging, fishing, and the tourist business as if she'd been doing so all her life, and always kept an eye on the weather. She never mentioned Astoria or her friends there, except to observe she was happier here. The boys were doing well in school and both had managed, by being the early birds on the scene, to get employment for the summer in Cannon Beach. Though I was sure they were sacrificing income to spend the time with me, they pointed out I charged no room and board. And I wasn't forceful in urging them to work in Portland or Corvallis that summer. Too soon they'd be looking for jobs, and in the depression, that might take them anywhere.

One morning just after Bunny had gone out the door to school, Chin dropped one of his precious San Francisco Chronicles on the table beside my coffee. Having been born and raised there, he got the papers in the mail and was quite stingy with them.

Pointing to a center column he said, 'She died.'

'Oh, my lord, Great-aunt Hester,' I gasped.

'No inheritance for our Miss Bunny,' he said pragmatically, sliding his finger down the column.

I began to read. He'd told the truth. Great-aunt Hester had left every penny of her considerable fortune to a small group of Russians who believed that the entire royal family—the tsar, empress, and all the children—had escaped the Bolsheviks and were hiding in exile somewhere, waiting for the right moment to turn Russia back into a monarchy.

'She never knew how close she was,' I murmured.

Chin took back his paper.

And with that door closed I was looking forward to our summer without reservation. Though I'd realized when she came I could deal with any trouble Hester made, it gave me a sense of peace to know she'd not return.

The school year went into its last months and the weather

grew warmer each day. The angle of the sun mounted and the hours of daylight increased. I spent more and more time out-of-doors, trusty Pal at my heels. And I realized one afternoon as I ambled along the beach, how much I had to look forward to. For the first time since the day Henry had gone missing I was actually living my life instead of just going through the motions.

I saw in this spring a new beginning for all of us. And that night, as I always did before I got into bed, I went to the window to look out over the water and watch the Tillamook Light sweep the waves. My prayer, my mantra, came to my lips. 'He shall give his angels charge over thee, to keep thee in all thy ways. They shall bear thee up in their hands. He shall cover thee with his feathers, and under his wings shalt thou trust.' And then I added, 'Come home to me Henry. I miss you. Please come home.'

.   .   .

'Come on then, Pal,' I called. 'Time to go.'

My companion was dashing fruitlessly after yet another seagull. Shading my eyes, I watched the little dog tear blindly over the sand but stop short just before he got wet. Since the day I'd rescued him from the rolling pin he'd demonstrated a profound dislike of water. And I wasn't sorry he didn't care for the surf as Tar and Pete had.

He raced ahead as I started up the dune, and as I looked toward the house I saw Bunny waving frantically from the upstairs porch.

I returned her signal and she disappeared into the house. Quickening my steps I met her on the flags of the terrace.

'He's in Dutch Harbor!' she shouted jumping up and down, waving a telegram like a victory banner. 'I was right! I knew it! I always knew it in my heart!'

I saw her happiness. I knew what she was saying. But my

mind couldn't take it in. My thoughts spun like the chips of glass in a kaleidoscope.

Henry was safe and in Dutch Harbor... I'd been to Dutch Harbor when I came from Siberia... Henry was alive... It was on Unalaska Island in the Aleutians... Henry was in Dutch Harbor... I'd visited a beautiful church there, Holy Ascension Cathedral, a cruciform Orthodox church with ikons and art pieces donated by Catherine the Great... Henry was alive... The town had breathtaking views of snow-capped mountains and wild seas... Henry was in Dutch Harbor...

'Read it!' Bunny insisted, flapping the paper before my face. 'Read it! Read it! *Papasha* sent it!'

I took the paper, terrified the words I'd see would be different, would say something else entirely, might be for someone else, or would confirm what I didn't want confirmed.

'*Maman*? Aren't you going to read it?'

I opened the sheet and saw the words typed in capitals on the yellow surface.

'DARLINGS. ALIVE AND WELL. HOME SOON AS POSSIBLE. MUST CATCH TIDE. *PAPASHA*'

I read the words over and over, then said them aloud so I could hear the sound of them. But after all the months of waiting, I couldn't take in the tangible proof before my eyes.

Bunny danced into the house and only moments later I heard her joyous voice, shouting down the phone, telling the boys the good news. She was chattering and laughing, giggling with pure delight. It was the sound of her natural, girlish happiness, so honest so genuine, that somehow let me know it was true.

I sank into a chair and my eyes roamed the waves, mindlessly watching them roll and break along the sand.

Bunny ran back out to me. 'We have to get ready,' she bubbled. 'Oh! Dear! He doesn't know we're here. He sent the telegram to Astoria. How will we let him know?'

'It could take a month or more for him to even reach Seattle,' Chin said matter-of-factly.

'And he could be there in two weeks,' she laughed. 'He could
be here in less than a month! Maybe we should go to Seattle and
wait for him.'

'And how will you know which ship he will be on?' Chin
asked. 'Unless there is another telegram, we will have to wait.'

'But he's going to the wrong place,' she insisted. 'We have
to do something. *Maman*, why are you just sitting there? Aren't
you happy, don't you want him to get here soon?'

I looked into her bright and shining eyes unable to re-
spond. I felt as if I might shatter into a thousand pieces, or that
the whole dream that was coming true around me would vanish
if I moved or spoke.

Chin took a seat on the small stool before me and my eyes
fell to where his slender fingers rested quietly on the back of
my hand. He'd never touched me before, never crossed the line
between servant and mistress in all our years together. I raised
my eyes to meet his dark and slanting ones.

'He will come, Mrs. Captain,' he said gently. 'You were
right to believe. He is coming.'

I nodded and tears filled my eyes. He produced a fine large
and perfectly clean handkerchief, as if he'd been anticipating
this exact moment.

'Thank you, Chin,' I managed to say before my tears of joy
and relief consumed me.

Bunny sank down on the arm of my chair and hugged me,
whispering comforting words. When Chin appeared with a cup
of steaming tea I was much recovered.

'We'll simply have to wait,' I said sensibly, and blew my nose.

Seeing I was once again myself, Bunny renewed her concerns. 'But he'll go to the wrong place.'

'Not for long,' I assured her.

'But...'

'What will you do?' I chided with a smile. 'Go and camp on the corner of Eighth and Duane and wait for him?' Thinking I wanted to do exactly that.

Bunny smiled ruefully and nodded. Then she jumped up. 'How can I wait? This is like Christmas times a million!'

'It's only the last week of May,' I reminded her, and myself. 'The boys will be here by June 10th. We'll all be here at home when *Papasha* arrives. I know you want it to be sooner, but July is the soonest we can really start to expect him.'

But the ever-optimistic Bunny, and all the rest of us though we tried to be less obvious about it, jumped up to run to the window at the least sound. Will was out most days taking summer tourists on horseback rides all over the area, and rushed home every evening, sure he'd missed the important moment. Joe was working at Himes Grocery and had a good vantage point to the main street, but as the summer grew busier couldn't keep an eye on everything, and he too began racing up the hill at the end of his shift only to find nothing had changed.

But then, of course, when we weren't expecting it, the miracle happened. It was late afternoon and we were all completely involved in an old jigsaw puzzle, laughing and joking as we stole each other's pieces and triumphing when we found a fit. Pal barked, as he often did when he thought one of the summer people was coming too close to our porch, and though the children ignored him I looked up to see a gaunt scarecrow of a man standing in the front doorway, hand on the knob, watching us.

He was bearded and had a scar that shot from his right eyebrow into his hairline where it left a silver streak. His clothes were ill-fitting and shabby, obviously not his own. And there was a sense of hesitancy about him, of uncertainty, as if he wasn't sure he belonged in this moment.

As our children continued their banter I met the gaze of my husband over their heads and no amount of illness or injury could mask the smile that warmed his eyes. My glass of lemonade slipped from my fingers and the children, alerted by my inadvertent signal, jumped into his arms. He embraced them, kissed them, and his eyes never left mine as I happily waited my turn.

And when he took me against him, the smell of him, the sound of his heart beating, his breath coming in and out against my neck, along with the weight of his arms around my body, was all I could ask for. He kissed me, not the hungry passionate kiss that might have been expected, but a soft lingering caress, as if he was tasting something sweet and rich and wanted to savor it, not gobble it down.

'I knew you'd come,' I whispered.

'How could I leave you?' he replied.

I touched the scar gently. 'Almost though.'

'Mmm. Almost.'

His arms crushed me against him and I knew completely, without a word of his untold odyssey, how terribly close he'd come to death, and how hard the battle to get home to us had been.

. . .

We gathered on the upper porch. Henry had spent an hour in the bathroom and then Chin had been called in with his straight-razor and scissors. The result was quite amazing and Bunny flung herself at her now completely recognizable *Papasha* with renewed vigor. The clean clothes and naked chin, however, showed even more clearly how thin and drawn my husband was. While his daughter chose not see those things, his sons and I would have been deeply concerned had we not been able to see he was strong and in good spirits. Though despite seeing he was well, Chin and I had been pushing food on him constantly.

By evening, when we'd all hugged and kissed him completely, simply basking in the delight of his presence, he settled on the upper porch in the summer breeze to tell us his story. The fading light softened the scar on his temple and his smile counteracted the sharp planes of his face.

'We'd picked up a hundred caribou and they were hard to come by. The Chukchi don't like to part with their livestock as it represents their wealth and provides for their survival in bad times.

'We saw the storm coming and had no way to avoid it, and I can tell you it was the trusty *Raven*, old as she was, that saved the few of us who survived. She fought that storm right along with us but it was so powerful even she couldn't win. The waves were so punishing that to be on deck was almost certain death from being washed overboard. But down below, men were thrown about so violently they were killed as well. And in the end, when we saw ourselves being driven onto the rocks of a small island, it was only the four of us topside who survived. Four men and six reindeer along with a large part of one side of the hull and a tangle of rigging made it above the surf line, due solely to the caprice of the storm and no skill on our part. It came down to luck, fate, or heavenly intervention; whatever you want to call it.

'Thinking it might save some of the men, I'd managed to maneuver us between a small island and a larger one. In that tiny respite from the chaos, our doomed ship was driven for the larger of the two. These islands were barely more than piles of rock, and no more than shadows in the blinding storm. We crashed so hard that even over the howling of the wind, I could hear the *Raven* screaming as she was torn apart. Then a huge wave took the upper deck and a part of the hull and cast it far up into the rocks. Had another such wave come along we'd have been swept right back out.

'We huddled in the rocks, soaked to the skin, and waited to die. But the fury of the storm began to abate and after twelve bone-chilling hours we knew it was going to end. The only reason we didn't freeze to death was because that monster storm had been spawned in the tropics, some kind of typhoon or hurricane, and had warm air in it.

'But when we were able to look about and assess our position, we weren't sure we were glad we'd been spared the quick death of the arctic waters. We were all alone in the ocean on a small island. Where we'd come ashore there was a rocky beach, but the other end of our domain rose in sheer cliffs a thousand feet above the sea. As we looked down over the edge I felt again the hand of fate. If we'd come ashore there, we'd all have been smashed to bits on those ramparts.

'As we continued to explore, Arctic foxes watched us. No one had come to prey on them and make them wary. Though later in the summer we did discover remains of a long-ago Russian occupation. We speculated on what became of the men who'd lived in the ruins of the rude driftwood hut we'd found, and the alternatives weren't very hopeful. Though it was a good sign we didn't discover any human bones. I was feeling a little down when I came across a Russian Orthodox cross in the rubble.'

Henry showed the sturdy, simple gold cross he was wearing around his neck on a piece of leather. 'I decided it was sent by my Neddy to remind me to get home. I took it as my luck piece and started wearing it.'

'And it was!' Bunny said. 'It was!'

The boys shushed her and told their *Papasha* to continue.

'We built a shelter and were grateful to see six reindeer grazing on the scant grass and mosses. Since they were too large for the foxes to bother, we looked about a bit and discovered there was also some kind of mole or vole on the island that provided their main source of food. Every day we checked on those reindeer, knowing what they might mean to us in winter.

'As we explored we found a small lake that had Chinook salmon and Arctic char. I'd learned from a Russian sailor years before to boil grasses and make a sort of tea to keep away scurvy.

So all in all we thought ourselves fairly lucky.

'We improved our shelter over the warm months and collected heaps of driftwood for a beacon fire. We could guess fairly well where we were by the sun, and I was certain we were far south of Nome and quite likely below where the pack ice would reach. We set up a watch for passing ships and tried to keep ourselves occupied. I urged the men to fish, as the flesh of salmon and char were abundant in necessary oils, and I wanted to save the reindeer. I got no arguments and one of the men began keeping close watch on our herd of six so we'd always know where they were.

'Things were beginning to look bleak when we reached late August. With the weather turning cold we were facing the prospect of winter on the island. And then we saw the ship.'

At this point in the narrative we were all riveted. There was a collective sigh from the children and Bunny clasped her hands over her heart. But since he'd not mentioned being injured in the shipwreck I knew there were harrowing events yet to come.

'I grabbed a brand from the fire and started up to the height where we'd laid the signal. But the man who'd been keeping such close watch on the reindeer stopped me. He said I shouldn't let the men from that ship come ashore as they might steal our reindeer and we'd starve. I tried to tell him they were coming to rescue us, but couldn't persuade him. The other two sailors had to wrestle him to the ground and he was screaming his dire predictions as I ran.

'I made it to the beacon and set it alight, reveling in the leaping flames that I was sure would be our salvation. I watched the ship willing it to come our way. It was almost dark when I heard someone coming up the path and turned to share the joy I was feeling. But it was only the man who'd been worried about the reindeer. I saw blood on his torn clothing and his eyes fairly glowed in the firelight. I should have known, should have been more wary, but was too intent on bringing in the ship.

'Without warning he attacked me, stunned me, and when I came to he was scattering the fire. I leaped at him, pushing him away from his task and then he came at me in earnest. He was insane and had no fear. But I had a force behind me, too, because I knew if I let him douse the fire I'd die by his hand. I was sure he'd killed his shipmates—how else would he have gotten away from them?'

Here Henry paused, seemed to be looking away over the water into the night.

'Is that the end?' Bunny asked. 'But how did you get home?'

My husband shook his head and sighed, then smiled at her. 'No, that's not the end. I did manage to best my demented shipmate and though I was battered and wounded, kept the fire going through the night. In the dawn I saw that the ship was close and went down to our camp. One of the other men was still alive. I begged him to hang on and did what I could. He took courage knowing rescue was coming.

'The ship was Russian and when they saw my cross they took me for one of them. But when they discovered I wasn't, it didn't matter. With my basic knowledge of Russian I was able to grasp we'd wrecked on St. Matthew Island and our rescuers were bound for port on the Kamchatka Peninsula. The last thing I remember clearly was being in a small boat, dipping and rising with the swell, and each time we came to the top of the wave I saw the reindeer who'd escaped being eaten standing on a small promontory as if bidding us farewell.

'When they got us on board my last shipmate was more dead than alive, and once I saw he was in good hands I had to admit I wasn't much better off. Both of us, according to the captain's later account, had been given up for dead more than once.'

'But, why did it take so long to get home, then?' Joe, the mathematician, asked.

'Because the Bering Sea wasn't finished with us,' Henry said with a shake of his head. 'That's why.'

'Tell. Tell,' Bunny urged.

'Racing before another storm we were almost wrecked again on the coast of Kamchatka and spent the winter with a band of nomads living on dried salmon, reindeer, and some kind of drink with tea and butter I hope never to taste again.'

Here I laughed. 'Kuzma drank it, but I never could after the first taste. Oh, my poor Henry.'

'But they were good people. Kind and caring. The houses they made were half underground and very snug. I think it took me a month to get the smell of smoke out of my hair. But it was too cold to shave even my beard, let alone my head.'

Now it was Bunny who laughed. 'Oh, *Papasha*, we'd never have known you with no hair!'

'You were the one with no hair,' Joe teased. 'We thought you'd look like a cue ball all your life.'

'Enough of that old joke,' Will ordered. 'What's the rest of the story *Papasha*?'

'With spring we made our way down to Petropavlovisk. There the kind men who'd rescued us passed us on to another Russian ship that was headed for the Aleutians. And all of this for not one penny of compensation, though by the time we left Kamchatka my shipmate and I were both strong enough to do our share of the work. It was a rough crossing being early spring, but we'd had to take our chance of a berth where we could get it.'

'Where's your shipmate,' Joe asked. 'Did he come to Astoria with you?'

Henry smiled. 'He touched ground at Dutch Harbor and refused to go on. He'd decided to stay the rest of his life on dry land and was only waiting to be back in America to do it. He told me he was going to get him a fat wife and never set foot on a ship again, and urged me to do the same. But he didn't know what I had waiting for me and so couldn't understand that I'd have gotten into a canoe and paddled my way home if I'd had to.'

Bunny jumped up and welcomed him home all over.

'Now, my darlings,' Henry said, 'you've heard all my adventures. Tell me yours.'

The children happily competed to tell him of our minor adventures. I was the heroine with the secret Russian nest egg. Pal trying to steal Great-aunt Hester's giant ruby made the children laugh but I saw my husband was strangely pensive about it. Then Chin got his praise for saving the painting of the *Denali Princess* from the grasping Bertram Holden-Peters.

But at this I had to interrupt. 'Mr. Bertram Holden-Peters, that grasping South Seas pirate, sent on *Papasha's* telegram and then sent him to the train station in his grand car.'

'I suppose we shall have to refer to him as a kindly pirate from now on,' Bunny said with a yawn.

Then she and her brothers bid us goodnight.

. . .

But as soon as we were alone in our room, Henry confronted me. 'Hester was here again?'

'She thought I was some sort of Bolshevik and she could get Bunny from me. But Chin and I sent her off. She died not long afterward. She's no more to the children than a funny story about the dog. They weren't here. They didn't see her.'

'But you did. And I'll wager she thought she had you where she wanted you when she heard I was dead.'

'Don't say dead! I never believed that. Never!'

He slumped on the bed. 'And you sold all of the nest egg?'

'I wanted to know what we had.'

'That damn dealer probably cheated you.'

'He did not! I know the value of a diamond, Henry Tilton. And you'd have done the same. I had to know how much we had in case... It was the only way I could feel safe.'

'I just feel like I let you down.'

'The only way you could have let me down was if you'd decided to take your shipmate's advice and stayed in Dutch Harbor with a fat wife.'

He smiled.

'Good. Then come to bed, husband,' I ordered, as I started to take down my hair.

He pulled off his shirt and I saw the real scars from his battle on St. Matthew Island. He'd been burned as well as stabbed and the scars were still quite livid.

I gasped, and distress showed on my face.

He looked guilty and shamed, quickly trying to cover the offensive marks.

I stopped him. 'The scars don't repel me,' I assured him, laying my hands on the puckered flesh of the burns and poor suturing of the cuts. 'They're the clear evidence of how hard you had to fight to get home. But they also tell me how close I came to losing you.'

He put his arms around me and let out a deep and shuddering almost-sobbing sigh.

'Tell me,' I murmured. 'If you say it aloud you can let it go.'

His fingers gripped my hair. 'I had to kill him. There was no other way. He was going to kill me.'

'And all for nothing, for his crazed fantasy,' I whispered. 'He lost his life through his own madness.'

'I didn't even have the strength to move the body when he was dead. He lay there, beside the fire, his empty eyes still seeming to glow with that wild light I'd seen when he came up the hill. I felt as if he was watching me from beyond death, hating me for every log I threw into the flames, cursing me from hell for giving up his reindeer. If I didn't have these hideous reminders I'd think it was some kind of macabre nightmare.'

'I was a nurse,' I consoled him. 'I've seen worse than this.'

'I've gotten used to them. They were so much worse.'

'I can see you had some good nursing. These burns are well-healed.'

'Remember the foul tea?'

'Too vividly.'

'Well, whatever that kind woman slathered on me night and day smelled worse!'

'She knew her medicine, but I'm surprised she was such a poor seamstress.'

'That was the old seaman on the Russian ship who put me back together,' he said with a chuckle. 'Told me before he started he'd begun his life at sea as a sail-maker. I think it was supposed to make me feel better.'

'Surely they gave you vodka. That and garlic are the medicine of the people. Though, it looks as if maybe he had a bit too much of it while he worked.'

'End of the trip,' my husband said with a grimace. 'All they had left was the garlic.'

I kissed him, a deep and yearning kiss, allowing myself now that we were alone to show him how much I'd missed him.

'Now that's what I came home for,' he murmured.

'I'll never let you out of my sight again,' I informed him as I led him to the bed.

'I can live with that.'

. . .

For a year Chin and I restored my husband's health and he settled into life on the coast with ease. It was, after all, the place he'd chosen long ago to spend his days on land and now he was getting to do just that. He repaired and restored the house, though in Chin's capable hands it hadn't needed much work. But he had fun repainting and fitting the place up with extras for the weather and lots of little conveniences for me in the bathrooms and kitchen. He even found a coal stove small enough to tuck into his study and provide himself a cozy retreat for winter.

He also crewed for local salmon, halibut, and crab fishermen, which gave the sailor in him the opportunity to get out on the water with no outlay of cash. He required no pay but enough of the catch for our own pot, and was much in demand for his skills among the captains, who were barely making ends meet.

An examination of our accounts had set his mind at rest that our situation was secure if not lavish, and with time he came to understand I was happy cooking and caring for our snug home on the Pacific. Still, he didn't pass up a chance to add to the larder or labor for a little cash.

I'd never have demanded he leave the seagoing life, and had he received an offer to captain a ship without having to buy in, he might have accepted it with my blessing. As to the dangers he'd face, I knew only too well that no place in the world was safe—not even the palace of an emperor. But in the depression it wasn't likely he'd get to sea and I know he enjoyed the time with Bunny and the chance to see the boys more often.

The months slipped away and it was June of 1933. Full summer, with tourists and bustling streets, was already beginning. The hard times kept people from taking long trips, but an escape to the beach could be quite reasonable and always fun for the whole family.

Soon, Bunny would be out of school for the summer and going fishing with her *Papasha*. She'd shown a love of the water from childhood, but now relished the chance to dress up in boy's clothes and accompany Henry when he crewed. She soon proved herself fearless and competent, gaining the respect of the other hands. And I loved to watch them coming home for dinner together, all smiles in yellow slickers and pants, with their catch as their pay.

Joe was about to graduate from his engineering studies and was already searching for work, but hoping to be involved with the creation of Ecola Park. This beautiful area along the coast was about to become a reality through the generosity of some longtime Cannon Beach residents, who donated land, and also thanks to the shrewd political bargaining skill of Samuel Boardman, Oregon's first superintendent of parks, who somehow got the state to put up the needed cash in 1932, when the depression was at its height.

The park needed a water system, parking lot, roads, trails, viewpoints, picnic tables, restrooms, and shelters. The CCC (Civil Conservation Corps) was providing the labor, but there might just be a need for a young engineer with local experience and excellent grades.

Will was already teaching in Portland and so would be with us for the summer, returning to his job at the stables. But having been told that our dear Miss Radford was getting married, he was going to try for the job right here in the fall. I was too prudent to count on having all my chicks so near, but the idea was delicious. My husband and I let ourselves savor it from time to time that spring, along with the softening of the weather and bursting of my daffodils.

On a particularly nice morning Henry and I were on the upper porch when the front bell sounded. Pal, ever on guard, dashed down the stairs.

'Barely ten,' Henry said lazily. 'Who could it be?'

'And who would come to the front door?' I asked, thinking for a moment of Great-aunt Hester.

Chin stepped out from the upper hall. 'A gentleman and a lady to see you, Mrs. Captain. He would not give his name. I put them in the parlor.'

Since there was only one room downstairs, the use of that word, coupled with Chin's punctilious manner, put me a bit on guard.

'You let strangers into the house?' Henry asked feigning shocked surprise.

Our manservant had been known, both here and in Astoria, to leave unexpected visitors cooling their heels on the front steps until Henry or I gave permission for them to enter.

Chin shot my husband a withering glance and extended his palm to me. In it lay a green jade egg with a tiny white flower affixed to its smooth surface. 'The gentleman had your treasure, Mrs. Captain. He said he wanted to return it. And he was very clean.'

Tears filled my eyes. It seemed so long ago since that trip to San Francisco. And though I'd been right to pawn it, and it did bring a good price, I was delighted to see it again.

'Damn it!' Henry cried, snatching the egg from Chin. 'So even this was sacrificed? I'd never have let you give this up.'

'I know,' I said smiling. 'That's why it was so easy.'

He put it gently into my hand and I opened it to see that the four little bunnies still slept in their nest.

'Shall I make tea?' Chin asked, bringing us back to our guests and social responsibilities.

'Please. And tell the gentleman we'll be right down,' I said, arranging my shawl.

'Yes, Mrs. Captain,' Chin replied and gave me a slight bow as he left.

'Do you know who it is?' Henry asked.

'Since Hester stirred the pot, I've been expecting something, though I don't know what. But the egg, in the hands of someone who knew its provenance, would definitely give me away. The question is, to whom?'

'And if your secret's exposed?'

'Nothing and no one will persuade or force me to leave you. That simply isn't possible.'

Henry went back to the bedroom, deposited the egg in the leather box, took the small revolver I'd threatened him with the night he proposed from the dresser, and slipped it into his pocket.

I hesitated; for all my firm words, I felt the specter of my past close at my shoulder.

'Past or future,' he assured me. 'We face it together.'

I took his hand and he led the way.

When we reached the bottom of the stairs my heart skipped a beat as I saw a small, prim, and slender gentleman of about fifty standing by the fireplace. His foot touched Nadezhda's cleaning bucket, now filled with kindling, and in his hand was a book. By the lettering on the spine I could see it was one of the Russian ones Henry had picked up for me in his travels.

'I see you're keeping up with your Russian, Princess,' he said politely.

'Thank you for returning my treasure,' I replied, bemused and more than surprised. I'd not expected a friend, someone who would call up such old, dear, and terrible memories all at the same time.

Then I heard a gasp, and a plump little woman dropped into a deep curtsy, and began to weep.

I rushed forward, taking her hands, and helped her up. 'Dear Shura, no more of that. Those days are gone for all of us.'

'You will always be my princess,' my former nurse sobbed in Russian, kissing my hands. 'Always, always my princess.'

As I assisted her to a chair, I met the grey-blue eyes of the man at the fireplace. 'Monsieur Gilliard. I think you were the last person I expected to see. Yes, the very last.'

He closed the book and folded it against his chest as he tipped his head quizzically. 'Ah, but I hoped against hope it might be you when I held your father's gift in my hand,' he replied in his careful English. 'But then,' his toe touched the beautiful bucket, 'I convinced myself it would not be so.'

His grip tightened on the book and distress marked his usually bland face. 'I stayed after the Whites came. It was only eight days... I couldn't give up hope. Much later Sokolov showed me some things, junk really; three nails, some tinfoil, a few copper coins, and a small lock...'

'From Alexei's pockets.'

'How could I not recognize them? They were his treasures, the only things he could call his own. Except for his little dog, his Joy, who was with us for seven more years.' Here the little man sighed and collected his thoughts. 'There was also *Tortino's* collar, the empress's emerald cross, and the emperor's belt buckle.'

'My dear husband, stop,' came a faint pleading voice from the chair.

'You're right, my love,' Pierre Gilliard said with a sharp nod of his head. 'This is a joyous time.'

Caught in the memories and emotions of another world, of another life, I felt outside myself, displaced, detached from the woman I'd become. My former nursery maid kept patting my hand, and my childhood tutor and hero regarded me with calm affection. And I felt as if the life I'd come to treasure would vanish, that I'd be swept back into the world of shadows and dreams I'd left so far behind. But then my eyes found Henry's and my tottering reality righted itself.

I introduced him, and that small natural act brought me completely back to myself.

Chin brought the tea tray. 'Tea, Mrs. Captain?'

'Let me get you a proper chair,' Henry said, and while I directed the Gilliards to comfortable seats around the low fire, he fetched me a straight chair, dropping the pistol unobtrusively into a drawer of the small sideboard as he passed. He took a place by the mantel near me but not hovering, giving me confidence.

'Do you still take lemon, Monsieur Gilliard?'

He nodded with a smile.

'So, Shura,' I teased, 'you always said you'd marry Monsieur, and you did.'

'I never knew you set your cap for me,' Pierre Gilliard

exclaimed.

His wife blushed and smiled as she dried her tears.

'From the first week you came to the palace,' I revealed with a chuckle. 'That was why she asked you to teach her French, so she'd be ready to return to France with you.'

'Shura,' my former tutor admonished with gentle delight, 'you never cease to amaze me.'

Shura began to reminisce and once started there was a flood of recollections about Tsarskoe Selo, Finland, and the Crimea. Bright images of my childhood flickered before my eyes and the three of us chatted as if we'd never been torn apart by dreadful events and more than fifteen years of separation.

But after some time Monsieur Gilliard observed, 'I can see that Captain Tilton is puzzled by our intimate talk despite your excellent translations.'

'I'd hoped I was hiding that better,' Henry said easily.

'Do you mean he does not know who you are?' Shura demanded with astonishment.

'Of course he knows who I am,' I replied, turning my eyes to his. 'I'm his wife, and the mother of his children. What he doesn't know, and does not matter, is who I was before.'

'Children?' Shura whispered, her mind suddenly turned in another direction. 'But...'

'We have two sons and a daughter,' Henry said, producing a photograph.

'And the boys?' Shura asked, fear in her eyes as she touched the faces in the frame.

'Monsieur, you didn't have to keep my secret from Shura, she's your wife.'

'It was not mine to tell,' he replied simply.

'What? What can you have kept from me?' Shura demanded.

'I can't have children.'

Shura's innocent face grew puzzled and she looked from me, to her husband, and finally to Henry.

'They're the children of my brother and his wife who both died,' Henry said, rescuing her. 'Neddy came to be their governess and tutor. Our Bunny was only a few months old then.'

Shura frowned. 'Who is Neddy?'

'I am. Nadezhda. But the Americans have a hard time saying it so I became Neddy.'

'I suppose you needed this alias, but surely you weren't a mere governess.'

'And a tutor. I even got my Joe, my oldest, through Latin,' I said with pride.

'But you are a princess, a grand duchess, not a servant. You are the last of a dynasty, the last Romanov.'

'I'm Neddy Tilton now,' I said, wanting her to understand and accept. 'I have a family and a life here. The past is over for me. Gone.'

'But your subjects. You can't deny your destiny. You're their princess. They wait for you.'

'Let me guess,' I said, taking her hand. 'They live in Paris in shabby but elegant rooms cluttered with all the little gewgaws they brought when they escaped; snuff boxes, orders and medals, candlesticks, and pieces of mismatched imperial china. Within a now-meaningless class structure, they cling together pretending they can restore the magical world of the monarchy they remember as being perfect. They sip endless cups of tea while they plan and pretend as the real world passes them by.'

'But if you went back to Russia—'

'Russia is never going to be like that again,' I said. 'And I refuse to perpetrate the fraud those people think is true. I'll not be party to that kind of charade.'

'Now you sound like him,' she said, pointing an accusing finger at her husband.

'Because it's so,' he said frankly. 'You know it is.'

'It's over, dear Shura,' I said, seeing surrender and disappointment on her face. 'Don't tell me you and Monsieur spend your days with those poor deluded people.'

'Pierre is a respected professor at the University of Lausanne,' Shura said proudly. 'Though he still helps, especially when discretion is necessary.'

'Discretion,' Gilliard said with derision. 'Every dealer in Europe knows the people in that circle who have money. I received a call from one who knew I often acted as a go between with the Russian enclave in Paris. When he showed me the egg I convinced him it was a good forgery and bought it, but not until I'd learned the path it had traveled. And from San Francisco and the misguided woman who'd bought it there, it was an easy path to your door. But do not worry, I gave away nothing to those silly fools she left all that money to. You know I would never betray your trust.'

'Tell the truth, Pierre,' Shura insisted. 'You thought to find that servant girl and not our grand duchess.'

'And so, in a way, it was she you found,' I murmured.

The little Frenchman jumped to his feet, suddenly understanding it all. 'Of course! In Ekaterinburg you implemented the plan.'

'On the very afternoon before the massacre. I was to meet with the partisans overnight and return for breakfast to reassure my mother. But they never came. And when we went back...'

'Oh, Tanushka,' he said, taking my hand and using the name Olga, my Olenka, had always called me. 'Such a road you've traveled.'

'Yes my friend, my good friend Pierre,' I said warmly, using his Christian name for the first time, 'it's been a long road. But at the end I found all I'd dreamed of and more.'

'But you're a princess,' Shura insisted, unable to give up her fantasy of me. 'You should be living in the Winter Palace, holding court, not keeping house in this, this... cabin.'

Trying not to laugh, I began stripping off my shoes and stockings. 'Take off your shoes,' I ordered. 'You take them right off and come with me.'

The Gilliards stared at me, bewildered. Henry, laughing, quickly followed my lead.

'I'm a princess—you insist it's so,' I reminded Shura. 'Now you must do as I say.'

Still confused, they did as I'd bid and followed as I led them out to the back terrace and down through the beach grass.

While we'd talked, the sun had risen high enough to send dazzling sparkles over the magnificent blue water, and Haystack Rock rose against a calm sea.

I dashed across the hot sand, threading my way around the groups of summer people enjoying the beach. As I reached the waterline a flight of pelicans skimmed over the waves and seagulls laughed in the sky over the rock.

I made Shura step into the water and she gasped because it was so cold. 'What does this remind you of?' I laughed.

'Finland,' she answered promptly with a smile.

'And, my adored Shura who knows me so well, where was I always the happiest? Where did we all have the most fun? Where did even *Maman* sometimes smile?'

'Finland, those summers in Finland,' she said warmly. Then she caressed my cheek and added in Russian, 'All I want is for you to be happy, for my baby to be happy.'

'Look, Shura,' I said. 'This is my kingdom. I'm the sovereign of each and every one of my days. And I spend those days in this magnificent place surrounded not by sycophants and assassins, toadies and gossips, but by the people I love who love me as well.'

I felt Henry come to stand behind me, his broad strong body my rock and mainstay backing me up as always.

'Here is where I reign, with this man who loves me for who I am; not what I am. I fell in love with him on this beach. We were married up at the house. And here was where I waited for him to come back to me when he was lost at sea. This is where I belong—where I'll always belong.'

'No regrets?' Shura questioned, her knowing eyes probing those of the child she'd practically raised.

'Tell me the truth,' I asked seriously. 'Would you trade your Pierre for the tiara of a tsarina, for the life of my mother?'

Shura shook her head sadly. 'No.'

We embraced. 'You've come so far from where we began,' I said. 'And so have I. Let's forget the past and go on as friends from here.'

'But you must tell the story,' Pierre said firmly. 'For the historical record. For the future.'

'He's right,' Henry concurred emphatically. 'If you don't want to jeopardize your sanctuary here, write it down for the children. Let them know all about the woman who was their mother. There's no blood tie; they can have no backlash from the truth should it come out after you're gone. But you must preserve it. Neddy, you must.'

'And you must begin at the beginning,' Pierre insisted. 'You owe this to your father's memory. He deserves his due. People need to know he was the prisoner of his fate in a world he knew was vanishing like mist burned off by the sun. He was sure change must come, but like so many of his predecessors he truly believed it had to come from the top. And had he found a man he could trust, who had Russia's interest at heart to advise him, he might have managed that change.'

'Rasputin,' I whispered and shivered, chilled by the shadow in even the bright sun of this grand day.

'The fatal influence of that man was the principal cause of death to those who thought to find in him their salvation,' Pierre said heatedly. 'He was a madman and a monster the like of which I hope I never see again.'

'I'll do as you say,' I promised. 'All of it. Beginning to end. But it won't see the light of day until there can be no repercussions.'

'That's all I could ask for,' Pierre said warmly. 'Just to know you're safe is more than I ever dreamed.'

'And in the protection of such a handsome captain of the sea,' Shura said, capitulating completely because she was finally convinced of my happiness.

Henry kissed her hand. She blushed and curtsied barefoot in the sand.

'Then we shall go,' Pierre said, smiling at his wife.

'Oh, but not before you meet the children,' I insisted. 'Bunny will be here this afternoon and the boys will be home in only a week or so. Please?'

'You've come so far,' Henry persuaded. 'Surely you can stay for a while and enjoy our paradise.'

'And who will you tell your children I am?' Pierre asked, with that face he always assumed when setting me a problem.

'My former tutor,' I answered instantly. 'And you see if my Joe doesn't tell you how well I did in Latin!'

'I'll have to be completely honest and reveal the truth,' he replied shaking a reproving finger. 'You my dear, ah, Nadezhda, could have done much better had you applied yourself more diligently.'

'Please, please, say you'll stay,' I begged.

The Gilliards looked at each other.

'I command it,' I said imperiously.

'Who are we to deny a royal command?' Pierre said, giving me his small meaningful smile. 'Especially from such a dear friend.'

'Let us walk among your subjects, Highness,' Henry said, giving me his arm. 'Shall I send a footman to inform Chin we'll return for luncheon at one o'clock sharp?'

'Instruct him to use the imperial china,' I laughed. 'Nothing but the best for the Princess of Cannon Beach.'

RELATED BOOKS
OF INTEREST

Karen L. Leedom, *Astoria, An Oregon History*

Marie, Grand Duchess of Russia, *Education of a Princess*

Robert K. Massie, *Nicholas and Alexandra and The Romanovs*

Terence O'Donnel, *Cannon Beach—A Place by the Sea*

Edvard Radzinsky, *The Last Tsar*

COLOPHON

The author creates but it takes much more than an idea to proffer a book. The Princess of Cannon Beach would never have seen the light of day without the help and cooperation of the following:

Editing: Sarah Cypher—The Threepenny Editor

Cover Design & Text Layout: Kristin Summers—redbat design

Friends who read with honesty and insight: Heidi, Cami, and Jean

My best friend and husband: he never lies to me—
    even when I want him to.